Beneath the Texas Sky

Beneath the Texas Sky

Marilyn Read
Cheryl Spears Waugh

Tranquility Press
Georgetown TX: 2020

For information:
Tranquility Press
723 W University Ave #300-234
Georgetown TX 78626
TranquilityPress.com
TranquilityPress@gmail.com

This book is a work of fiction. Historical figures are used fictitiously, and any scenes, situations, incidents or dialogue concerning them are not to be inferred as real. Any other similarity to real persons, living or dead, is entirely coincidental and not intended by the authors.

Cover image by Rob Greebon, ImagesfromTexas.com, used with permission. Longhorn image from pixabay.com.

ISBN: 978-1-950481-19-4
LCCN: 2020935067

Publisher's Cataloging-in-Publication data

Names: Read, Marilyn, author. | Waugh, Cheryl Spears, author.
Title: Beneath the texas sky / by Marilyn Read and Cheryl Spears Waugh.
Description: Georgetown, TX: Tranquility Press, 2020.
Identifiers: LCCN2020935067 |
ISBN (hardcover) 978-1-950481-21-7 | ISBN (trade)
978-1-950481-19-4 | ISBN (e-Book) 978-1-950481-20-0 Subjects:
Texas Hill Country (Tex). | Cowboys--Fiction. | Texas longhorn cattle. |
Man-woman relationships--Fiction. | Family--Fiction. |
Outlaws--Fiction. | BISAC FICTION / Historical / General
Classification:LCCPN34412020 | PS3618.E2242S442020 | DDC
813.76468--dc23

To our strong Texas men

Jim Bob, Taylor, Brooks,
Kade, Tyler, Tanner, and Jack

Other states were carved or born;
Texas grew from hide and horn.

From “Cattle”

a poem by Texan
Berta Harte Nance (1883-1958)

Authors' Note

Print English is a wholly fictional character, as are all of the characters in this book. He is an amalgamation of the old-time cattlemen of early Texas, a rugged breed of men.

San Simon is also a fictional county in Texas, but all of the pivotal events of *Beneath the Texas Sky* are based in history. The years following the Civil War in Texas were filled with violence, simmering feuds, and large cattle drives. "Red gold," the beef of wild Longhorns, furnished fortunes to men hardy enough to hunt them.

Details of open range longhorn ranching are as authentic as we are able to provide through research and the first-hand input of Marilyn's husband, Bob, taken from his years as a cattleman. As a boy, Bob soaked up stories of old-time cattlemen from his great-grandfather, who began ranching in Texas in the 1880s. Bob encouraged Marilyn to try a novel instead of the biography and historical articles she usually wrote, but he did not live to see its completion.

God sent Cheryl Spears Waugh to come alongside and add her insights and wisdom to complete this story, and to help create the others we write to the glory of God.

Cheryl and Marilyn

Chapter 1

May 1860, San Simon County, Texas

"At least Father sees I'm a woman," Julie Denton proclaimed to her canine companion. "But fifteen, almost sixteen, isn't enough for Mother. She wanted Uncle John to come with us. Called it 'a raw frontier town.' As if I'm not perfectly capable of walking a mile by myself to sell a basket of eggs at the mercantile store."

Julie took off her bonnet and laid it in the basket. She loved Mother and admired her ladylike ways, but sometimes her obsession with bonnets and endless rules for proper behavior were stifling. It was a wonder she hadn't insisted on gloves.

The small dog romped along beside her. Of course, Risky hadn't been listening to her tirade. He stopped to sniff once more. Julie laughed when he jumped back at the menacing buzz of a bumblebee. He didn't hazard another, seeming to understand he had dodged a bullet.

"You're a lucky pup, Risky. Bumblebees are iffy insects. They resent inquiring black noses. Better stick to beetles and butterflies, although I do understand."

Some things, though Mother would never agree, were worth a bit of daring. Like risking a freckle by taking off a bonnet, or a careful sniff at an unknown insect in a dog's world. Truth be known, Julie considered herself to be sensibly daring.

Along the country road, trees quivered with new life. Bluebonnets spilled from beneath, punctuated by pink evening primroses at the edges of the lane. The delicious breath of last night's rain and a perfume of blooms hung in the air. Wildflowers blanketed the hills beyond in a riot of color.

"A painting come to life, Lord. This day offers a hint of heaven's garden," Julie whispered.

Nothing could spoil this glorious afternoon. Not even Mother's worries about her being on her own in a county where rough men plied their illicit trades. Cattle rustlers were a constant threat to ranchers, but Uncle John said she'd be fine on a public road and Father agreed. After all, she was almost an adult and filled with the good sense godly parents had instilled in her.

She stopped to remove a grass bur from Risky's paw. He offered a grateful kiss and trotted ahead.

The land rejoiced with her with the songs of birds and insects. Their melody matched the song inside her, the one that often welled up in times like this. It had no words, but her soul pulsed with its rhythm. Julie's spirit hummed as she worshiped the Creator through her senses.

She could be quite happy here in San Simon County; but Father, being a lawyer, needed the opportunities of a larger town.

If only Father would approve my plan to become the first woman lawyer in Texas. What a world of good I could do for people.

"I could work for women's rights, Risky, and help abolish slavery. Always been my dream. So much I could accomplish." She sighed.

Father believed in education for women and promised schooling "back East" if she wanted, but he drew the line at studying law. He and Mother insisted she should have marriage instead of a career. They'd even offered a list of exactly what kind of man she needed, and said church was the place to find him.

"Mother's rule number umpteen-twenty-something, Risky: it's the duty of a respectable woman to defer to her husband's judgment. I can't see myself giving in to some man's ideas. My brain is as good as any male's."

Her parents loved her, but sometimes Julie felt hedged in. Bert's brotherly teasing annoyed her. Only Father seemed to understand, yet even he couldn't believe in the lawyer dream.

Risky's ears went up as he spotted movement behind a nearby algerita shrub. Julie laughed as they drooped again. Cows were not always friendly to playful pups.

Julie marched along, deeper in thought. Marriage was for life. She intended to follow the counsel of her parents. First and foremost, her husband would be a man who loved God and made decisions based on His wisdom—just as Father did.

"My husband will be brave, of course; but more importantly, he'll be smart. Father says I have a quick mind, so my husband will need one, too. He must enjoy laughing and not take life too seriously. A man needs a sense of humor. Father certainly has one."

Risky's bark alerted her to the rumbling of a wagon out of sight over the hill. She was nearing town. A few more steps and Julie could see San Simon City, drowsing just down the slope.

The nearest building was her target—Mr. Bowden's mercantile store, which also housed the post office. The Bowden family lived upstairs. Two horses stood tied to the hitching rail.

Next door was the saloon, which Uncle John called a den of iniquity. Not one of the no-good loafers that Mother worried about exhaled whiskey fumes on its long porch.

A wooden trough with an iron hand pump occupied the middle of the empty street. On her last visit Julie had watched a dusty cowboy fill his ten-gallon hat and pour the water over his head, while his horse guzzled thirstily. No one was there now.

The single stone structure in town, a narrow two-story office building, occupied the other side of the street. It was shared by a lawyer and the county's only doctor, both friends of Uncle John. A few other structures on Main Street and some houses on a back street comprised the town.

Julie's hometown of Paris, Texas was older and larger, and its architecture more refined, but she liked the frontier appearance of San Simon City. The unpainted frame building of the courthouse had not yet weathered to the gray of the saloon.

Small towns made full use of each structure until funds were available to build more, so the courthouse also served as a school and a meeting house for the faithful on Sunday morning.

Uncle John had told Julie the first church services were held under an oak tree on Main Street, and moved indoors to the saloon on cold winter days, until the courthouse was finished. The saloon owner closed down the bar on Sundays to accommodate the sensibilities of the ladies of San Simon City.

Aunt Betty's lips had thinned when he told the story. "John, that's not a fitting story for Julie," she said. Mother, too, appeared disapproving.

But Father laughed. "Truth is truth," he'd said.

John Denton was a county commissioner, and now that the settlement had become the county seat, he had great hopes for it—if war didn't come. He and Father spent a lot of time talking about the probability of war.

Most people lived on farms or ranches, or in a couple of other outlying settlements in the county. Even the church Uncle John and Aunt Betty attended, the Crossroads Community Methodist Church, was a couple of miles north of town. It was in an older but smaller settlement, and the attending families met in a whitewashed board chapel that also served as a school. Julie found the services comforting—like being surrounded by a large family.

Risky had fallen behind, and Julie waited for him to catch up. "Keep up, Risky. I know it's hard for a pup not to dawdle and sniff, but we have an important task to finish."

Risky appeared unimpressed by the settlement, but its scents were a different matter. His nose once more to the ground, he turned back after a dung beetle rolling its prize.

Julie balanced the good-sized basket on her hip and walked on, leaving Risky to his adventure. The basket was heavy with the fresh eggs Aunt Betty gathered each morning. The money they brought would be welcome.

Hoof beats pounding behind Julie broke her reverie. She whirled. "Risky, come here!"

Too late. One of the two horsemen thundering

down the lane swerved to tangle the puppy in his mount's churning hooves, rolling a yelping Risky off into a mass of tall thistles.

"Horrible man!"

As the offending rider drew abreast, Julie dropped the egg basket and snatched up a fair-sized rock, which she sent speeding through the air. The rock connected unerringly with its target. Bert had taught her well. She didn't throw like a girl.

The rider yelled an oath and dismounted. His ear dripped blood as his jaw turned red and swelled. Glaring at Julie, he growled, "You brat! I'll turn ya up and give ya a lickin' ya won't forget!"

He strode toward her, mouthing unpleasant promises with each step. The other ruffian stayed on his horse, laughing and encouraging him. They were young, but too old to be acting like this. The sight of pistols hanging from their belts curled Julie's lip. She despised guns. She squared her shoulders and stood as tall as five feet, two inches could reach.

"Bullies! You two should be ashamed to pick on a woman and a defenseless puppy!"

She stood glaring at her older and much taller antagonist as he neared, not at all slowed by her words. The tormentor pressed closer, forcing her to step back. Julie's heart raced. *Maybe the rock was a mistake.*

The man's pale gray stare devoured her in a most unpleasant manner. His eyes were heavy-lidded, frozen into a permanent squint. He reeked of stale tobacco, perspiration—and danger.

"You're not as young as I first thought," he drawled. "I reckon a spanking's not what ya need, missy. I've got several ideas how to deal with a female who don't act like a lady."

He reached out a large hand, and Julie, despite

her brave intentions, took another backward step, her stomach in a knot.

"Cully, you'd best—" The one still on his horse didn't have time to finish before a big bay gelding shoved into the midst of them.

Where did he come from?

Its rider leaped to the ground. A hand grabbed Cully and spun him around. Over Cully's shoulder, Julie came face to face with a lean, clean-shaven man. His mouth formed a grim line, and he watched them through narrow slits.

"That's enough, Cully," he growled. "You're not going to touch her. You and Tru take off, and I'll pretend I didn't see you bested by a child."

Child! But this was not the time to argue.

The newcomer glanced up at the man still astride his horse. "What're you doing out with this bum, Tru? Bet Frank doesn't know where you are."

Cully bristled and the stranger gave him a shove, sending him reeling. Confronting Cully was a man near his age—one who stood firmly planted, his fists now clenched.

Cully's hand moved toward his pistol, but stopped mid-draw as the intruder's hand hovered near his own. His gaze never wavered from Cully's.

All three of them wearing guns...this could be very bad. What have I done?

Julie's older brother had insisted she learn how to fish and how to fire a gun. Bert had slight use for squeamish females, and Julie was determined not to be one. But guns horrified her.

"Cully, Con's outside Bowden's store with a rifle," said the one called Tru. He fidgeted in the saddle, his hand hovering near his scabbard, as his attention darted from his partner to the store.

The tightness around Cully's mouth eased.

He rubbed one hand down his pants leg, spat, and backed toward his horse. He mounted and cast a last malevolent glare at Julie and her champion. Then he and his partner trotted off.

After they were some distance away, Cully hollered, "There'll be another time, Mister High-and-Mighty, when your brother's not backin' you up."

High-and-Mighty didn't even glance Cully's way. He waved to the man on Bowden's porch, who lowered his rifle. Then he turned to Julie and removed his hat, revealing coal black hair and intent eyes the color of dark coffee. His scowl softened as his gaze rested on her face.

"Cully North and Truman Evans are not men to be messing with. They might have done you real harm if I hadn't spotted you as I came out of the store. Why'd you throw that rock?" His voice was curt—several degrees less than friendly.

Julie glared up at him. *Don't need him to tell me I was wrong.* They stared at each other for what seemed an eternity before he grinned.

"Good throwing arm for a girl. Cully'll have a sore jaw for a while. Maybe he learned something, but I doubt it."

Julie didn't return his smile. Instead she turned dismissively and searched for Risky.

What a mess! Beside the basket, shattered brown shells and golden yolks oozed a trail over the moist earth. Julie stalked over to pick up the tail-wagging puppy lapping up what remained of the eggs. Risky greeted her with a slimy lick.

Thank heavens, no blood or broken bones. She let out a breath and set him down, then stooped to pick up her egg-stained bonnet and toss it into the basket.

Hands on hips, Julie turned to her rescuer. He

needed to be set straight, blaming her for the whole thing. "Did you see what they tried to do to Risky?" Her voice was laced with indignation.

He squinted and bit his lip.

He better not laugh.

"Risky is the best of the litter, and this is his first outing from Uncle John's barn and I'm responsible for him." Julie pushed at a pesky wisp of hair. "Those two made me drop the basket of eggs I was going to sell for Aunt Betty. I wish I'd knocked that ruffian's teeth out!"

Her voice trembled when she mentioned the eggs. Bad, that rock business. Mother would have a fit if she found out, but it was Julie's affair, not this man's.

High-and-Mighty's mouth tilted upward, but he didn't laugh. "You must be John and Betty Denton's niece. What's your name?"

"I'm Juliet Booth Denton from Paris, Texas, but I like people to call me Julie. We're here for a visit. I've come several times before, but I don't remember seeing you."

Good. That sounded more composed. Don't want him to think he's dealing with a child.

High-and-Mighty nodded encouragingly.

"It's not right when a lady is minding her own business for a couple of seedy-looking ne'er-do-wells to come along and try something like that."

The rock aside, I do usually act lady-like.

He didn't smother the smile in time. Julie frowned. *Botheration! He does think it's funny.*

"I'll have you know—"

"My name is Print English." He cut in before she could give him a piece of her mind. "I know your Uncle John. He and my dad are friends. You must be Albert's little girl. You have his red hair, but you sure as tootin' don't have his calm disposition."

"Auburn—my hair is auburn," she said through her teeth. "And I am *not* a little girl. I'll be sixteen in a few weeks. And Mother says polite people don't say things like *tootin'*."

Print seemed to have some trouble with his hat. He turned it around in his hands, staring down at it. Julie watched him, searching for any sign of amusement, but he seemed quite serious.

She'd heard only good things about the English family. They had a ranch near the Crossroads Community, and she had probably been in church with them on earlier visits. She liked the clean-cut appearance of Print English, even if she couldn't appreciate his sense of humor. The tilt of his dark eyes drew her—melancholy, that was the word. Was he hurt by her sharp words?

He could have been killed, coming to my rescue. She shuddered, remembering the hateful expression on Cully's face and his hand reaching for her.

"I've heard my aunt and uncle mention your family, and I'm obliged to you for coming to help." She used her most charming voice and gave him a coy smile. Print English returned her effort with a grin of his own. He put on his hat and remounted.

"Well, almost-sixteen-years-old Juliet Booth Denton, you'd better hand me Risky. Grab your basket and climb up here with me. You shouldn't be out on this country road alone. Cully and Tru may be waiting. I'll take you home."

Print stood in the stirrups and fished a coin from his pocket. "Tell your Aunt Betty you sold the eggs before you got to the store."

She took the coin and with a sincere "Thank you," gently handed Risky to him. Then she took his extended hand to hoist herself up behind him.

"Hang on," he said, as he guided the horse with one hand and held Risky with the other.

His muscles were firm beneath her arms. *Must be a hard worker.* Maybe marriage wasn't such a dubious future. Especially if the lawyer thing didn't work out. It suddenly seemed a more attractive possibility. Father said a wise person collected evidence, weighed it, and made a decision. And Mother said a woman needed a mature man—a settled one, well able to provide for a wife.

Julie rode along quite contentedly as one tired pup snoozed in her champion's lap. Print talked easily of the times he'd spent with her father and Uncle John. He shared a recent adventure of rescuing an injured white longhorn calf he named Cotton from the banks of the San Simon River.

Print English captured Julie's interest, for sure. It might be all right to be a wife to such a man—especially after she persuaded him to get rid of that pistol.

He could be just the man for me. She considered her own checklist: *handsome—very handsome. Brave. Has a sense of humor—possibly a bit too much for my taste. Well, I can repair any shortcomings.*

Print English was a man to consider. She'd have to find out more about him from Aunt Betty and Uncle John. Just possibly God's intention for Julie's future had presented himself on this afternoon walk to San Simon City.

She dismissed from her mind the two ne'er-do-wells she'd encountered. *Probably never see them again.*

Chapter 2

"Juliet Booth Denton, indeed! That red hair matches her spirit," Print mused as he rode back to the store. "Have to tell Jonas about her. He's more her age. Not many like her out here. If I were a year or two younger and looking for a wife, nothing would stop me."

No time for that kind of thinking now. He was twenty-two. If the English family was going to make the Reverse E ranch the biggest ranch in Texas, he didn't have time for anything but gathering longhorns. Marriage would have to wait.

Everything depended on the war. Father and Julie's uncle, John Denton, didn't see any way a war could be avoided with the way things were going in Washington. Why couldn't politicians leave things alone? Each state should be deciding what was right for its citizens, not a bunch of politicians far away from real life.

John Denton said railroad barons were the hidden actors behind the scenes. They needed a central government to work with—too expensive to deal with individual states. The slavery issue had presented a perfect front. Most rational people were against slavery these days, including the English and Denton families.

He'd never held any truck with it. Aunt Maizie would have thumped that idea out of him before he could walk. Her philosophy of child-rearing was a generous helping of unswerving devotion and a kick in the seat of the pants when she thought one was needed.

"A free woman of color," he said aloud, with a laugh. "Unmarried and uninterested. That's my Aunt Maizie."

She'd grown up with Mother in a preacher's home in Georgia, two orphaned girls rescued by a godly couple. Maizie and Louisa English were as close as any two women could be, given their differences in makeup and their stations in life.

Aunt Maizie had even adopted the English name as her own and gone with Mother and Father after they'd married, grumbling every step of the way that Jacob English had a fiddle foot and would never settle. Print grinned, thinking of the story Mother liked to tell about Maizie moving to Texas with the family in the 1850s.

"Louisa," she'd said, "that man of yours is gonna' cost me my hair. Texas means wild Indians and more hard work than the law should allow. Only reason I'm going is the promise of a cabin of my own."

Aunt Maizie now had her cabin in Texas, snuggled up near the larger one of the English family. She'd been right about the hard work and even skirmishes with wild Indians...

"Hey, Print," Conner English called. "I could see that cloud of red hair from here. How old is she?"

"Just right for Jonas. Fifteen, soon to be sixteen, and her hair is *auburn*, not red, she'll tell you. The niece of John and Betty Denton. A spirited young beauty. And, she'll have you know, polite people don't say things like *tootin'*."

Conner's eyebrows rose. He stared at Print a moment, then shook his head. Finally he said, "Jonas can pay a visit. Go after some eggs."

"Yeah. We always need eggs. As long as Aunt Maizie is around, the English family will have no chickens."

They laughed, remembering Maizie's complaints about messy, squawking birds.

Conner scratched his chin. "Why in the world would you say *tootin'* to a young thing like that? Father taught—"

Print frowned. *Don't need my brother questioning my manners.* "It just slipped out. Forget it. We should get these things to Maizie and Mother for dinner."

Soon be dinner time, and that meant the whole family around the table with Mother and Aunt Maizie setting out a feast. As usual, Print's best friend Frank Evans would be there, and Father would preside over the table with a prayer and lead a serious conversation.

Maybe there'd be a couple of Aunt Maizie's pecan pies. She'd planted one of the first pecan orchards in the county and was refining her product from a wild nut she'd picked up when they were still living in the covered wagon. She was a wonder.

As usual, the dinner conversation settled on the topic of war. Aunt Maizie's face was less than pleased. She'd have something to say before long.

"Oh, Jacob, do you really think it will come to

a blood-letting?" Mother's expression was stressed as she glanced at her husband. Then she turned to each of her four sons, love and worry showing in her dark eyes.

Print's chest tightened. Mother had been through enough hardship in her young days. Her Cherokee mother had died on the Trail of Tears, leaving a seven-year-old daughter. Mother had never known her French fur-trapper father. If that kindly Methodist preacher hadn't taken her home, Louisa English could not have become the wise and wonderful mother he loved.

Everyone waited for Father's answer. He never spoke in haste.

"I do, darling," he finally answered. "The division is not to be reconciled. Anyone who tries to see both versions of the issue, as we do, will be in danger from both sides. There's no right way in this thing except God's way, and no one's looking for that. Fortunes are at stake and men get crazy over money. If the people of Texas are smart, they won't see a need to get involved."

Frank shook his head. "The Yanks may need a lesson about mixing in our affairs. I'll fight 'em." He sat taller, a wry grin on his handsome face. Frank loved a good fight, usually after he'd had one too many nips from a whiskey bottle.

Print said, "I say leave it to the real cotton states. It's their war. Wasn't that why we left the Boot Heel of Missouri? You saw it coming. Cotton demands too many willing or unwilling hands, and brings more trouble than it's worth."

"East Texas has some big plantations, and the men who own them have a powerful voice," Father said. "Governor Sam Houston is firmly against war. He knows that both planters and their neighbors who own no slaves will be ruined in a war that favors the industrialized North."

Jonas, the quiet sixteen-year-old, said, "There'll be conscription. You won't have a choice about joining up. It's not our war, but Print and Con will have to fight. My heart murmur will probably keep me out."

Frank may have wanted to add something, but a glance at Louisa's and Maizie's faces kept him quiet.

"Land sakes, let's not even think about that," said Aunt Maizie. "No way I'm giving up any of you boys to fight a bunch of secessionists."

Dinner finished with more talk of war. As Aunt Maizie brought pecan pies and whipped cream to the table, she put her hands on her hips and declared, "This kind of talk makes my head hurt. Why don't you get your fiddle, Jacob? Frank didn't show up tonight to hear all this war malarkey. He and Print need some relaxation before they get back to the longhorn hunt in the mornin'."

"Yes, ma'am," said Frank. "I'm always game for a fine meal and a dance. Seems like I eat here more than I do at home. Don't ever tell Maw, but the food is better, too. I'm much obliged. Can't wait for a taste of that pie."

"You know you're always welcome, Frank," Mother said. "It's only fitting that we feed you. You've been roping longhorns with Print since you two were knee high to a grasshopper."

Hamilton, the youngest, piped up. "Can I go on the cow hunt tomorrow, Print? I'm more than ready."

"Not yet. Twelve is too young to start wrestling longhorns. But we'll practice with our pistols when I get back. Just a couple of days—no more than four—for this hunt, and I'll be home."

Print glanced at his mother, registering the disapproval in her expression. She didn't like pistols, but a man had to learn early how to take care of himself on the Texas frontier. Guns were on almost every man's hip. Ham would need the skill.

"How is your mother, Frank?"

"Always sickly, Miz English, but she does the best she can."

Maizie muttered, "An' without much help."

Print's lips thinned. Mr. Evans was a careless husband and father at best. And his other sons were worthless. They should have been gathering cattle and building their own fortunes. Instead, Tru was hanging out with Cully North and up to no good, as his encounter with Julie Denton showed. Buck was somewhat better, but he showed no interest in the home place.

Frank was different. A good friend, and the top man to have along on a cow hunt. *Hard- working and concerned about his mother.*

"I want to send some things home with you, Frank. It's what neighbors do."

"Thank you, Miz English."

Always being on the receiving end must stick in Frank's craw. He had his pride, and the shoddy antics of his father and Tru must shame him. The money Frank earned from the cow hunts went to his family, but most of it was probably spent on whiskey for his father. A frustrating set-up for a man.

"Who's ready for some music?" Maizie said as she held out a hand to Frank.

Print took his mother's hand and the square-dance began. The other three brothers formed their own group and followed Jacob's calls. Print's feet kept the rhythm, but his mind wandered.

Family is what it's all about. I might be overly

ambitious—never satisfied, Mother sometimes says—but it's all for family.

His reputation as one of the best cow-hunters, or *mavérickers*, as the old-timers called them, was a source of pride, hard-earned after years of practice. He'd been at it since before he was Ham's age, but he was stronger-built than his youngest brother. Ham's time would come.

"Enjoy yourself tonight," Frank said as he and Maizie sashayed to the middle of the square. "Tomorrow it's back to brush-popping, wrestling longhorns, and living on beef and corn dodgers."

"Tige has been whining at my heels," Print replied. "He's as ready as I am to get back to work."

A good catch dog was as necessary as a good horse. A few whistles were all Tige needed to single out a maverick and hold it by the nose until he or Frank could rope it.

Frank often said, "I think he can read brands."

Fifty cents a head, Frank's wage, was a generous chunk of the two-dollar sale price of a steer, but he would have helped without pay if asked. His harmonica and good singing voice helped pass time out under the stars.

Like another brother, but one I've never fully understood. There's a reserve in Frank. But I guess anyone could say the same of me.

Mother stopped mid-step and said, "I know you're a thoughtful man, son, but please get your mind off those longhorns, and back into the dance, or you'll have our square on the floor." Her smile made it obvious that she really did understand his preoccupation.

Everyone laughed, and Print managed a rueful grin. "You've got me. My mind did wander."

The best of the wild cattle that roamed San

Simon County were destined to bear the brand of the Reverse E. Print didn't appreciate any other rancher beating him to a good one, but he was careful to take only *slicks*, the unbranded ones.

Others in the area didn't share his outlook. On unfenced ranges he'd found more than one cowhide with the English brand on its hip, left by a poacher who wanted the meat. Father wouldn't talk about retaliation.

"Cattle are numerous and the poaching is small," Jacob said last week when Print complained about a loss. "Some men love the taste of another man's beef. Amassing wealth is only one thing we're cut out for, Print. Another is getting along with our neighbors, even if they are somewhat lax in their views of ownership."

Print suspected one of the beef-loving neighbors was Frank's father. When the place was really his, he'd put a stop to the rustling.

The dancers paused for a rest and some of Maizie's good apple cider. Print brought glasses for Mother and himself. Ham joined them, his features settled in a pout.

"Mother, can't you make Print and Frank let me go with them tomorrow?"

Print laughed and reached out a hand to tousle Ham's close-cropped, wavy light-colored hair. "I'm too old for a paddling, baby brother. Might be hard for anyone to make me do something I don't believe is a good idea."

"I'm not a baby. I'm half-grown and ready to do some cow catching."

Frank joined them. "Ham, your day's coming. When you're out there eating dust and too tired to crawl down out of the saddle, I'm going to remind you how eager you were."

"Aw, Frank. All I want is a chance to show y'all what I can do. I'm almost as good with a pistol as Print. Isn't that right?"

"You're good. A natural shot," Print said. "One day before long, you'll be better than me."

Louisa sighed. "You book-ends," she said, nodding to Print and Ham, the oldest and the youngest. "You two are the cause of my camel's knees."

She claimed her knees had roughened in the long periods she spent kneeling before God, seeking wisdom for her sons. Print could leave the praying to Mother and Aunt Maizie, bless their faithful souls. He'd probably been the recipient of a few minor miracles because of their prayers.

Chapter 3

A couple of days after Print returned from the cow hunt, he herded his brothers into the bedroom.

Louisa followed.

"Why aren't you boys at school?" She stood glaring, hands on her hips. "You can't afford to miss an opportunity to learn from books."

Sixteen-year-old Jonas had been begging to leave school for full-time work, saying he'd learned what he could from the San Simon country school. He was of age, and Jacob was considering the proposal. Jonas was interested in reading law. Attorney Truly in San Simon City had offered a position, when he was ready. But both Ham and Jonas had been sent to school today.

Print handed her a note as they watched the boys change into work clothes. "They found it nailed to the schoolroom door."

Louisa read aloud to Maizie, who stood in the doorway: *I have become heartily tired of my job and decided to wander around some.*

She rolled her eyes. "Another school master into the wind. Took what was left of the tuition money, likely as not."

Schooling was never a certain affair in San Simon County. The boys attended as they could, but depended upon Jacob to fill gaps in their learning provided by the small school that met in the Crossroads Chapel. The four-mile ride to the bigger school in San Simon City wasn't practical.

Louisa caught Hamilton's face in her hand as he tried to follow Print.

"Another black eye. I talk patience, Maizie, till I'm blue in the face, but I don't mention turning the other cheek. I know they won't hold still for that."

Conner said, "There are always school bullies. A guy can't back down."

"That'd be a waste of fruitless effort," agreed Maizie, putting her own twist on the maxim. "These boys are scrappers and they hang together. It won't take many more lessons from the English brothers till the toughs decide to hunt elsewhere for someone to pick on."

The women watched the young men climb the hill, Ham one step behind his idolized eldest brother. They were moving Print's belongings from the main house to his new cabin.

"I worry about Ham's attitude, Maizie—too many schoolyard scraps. I know I indulge him more than the others, but he has a troubled soul. Print is closer to him than I am, and I don't agree with the direction he's taking Ham."

Hamilton was impatient with the counsel of his father and said Louisa treated him like a baby. He chafed at being the youngest, thinking Con and Jonas took advantage of him, and turned to Print as the arbiter in any dispute.

"Print gives him too much leeway," Louisa continued, "especially where guns are concerned. Ham tries to imitate Print's every move—most of all, his interest in longhorns and pistol practice."

She sighed and fell silent for a moment. "He's obsessed with that pistol. You've heard him claim he'll be the best gun-handler in the family within another year. Wisely, Print keeps that revolver under lock and key until he's ready to practice with Ham."

"Don't worry about Ham, Louisa. He'll grow up with his father's good sense and Print's skills. Print is a born stockman. He seems glued to a horse when he's closing in on a longhorn. Ham will learn from him, and one day they won't need pistols in this country."

Louisa nodded hopefully. "Print found his dream on his first cattle drive, the year he was fifteen."

"I remember," said Maizie. "He came home unable to talk about much else."

Louisa smiled. "I think Jacob is right when he says Print can think like a longhorn."

Dislodging three or four long-horned freedom fighters from their brushy defense might be considered a respectable day's work for any cow hunter, but her son was never content with less than five or six. There had been days when he brought seven or eight to the Reverse E brand.

"I look forward to the day Print can take over the cattle raising, and Jacob and I can concentrate on running the store," Louisa said. "It's almost finished—Jacob's dream. He'll be happy to turn over a demanding outdoor life to his sons and spend more time with me, his books, and puttering about the place, trying out his ideas for improvements."

"He has an inventive mind. Take that shower bath he and Print rigged up for the cabin," Maize said. "It's great for a man who doesn't mind cold water."

"If only war doesn't intervene."

"I can't think about it." Maizie appeared close to tears.

"Jacob hears men in the county talk about the war in positive terms. They seem to think the southern states should secede and form a nation of their own. See how the industrialized North gets along without the agricultural input of the South, they say. But not a single mother I know has expressed any enthusiasm for war."

"Women should be able to vote."

Finished...and it's all mine.

Print and his brothers carried his belongings inside the new cabin. Then they walked all the way around, searching for construction flaws on the outside, but found none. They'd done a good job. It was a one-room log structure with a good well on one side and a shower bath tacked onto the rear—a real bonus. The outdoor privy was close, but a safe distance from the well.

The house faced east under the brow of a hill about a quarter mile from the home place. Corrals, a large barn, and a granary were shared with his parents' headquarters home. This would be his first night in his own cabin. And the setting was just as pretty, with a big oak tree spreading its shade on the rear west side of the house, and smaller ones grouped a few hundred feet from the front step. One day he'd build a porch.

He needed the privacy. No one to tell him to go to bed instead of sitting into the wee hours writing and drawing in his journal. Planning took time and space to sketch out ideas that came to him. He meant to turn a county full of wild cattle into an empire. A realm erected on red gold, the beef supplied by the seemingly limitless longhorns thriving in the brush.

Print liked what his father said about the cattle. "They're not a breed, but a *kind*; rugged and self-reliant, like the men who seek them."

Conner said, "One of the cowboys is riding in, in a big hurry. We'd better meet him. Something's not right."

Print and his brothers sprinted down the hill to the corrals.

"What's up, Rodrigo?"

"Two poachers, Señor Print. They have a steer down, skinning him. I was alone, and I could see a rifle on the wagon seat, so I come *muy pronto*."

"Don't even think about sending me home," Ham said.

"No. You can come. Let's head over there." Print and his brothers soon were in the saddle, riding with Rodrigo to the scene of the theft.

"Uh, oh. I know that rig," Print said as soon as they came in sight of the rustlers. "It's Frank's father, Tom Evans. And he has Tru with him."

The English brothers surrounded the two men, who had the animal skinned and were loading the carcass into the wagon. Tom and Tru continued with the job, as cool as if it were an everyday affair.

Print dismounted and kicked at the abandoned cowhide. "Tom, that's a Reverse E steer." He picked the hide up and threw it up behind his saddle. *Worth a few cents.*

Tru suddenly grabbed for the rifle on the wagon seat, but Print's pistol covered him before he could reach it. Just then Jacob English and Frank Evans rode in and dismounted.

"Frank—" Print began.

"I spotted them, and caught Jacob coming from the post office. Intended to deal with them with Jacob's help."

"The Evans family have been our neighbors for a long time," Jacob cut in. "It'll take a while, before old-timers like Tom change their ways. Long-horned *cimarrones* have roamed the brush since the 1600s. In the old days, they were all there for the taking whenever a man needed meat for his family, and were considered game animals."

Print snorted. "That time is long gone, Father. Men in this county know not to kill anything wearing a brand, nor to brand any animal under a year old, and nothing following a branded cow. If we're ever to get ahead, we're going to have to hold onto what we have. Keep the cattle from scattering too far, show up at every cow hunt, and discourage rustlers in any way necessary—including a neighbor and the father of my best friend."

Jacob stood silent.

"Cow-hunting is hard work," Print continued, glaring at the poachers. "It took me hours in the brush, a rope, the nerve to use it, and a branding iron to add that young bull to our herd. Too much work for you, Tru?"

Tru sneered. "Not much of an animal."

Frank said, "I'll deal with him, Print. But my father can defend himself if he can think of an explanation for stealing your steer."

Tom Evans searched into his pocket and came up with a silver dollar. "I don't figger that steer is worth two dollars."

Print didn't move. His pistol was still pointed at Tom Evans' belly.

Jacob English reached out and took the coin.

"The matter is forgotten. A two-dollar steer is not worth alienating a long-time neighbor."

Print holstered his pistol. Blood rushed to his face and his hand shook. He narrowed his eyes, and stared into his father's face. "A silver dollar is not fair wages. I intend to defend what is mine." He took a step toward Jacob. "Do not," he said, spacing the words, "ask me to repeat this transaction—ever."

"I'll keep an eye on my father," Frank said. "If I suspect any more thieving, I'll take him on. I'm bigger than he is now, so he can't use his fists on me."

Frank spat in the dirt. "He's never been one for hard work—always tried the easy way to what he calls a good life. Mother has been shamed by him on more than one occasion. I've only stayed for her. As soon as I can, I'm clearing out."

Tom Evans turned his back on his son. He and Tru climbed into the wagon.

"Me and Cully'll be seein' you, Print. He says he owes you one," Tru growled.

Print rode in silence with his father and brothers. Dismounting, he tended his horse, then without a word strode up the hill to the new cabin.

Near the window he made his bed and watched Aunt Maizie working in her garden. His mood softened with memories of earlier years when he and Frank worked beside her, and she offered her philosophy of life.

Like the time they got ahold of some of Tom Evans' tobacco and smoked it, pretending to one another they enjoyed it. When they returned to Louisa, as sick as two kids could be, she was very concerned.

Maizie bent over Print, smelled his breath, and

laughed. The miserable miscreants were left to suffer on their own, outside in the porch chairs, where Maizie said they could throw up to their hearts' content.

Frank's voice had sounded weak. "Print, your ole' dog, Tige, can't smell any better than Maizie. If she can scent tobacco that easy, we'd better never take a drink anywhere near where she can wind it. She might skin us."

Print could only nod. He didn't feel up to real words yet.

Glasses of cold water were the only medication they received from Aunt Maizie's hand, but she cooked them a good meal of beefsteak when their miseries were over. Some lessons were learned the hard way, and tobacco misery was one of them.

For Frank's sake, Print hoped that Tom and Tru Evans had learned a lesson today. Reverse E cattle were not up for grabs.

One day open-range stock raising would be over. Fences were what a man needed to protect his animals. Father said some Frenchman had come up with the idea of steel wire with sharp edges or points arranged at intervals. The idea had merit if it could be made strong enough to hold in longhorns. Doubtful. Maybe Father would retire soon to run the store he was building at the crossroads and leave the cattle work to him.

He doesn't have the temperament for ranching.

A couple of hours later, Aunt Maizie knocked on Print's door, bearing a big basket. "Heard all of it from Ham. Louisa and I figgered you wouldn't feel like dinner and discussion with the family tonight."

Print gave her a hug and took the basket. Peeking under the cloth, he said, "Thanks, Aunt Maizie. You always understand."

She looked around. "Nice place. Wait till I wash down that table top, before you put the cloth on. You must have spent a lot of time polishing that hard mesquite wood. Smooth as glass. I like the way you left the natural edge."

Print spread the cloth, then began unpacking.

"Fried chicken? I thought you hated those birds." He hid a smile. She ate as much fried chicken as anyone when it was on the table.

She eyed him for a few seconds to see if he was teasing. "Betty Denton brought them already plucked. Now that's a welcome gift. I don't mind frying chicken, once it's cut up and disguised by a coating of flour."

"I've helped Mother scald chickens and pluck feathers. The smell of hot, wet feathers makes me agree with you. Chickens are more trouble than they're worth—till they're fried."

"You've always been a beefsteak man."

"But I can't wait to dig into this meal: chicken, mashed potatoes and gravy, and your boot-heel biscuits. A meal fit for a king."

"And," Aunt Maizie said proudly, "hot apple pie—a treat for a man on the first night in his very own house."

Print lifted her off the floor and whirled her around as she laughed. He set her down and kissed the top of her head.

"Mmm. Your cooking makes a man glad to be alive."

Chapter 4

On a blustery day in February 1861, Louisa looked up from her biscuit making. The expression on Jacob's face made her heart drop.

"Texas has officially voted to secede from the Union and stand with the Confederate States of America," he said.

Maizie's hand went to her throat.

Louisa's chest was caught in a vice. She said, "Conscription is sure to follow. Our sons will be drafted into service, fighting for a cause that's not theirs."

"I hoped we'd left that foolishness behind in Missouri," Jacob said. "In 1851, Texas offered wide open land. A man had room to build a dream without someone elbowing into his business. But what seemed like political nonsense back then is now national insanity."

Louisa could hardly speak. "A mindless blood-letting, where neighbors will be killing neighbors, sons shooting at fathers—it truly is insanity."

"I'm heartsick beyond tears," said Maizie. "How can we offer our boys to such? How will we go on?"

Louisa stripped the sticky dough from her fingers. "We'll do as we were taught, Maizie. We can't talk this way. Preacher Cravens stressed that rehearsing troubles makes you experience them before they occur. God will strengthen us when the time comes. We'll pray and trust in Him and the boys' good sense."

Jacob nodded. "Amen," he said. "Prayer, not panic, you always say. Thank God for your rock-solid faith. I've learned from you and Maizie. I was a doubter till you two took hold of me."

"And you've taught our sons. Print and Conner are as prepared to survive as any young men can be. 'Vision, character, and commitment'—the boys have heard the words often enough from you."

Jacob raked a hand through his hair. "They're strong men. Print, especially, has no patience with laziness or laxness of character—he'll make a good soldier. Perhaps he and Conner can stay together if they enroll before conscription."

Silence fell. War was so much bigger than anything they'd ever dealt with. Even Indian raids hadn't presented a threat such as they now faced.

"Print English is a gentleman," Maizie finally spoke up, "like his father." Her voice shook, then strengthened. "He learned from you, Jacob: watches his language, especially in the company of women. Immaculate, even in his work clothes, and the cabin is always neat."

Jacob appeared thoughtful. "Con still takes direction from Print, but he's also a fine young man. They'll keep to their convictions, wherever they are."

Louisa's heart suddenly lightened, listening to Jacob and Maizie talk about her sons' strengths.

"Print admits to one big vice. And you know what it is." Louisa grinned. "He enjoys indulging his Aunt Maizie. You and Frank are the only human beings who ever hear him sing."

Jacob nodded, seeming eager to join the small talk. "Maizie brings out the best in him."

"I can coax a song or two from him, sitting by the fire after one of my fried steak dinners," Maizie said. "It's always a song he sings to restless longhorns on cattle drives."

She ducked her head and grinned. "And he's the only one who's ever seen me smoke my long-stemmed pipe. Print never smoked again after that one disastrous experiment with Frank." They all laughed.

Louisa said, "You and Print are much alike. Fierce in your loyalties."

"Maybe so. With Print, the work comes first. He doesn't suffer fools any better than I do." Maizie thought for a moment. "Talking too much causes trouble, he says. But just one glimpse of him should tell people he means business."

"Hard to put your foot into a closed mouth," Jacob agreed. "I suppose he learned that at my knee. I was taught a creed: a man takes care of his own, stands up for his friends, right or wrong, and doesn't back down from a fight. He minds his own business and expects others to do the same."

Louisa's eyebrows drew together. "But Print has added a pistol to it. When a situation calls for stepping up, he thinks it's more than all right to pull a gun on someone who keeps on coming." Her voice caught. "And he's teaching Ham to feel the same."

"I know. You've softened my flinty outlook, and Conner's," Jacob said. "Con is every bit the man Print is, but without the hard edge." He scraped his hand over his mouth and down his chin. "I want our sons to be real men," he said with a sigh, "but not self-centered or short-sighted. Other men have a right to their pride."

Louisa nodded. "Print has yet to learn. He focuses on a single objective. In army life, he may step on the toes of some undisciplined man who'll do him harm."

Maizie said, "Print needs the right woman. Like most good-looking men, he recognizes his effect on females. Uses those melancholy eyes and that little grin to advantage. Saved him a few switchin's from me when he was young."

Louisa nodded. "He hasn't had many encounters with women. Frank is more the ladies' man."

"They both need godly wives," Maizie said.

Jacob said, "Women don't offer Print the challenge of longhorns. They're too willing to go along with his ideas. He'll take his time choosing someone to share his life, as he should."

Maizie said, "He's waiting for one like Louisa. Not too long ago when I was twitting him about bachelor life, he said, 'My woman will have to be as special as Mother. She has a mind of her own, but she knows just how to keep it in check. She's wise and beautiful and I won't settle for anyone less.' I told him he couldn't do better."

Jacob placed his hand atop Louisa's floury one on the table. "Print's plan is a good one, but I don't think he or any of us left room for a war that will smash dreams and destroy lives all across this nation. Patience and tolerance are dead. The war I feared and fled in Missouri has pursued us, and is now reaching out for our sons." His blue eyes sought Louisa's, then Maizie's. "Forget the biscuits for a bit and pray with me."

The next morning Print stood outside Louisa's kitchen on the back porch, finishing a cup of coffee with Conner before breakfast. The air was fresh with last night's rain shower. It should have been a time for rejoicing, but a black cloud enveloped his thoughts. *War.*

"Frank says he's joining up this week," Print said. "I told him we'd wait as long as we can. Every day means more longhorns wearing the Reverse E on their hips."

He took another sip of the hot, strong coffee he favored. "I think his decision has more to do with his father's faded hopes than any political persuasion. Frank never found his dream. He's given up on the idea of a ranch."

Print paused for another sip. "I've told him I'd be there for him, just as he has been for me, but he needs more than my occasional help. His father's pig farm isn't much of a stock operation for a man who's one of the best cow hunters in the county."

"Don't take this wrong," Conner said. "I know he's your best friend, but Frank's usually spoiling for a fight, so maybe he feels different about this war."

Print nodded, biting his bottom lip. "I agree with him that no one is going to take away what I've worked for, but I don't go hunting a fight."

"He drinks too much and he won't keep his mouth shut," Conner added. "You had to pull your pistol not long ago to cover his hot-headed gun play. He wounded that guy. I suspect his early enlistment is a way to avoid charges."

Print pulled at his ear. Con was right, but Frank was his friend. "His drinking bouts aren't frequent. He needs an occasional release from his miserable home life, but I worry he might get in over his head in army life."

"Mmm," said Conner, squinting. "Speaking of Tom Evans and his pigs—there's one of his boars cultivating Aunt Maizie's garden again."

Before the brothers could chase the animal away, the back door flew open, and Maizie came charging out, shotgun in her hand.

"Uh, oh. It's going to take some tall talking to dissuade her." Print said. "I'd say have at it, but Father won't want her to kill it."

Eventually, Maizie surrendered the gun after Print promised he would deliver the riot act to Tom Evans again.

"Go this morning. Tell him if I find another one, the English clan will dine on pork chops."

"Yes ma'am," said Print, smothering the grin that threatened to show. "And I'll help with the butchering."

At breakfast Louisa studied her sons. Her dark eyes had passed to all four. They had her coal-black hair and olive skin, except for Hamilton, whose complexion was more like that of Jacob. But Ham's blond hair was beginning to darken at the roots as he neared puberty. All stood erect as young pines, lean and magnificently muscled from constant activity.

The English brothers presented a united front on the ranges or on the streets. They didn't seek trouble, but they gave a strong impression they wouldn't run from it, either. Her chest felt like it wore a band of iron as talk turned to war again.

"I was talking to Fred Maher at the store today," Jacob said. "A good man. But I can't fathom his thinking. There in the hearing of his sons, he said he favored war. He's ready to leave the Union and return to local rule."

Print said, "He has a point. The federal government has failed to protect us from Indian attacks and cattle raids. But I can't believe war is the answer to convince the North of states' rights."

Hamilton said, "No Yankee should be telling us what it takes. They never saw a Comanche on the warpath, or a bunch of armed rustlers stealing a herd of cattle. I wish I were—"

"Enough, Ham. You don't mean what you were about to say. If there were any way I could avoid this war, I'd take it, even if it meant giving up my dream. How many good men will have to die?"

Louisa spoke, heartbreak in her voice, "Please don't say anything more. I can't bear it."

"Sorry, Mother. I spoke without thinking."

Jacob said, "We've been in this county almost since settlement began. And we have as much to lose as any plantation owner. We started out crowded into the covered wagon that brought us from Missouri. It was a while before we were able to get a cabin erected and longer still until we could enlarge it enough to be comfortable."

"And build mine," Maizie said. "You and Louisa took some bullying over the years about allowing a black woman to sit at your table, but you've never backed down from God's Word and the Golden Rule. I'm still praying the issue can be settled without war."

"We mustn't give up hope, Maizie, but we'll have to live with the decisions of godless men," Jacob said. "As Print says, let's keep going for as long as we can."

"And that calls for cinnamon rolls and another cup of coffee," Maizie said, rising from the table.

"Amen," said Conner. "I can't think of an occasion that doesn't."

May 1862

There had been no word from Frank for almost a year. Presumably he was off fighting the nosy Yankees he resented. Conner marched beside Print down the main street of San Simon City. Ten of the finest young men of the county followed behind a uniformed military recruiter whose flag boot held an eight-foot pole and a Confederate flag. Men cheered and women wept as their loved ones paraded to war.

"We'll be back, Con. Now that the conscription law has passed, we're better off enlisting, no matter what we believe about this war. We'll be able to stick together and watch out for each other. In the meantime, Father can help the boys add smaller animals to the ranch."

Chapter 5

Julie Denton's entire body trembled as she listened to her beloved twenty-three-year-old brother. His plan sounded hare-brained and very dangerous.

Surely Father could talk him out of it.

Bert said, "We have no choice, Father, now that the county conscription board has formed. I have to take a stand. I can't take up arms against men who defend what I believe in."

"Oh, Bert," Julie moaned.

He reached out and patted her shoulder. "I'm not alone." Watching the faces around him, he added, "Eight of us will leave the state together and travel north to join Union troops."

Mother held onto Bert's arm as if she'd never let him go. She shook her head, her pale face distressed beyond anything Julie had seen.

"Men of reason can reach a peaceable solution to any problem. We must stand firm. Common sense will eventually prevail." Albert Denton used his lawyer's voice, steady and assured.

"I'm not so sure," Bert said. "Your men of reason lynched that Methodist minister and several slaves last month. Said the preacher was fomenting a slave rebellion and blamed him for those disastrous fires in the city. Claimed he was an abolitionist seeking to profit from breaking down the slave order."

Mother pleaded, "Albert, make him see reason. He cannot be out there among those wild-eyed men spouting secession. He'll be killed."

"She's right," Father said. "Confederate patrols roam the countryside spoiling for a fight. In this county it'll be impossible to keep your plan secret. If the wrong man gets wind of it, you and your friends face a kangaroo trial that the Home Guard calls a court martial. You could be lynched."

"We know all about the patrols, Father. We'll stay well hidden in daylight. Make a cold camp and cross the Red River under cover of darkness. We won't be caught."

"The Home Guard will pay no attention to boundaries. If they get on your trail, they'll follow till they catch you."

"My mind is made up. It's the right thing to do. We'll leave in three days. Meantime you can help me gather the equipment I'll need. I need to know you're backing me."

His brow now furrowed, Father nodded. "At least the Red River should have its normal flow by then. But you'll have to watch out for quicksand, so scout your route before you try to cross at night. If I can't dissuade you, I will do all I can to ensure your success. Let's join in prayer."

Mother's sobs almost drowned Father's words. Bert's arm was around her and he kissed the top of her head. Julie's heart was a stone within her chest.

Not Bert! How could rational men become

caught up in the senselessness of war? Bert seemed eager to go. Did he see it as an adventure?

An anxious two weeks dragged by with no news. Then one day in mid-July, an ashen-faced Albert Denton returned from his office in the middle of the morning. In a quavering voice, he delivered the details of what he had just learned from the county sheriff. An itinerant peddler had reported a grisly discovery in some woods near the Red River.

"He found a campsite," said Julie's father, "and the remains of several bodies. The sheriff believes they may be our young patriots."

Julie's mother fainted. When she revived, she begged, "Albert, go to the site. See for yourself. I can't believe Bert suffered such a fate. He's too intelligent to have been caught unaware."

"I agree. Some frightening rumors abound in times like this. I'll contact some of the other fathers to go with me. We need to see for ourselves."

Julie's father and four others journeyed to the wild, brushy site near the river. After three days, Albert Denton returned home. His gray face and his eyes mirrored the horror of what he'd found.

"The ravaged remains we found could only be identified by the personal effects scattered about. We buried the boys on a knoll overlooking the river and raised a stone over the single grave containing all that was left of our eight young idealists." His shoulders sagged. "Later, when it's safe, I'll bring Bert home and see to a proper memorial." Without even a glance in his wife's direction, he shuffled into his office and shut the door.

Mother collapsed. Julie pounded on the office door until Father peered out. The curtains were closed and the room was darkened behind him. When he caught sight of his unconscious wife, he mustered up strength to move her. He lifted her into his arms and wept into her hair.

It took Julie and their beloved maid, Annie, to settle Mother into bed. A nerve pill and warm milk had a calming effect, and Julie clung to her mother's hand until she slept. Father raised his head from across the bed where he had been praying. "I need some time alone, Julie." He stood and moved on wooden legs back into his office.

"I'll take him some coffee and sandwiches," Annie said.

"Wait a bit. He's too disturbed to think of food. I'm afraid of what this blow will do to his health. He came to Texas seeking relief from tuberculosis that plagued his lungs in Virginia."

"He's never sick now, Miz Julie."

Julie brushed back a wisp of hair from her mother's lovely face. "But the pressure on him was already intense from Mother's family. Grandfather Easton is a very influential man. He backed my father in establishing his own law practice years ago."

"'Scuse me, Miz Julie, but your Grandfather Easton and his sons ain't been exactly friendly with your father for years."

"Even before Secession was declared, they turned away. To a man, they favor the Confederacy. Father and Mother's friends have deserted them, except for a faithful few. I think they're afraid to be seen in the company of a Unionist."

"Well I won't leave you, Miz Julie. Not ever. Unless you pick up and move. I can't leave my grandbabies."

"Of course not, Annie. But we mean to stay here. Father believes it will be a short war. Secessionists will soon be overwhelmed by the stronger forces of the North." Julie suddenly dropped her face into her hands and cried as if she could never stop.

"I wondered when you'd finally break," Annie said, patting her head. "You're a strong woman, Miz Julie. We'll be all right."

Denton, Texas
August 30, 1862

Dearest Aunt Betty and Uncle John,

In my last letter I told you of Father's illness. It is worsening. Bert's death has taken away his will to live, and Mother appears helpless in the face of his withdrawal, unable to fight her own battle with grief and hopelessness.

Father's health has not once been an issue in all his years in Texas until now. His entire being, physical, mental, and spiritual, has faltered from the incomprehensible cruelty of Bert's death. Even his strong faith has crumbled.

"Where was God," he asked me, "on the night a noose strangled the life from Bert, a young man who loved the Lord?"

He refuses to talk about his feelings to anyone, even Mother. I'm not sure she could handle it, as lost as she is in her own grief. She sits at his side, staring silently at something that I cannot see. Her appetite is no better than Father's. Annie says it is a black depression that has seized them.

Father has become a pale shadow of the man who was such a vital force in the city—the strong figure who encouraged a venturesome spirit in me and Bert. Just yesterday he said to me as I was tying on my bonnet to go to church, "Don't leave the house, Julie.

Only the rough element of men will be on the streets. All the good ones have gone to die in this hated war." I have to sneak out to spare him worry.

He frets about his business, but cannot marshal the strength to go to the office or to interact with the few concerned friends who come to call. Father and Mother both seem to welcome the illness that has come upon them. I fear Mother will be bedridden within a matter of weeks.

Here a tear blotted the page and Julie recopied the last word.

...weeks. I long for the days of her pronouncing rules for proper conduct. My beautiful mother has lost interest in rules and everything else. She is wasting away before my eyes. I don't know what to do.

If Uncle John can spare you, Aunt Betty, I need you so much.

Lovingly,
Your niece,
Julie

Julie posted the letter, but it might be weeks before she heard anything from Aunt Betty and Uncle John. Annie was both her ally and opponent. Concerned and helpful, Annie had decided ideas about where Julie should find support in caring for her parents.

"Child, you need to demand help from your grandfather and your selfish uncles—that's what you should do. No matter what the Easton men think about secession, they're your mother's family. They owe you some help."

"I don't want them in the house; they'd upset Father. I've written to Aunt Betty and Uncle John."

Annie muttered and shook her head. The doctor came and went, trying one remedy after another, but nothing made a difference. Julie had her bed brought downstairs into the parlor to be nearer her parents' bedroom. Nights were not much different from days: endless trips carrying food, drink, and medications that went mostly untouched.

Within two weeks John Denton arrived with his wife. Distressed by the state of affairs in his brother's house, he said to Betty, out of Julie's hearing, "I can hardly take in what we see. Nothing seems to interest either Albert or Caroline—not even the plight of their remaining child."

Betty's hand covered her mouth. "I know. It's so troubling." Tears glistened.

John sighed. "I'll stay as long as I can, darling, but I can't leave the farm for more than a few days. Not with those ruffians over-running San Simon County."

"Of course, John. Albert will understand. The main thing is that I'm here for Julie. She is nearly out of her mind with worry, with no time to think about herself. Her every waking moment is taken up with nursing two beloved sick people." Betty reached for her husband's hand. "She's given little thought to what will happen to her if—no, when—her parents die. It's obvious to all but Julie that they will not live to see a new year."

"I'll return to you as soon as I can find someone to oversee the farm."

After the burial of Julie's father in late September, Julie's mother never spoke again before her own death three weeks later. John had returned to Paris before the funerals to address his anxiety. Betty and Julie's needs overrode worrying about his property.

Anti-unionist sympathy had reached fever-pitch in North Texas. Forty men were hanged in neighboring Cook County by a quasi-military court. Julie and Betty were not safe in the house of an outspoken abolitionist, even though Albert was dead.

Fear and revenge had become a contagion, and lawless men gathered in bands along the Red River, preying on travelers and outlying farms. Any suspicion of Union sympathy was enough for the bush-whackers to lynch a man. No telling what they would do to a young woman.

After her mother's funeral, Julie sat in Albert's office with John and Betty, seeming too drained to speak. John rose from the desk where he had been examining his brother's will and allowed a gentle smile to touch his lips.

"Julie, girl, your father left you a sizable sum of money, although the war will have devalued his assets considerably. It will be enough to enable you to pursue an education if that's what you want. Right now, however, your Aunt Betty and I want you to make your home with us. Leave this house for a time and come to us. Later you can decide what to do with it."

He didn't mention his apprehension at Julie living on her own in Lamar County, even with her mother's relatives nearby. Fear shouldn't be Julie's motive for coming under his protection. He and Betty loved Julie as a daughter. She would bless their lives in far greater measure than they could do for her.

He had to protect what trusting innocence remained in the mind of a young woman who acted with such fortitude and bravery in circumstances that broke the sanity of her parents. God was still in control, even if Albert and Carrie had given in to despair. Julie needed to keep her faith strong and sense the shield of the loving arms of God. He and Betty could help her.

Julie thought of the spacious, beautifully furnished house. It was now empty of the life that had made it home. She met Uncle John's gaze steadily enough, and in a small voice she hardly recognized said, "I think I'll do that, Uncle John. I seem to have lost any ability to act with success. I honestly believed I could force Mother and Father to get well, but I was not enough. They missed Bert too much."

"No, Julie, it wasn't how much they missed him. The shock of the circumstances of his death was too much for them to bear. I think the bitterness of losing a son in such a manner overwhelmed both of them. You know how much your parents loved you. They would want you to build a good life for yourself. They encouraged your choices. To come to us is a good one. We want you."

Aunt Betty rose and pulled Julie to her feet and into her arms. She stroked Julie's hair back, whispering, "Precious one, we not only want you, we need you. We were never blessed with children. We must keep the connection to your dear parents and to know that we can do something important for the daughter they treasured. Let us love you, darling."

Julie sobbed brokenly. John came from around the desk and embraced both women.

"Come to us, sweetheart, and let some joy seep back into your life. You can't believe it right now, but you will laugh again, and we want to be there to see it. We'll have a good life together in San Simon County."

Chapter 6

Julie stood on the front porch of Uncle John's farmhouse staring at a wintry countryside as bleak as her thoughts: claw-fingered trees, black against a sullen sky, and brown earth with barren ridges and furrows stretching into the mist. It had taken several months to settle affairs in Paris, but she was in San Simon County to stay.

If only time could be reversed and God would give her a second chance. Make it possible for her to return to happy days of earlier visits. She'd never be impatient with Mother or Bert again.

She spotted the old pear tree near the fence on the lane. Now bare of its foliage, it gave no hint of its summer perfection as a leafy retreat. She had spent hours reading, propped snugly in its branches, savoring many a juicy pear.

She replayed the adventure on the road to San Simon City when she first saw Print English. How many times had she done that? His actions and his words had become a cherished memory.

Over time, he'd become in her mind the man she would marry. There was no maybe now. Print English was the man for her. She'd met others—some handsome and wealthy, some charming—but no other man measured up. Print's brave stand on her behalf; his generous payment for a basket of broken eggs; his wicked little smile and dark, melancholy eyes that melted her resistance and caused her to trust him with an injured puppy and to climb up behind him for a safe ride home—all added up to form the character she wanted in a mate.

The bright world that lay at her feet on the spring day in 1860, when she met Print, appeared shockingly different two and a half years later. She was here, but he was on some distant battlefield, according to Uncle John. Her parents and Bert were dead. Print might die, too, in this hated war.

Stop it. Useless, destructive thoughts.

Julie shivered, acutely conscious of how cold she'd become in the early morning chill. She turned to go into her newly settled bedroom that looked out onto the porch. Her bed and wardrobe from the big house in Paris were in place, along with the small grandmother's clock that had ticked in the hallway.

A knock at the door and Aunt Betty entered. She added a log to the fireplace. "We need to brighten this space. I found some fabric that will work for new curtains," she said, holding it up to the wall. "And we can tie a rag rug for the floor near your bed. As the weather warms, we'll plant flowers outside your window in the box John made."

"My room is already lovely, Aunt Betty, but I'll help you sew and tie and plant. Staying busy helps my attitude. I must thank Uncle John for hanging portraits of Mother and Father and Bert on the walls."

"As soon as John finishes his chores, we'll go to

Mr. Bowden's mercantile store. We can trade some eggs for a new lamp for your bedside table."

At the foot of the bed Uncle John had placed the trunk containing most of Julie's treasures: her journal, her drawings and notebook of poetry, Father's Bible, linens embroidered by her mother's hand, and Bert's violin. Her mother's wedding dress hung in Julie's spacious wardrobe and two of her mother's favorite hats rested on its deep shelf.

The kindness of Uncle John and Aunt Betty was welcome, but there were times when grief would not be denied. That evening after dinner when Uncle John found her sitting in the swing, crying, he sat beside her.

Julie burst out, "How could God allow all this to happen? The war; young men dying; Father and Bert and Mother?"

He didn't answer immediately, and she hung her head. "I'm sorry, Uncle John. I know I shouldn't talk this way."

"It's natural, seeking to blame your grief on someone. God is big enough to listen to your anger, but you're asking the wrong questions, darling. What we need to seek is what God will do with the changes. He has a plan for your life, and we'll help you find it."

Uncle John's arms surrounded her. As she sobbed her frustration into his chest, his deep voice rumbled in her ear. "God's heart grieves with yours. His were the first tears that fell, precious girl. His cloak of mercy surrounds you, and He waits for you to allow His healing to begin."

In the months that followed, Julie discovered Uncle John and Aunt Betty were right—she learned to laugh. They saw to it that she had time to herself when she wanted it, but were constantly beside her when she did not, filled with ideas and invitations.

There were chores aplenty for the three of them on the farm; company often called; and it seemed they were inside the Methodist chapel near the Crossroads Community every time the doors opened. Julie told Aunt Betty, "I've found a friend in Charlotte Emory. She's only a year older."

"A pretty blonde. I like her, too. I think she's sweet on Conner English. It's sad that young men are so scarce, but most of them are serving military enlistments. What do you think of the two youngest English boys?"

"I like Jonas. He looks like Print. Ham is another matter, with his cocky, challenging manner."

"His mother, Louisa, says he's a subject for constant prayer."

Julie came to love the small, cozy Crossroads Methodist Chapel, so different from the formal Presbyterian church she'd attended in Paris. Women spread quilts on the splintery homemade pews, and lay others on the floor for sleeping babies. Occasionally, a wiggly older brother or sister stepped on a hand or foot and a loud wail interrupted the sermon.

The weather warmed, and one Sunday in May, Julie helped Aunt Betty prepare for an all-day singing at the chapel. Families would remain after church and enjoy "dinner on the ground."

"Help us, John," Aunt Betty said. "That basket is ready to go to the buggy. Be careful—three pies. Julie made the apple filling. Then come back for the one that has the fried chicken, ham, and cornbread."

When they arrived, Julie was surprised to see a milk cow tethered nearby. Children could have fresh milk, she supposed.

After the sermon, everyone went outside. A lengthy and heartfelt blessing was voiced as hungry children squirmed and whispered. Then everyone loaded up a plate.

When the meal was cleared away, the congregation sought the shade of the large oak grove, which also held the graveyard. Voices lifted praises in familiar hymns and Julie's clear soprano joined with Jonas English's tenor in a duet.

"I just wish Print and Conner could have heard you two," Louisa English said to Julie later. "Print will never sing alone."

Aunt Maizie laughed. "He sings for me. I'll bet he'd sing for someone as pretty as you, Julie."

Horrors. Julie felt her ears grow pink. Just the sound of Print's name did things to her. A woman of almost nineteen should be able to control herself.

"Have John bring you and Betty out to the ranch to visit one day soon," Louisa said. "Maizie and I are always ready for company."

"Thank you, Mrs. English," Julie replied. She wanted to get to know Print's parents and family. Maizie seemed like someone she could trust with questions. "Uncle John may allow me to drive the buggy. He's been giving me lessons."

Uncle John was a reader with a wide range of interests, just as Father had been. She and Aunt Betty furnished an appreciative audience as he read from scripture, or from Shakespeare or other books that lined the shelves of the parlor. If she closed her eyes, she could believe his deep, comforting voice was Father's.

Surprising how easily Julie recalled earlier lessons on the small pump organ in the parlor. Uncle

John accompanied on his fiddle and Aunt Betty's soprano lifted with Julie's own as the three joined in hymns.

The wise and nurturing love of her parents also existed in John and Betty. No Bert to complete her new life, but Uncle John encouraged her fishing skills. He took Julie on jaunts through the countryside, cautioning her never to go alone.

"There's a rough and unprincipled element in this county, now that so many good men have gone to war." He said they were thieves. "The county is in turmoil. My age keeps me from being drafted, but I have to keep a tight lid on my Unionist sympathies around other ranchers, except Jacob English."

"Do you have any news from the English boys, Uncle John? I was hesitant to ask Louisa when she spoke of them."

Amusement and disapproval warred in Uncle John's expression. "You mean Print English. He's been in Arkansas and is now in Louisiana, according to his letters. Conner is in the same unit. Letters to their parents are infrequent and don't tell much of what life is like fighting an unwanted war."

Julie was hungry for any words about Print. "What else, Uncle John?"

"Their ability with horses has them in a mounted cavalry unit. According to Print, that's far better than marching miles and miles."

Far from home, tired and probably hungry. Print wouldn't be frightened. Not the Print she remembered. He was so brave.

"Old man Tom Evans, the father of Print's friend Frank, managed a year ago to organize a unit of Home Guard troops in the county. He made up some nonsense about medical disabilities and drafted his married son, Buck, and youngest son, Truman, along with Cully North, a cousin to his boys. By serving in the Home Guard, they stay out of military service." Uncle John's grimace left no doubt what he thought about that fact.

"I met Cully and Tru, if you remember, and not in very pleasant circumstances. That's when I met Print, too; he came to my rescue."

"I seem to have heard that story more than once," he said, smiling. "But you should be forewarned. Print English is not an easy man to understand. He's ambitious and stubborn. I like him, but I'm not sure he's someone you need to be thinking about."

Julie said no more—at the time.

One day Cully knocked on the kitchen door and demanded eggs for the Home Guard unit. Aunt Betty sent a small basket with him and said, "Cully's manners are woefully wanting. That young man did not even thank me. I'm under no obligation to provide food for his unit."

"I don't really understand about the Home Guard. Why would Cully expect you to provide eggs for them?" Julie asked.

"The Home Guard unit in each county is supposed to protect residents from Indian raids and outlaws, who have increased in the absence of good men. But they can't legally requisition supplies like a regular army. The Guard also conscripts enlistees and patrols the county for deserters."

Returning from town, Uncle John heard Aunt Betty's last words. His expression troubled, he added, "As the war wears on, desertions increase. The hills and brushy ravines of San Simon County have become a hideout for disillusioned young men who thought the war would be a lark."

"They must live in fear," Julie said, "hunted by lawmen and the Home Guard."

John nodded. "A bad element is among them, causing problems for law-abiding citizens. The bad ones corrupt younger and better men. Outlaws have recruited deserters into thieving bands. Ranchers suffer losses almost every day."

He said law enforcement seemed unable to do much about the lawless element that gathered in a wild area known as The Bend—a rough, sparsely populated country in a deep bend of the Colorado River in the southern part of the county. "Men from The Bend are well-organized, able to move cattle and horses at will, according to Jacob English, without interference from our aging Sheriff Longworth and his single, near-sighted deputy. Jacob won't allow Jonas or Ham to try to protect their herd. Not worth the risk to their lives."

Julie said, "I don't think Print would allow rustlers free reign if he were here."

Aunt Betty's brow furrowed. "John, I hope local men don't take the law into their own hands. We saw that in Missouri. What about our Home Guard? Can't they do something?"

Uncle John's lips thinned. "The prime function of the Home Guard in San Simon County seems to be harassment of law-abiding citizens or fueling up at the saloon. With a drink or two under their belts, they become quarrelsome nuisances."

Julie shuddered. "I hope I don't see Cully again. I found him frightening."

She had not told either Uncle John or Aunt Betty that she *had* seen Cully again. He and Tru rode up last week as Julie watered flowers along the front walk. Cully slid off his horse, sweeping his hat from his head into a deep, mocking bow. The now-grown Risky barked furiously. Julie turned on her heel toward the house as Cully and Tru guffawed.

As he remounted, Cully called out to Julie's retreating figure, "Say, your ladyship, heard anything from your hero, *Prince* English? Or do you suppose the Yankees got him?"

Julie didn't answer, but it pained her to think of how little she actually knew about the well-being of Print. The day seemed long ago when a brave young man came to her rescue.

She remembered a handsome face, but she also remembered his concern for a skinny girl, as she thought of herself back then. He took on two men wearing guns, and showed no fear or tact in what he said to them.

He was a man now—five or six years older than her eighteen, and a force to be reckoned with, according to Uncle John.

Nothing will discourage me. I'll marry Print; but first I'll have to see him again.

Chapter 7

Julie yearned for news of Print. Uncle John said the capture of the Mississippi River by Union forces in mid-summer had dealt a fatal blow to the Confederacy. Worrying news.

But Print would find a way to stay alive. He wasn't afraid of anything, and surely if a man could keep his wits about him, he could evade a bullet.

Her friendship with Louisa—Mrs. English insisted on first names—and Maizie brought comfort. She occasionally saw Print's brothers. They weren't always with their parents at church. Uncle John said Jacob English believed it was right for the boys to make their own choices about when to attend church as they neared manhood.

Fifteen-year-old Hamilton English was an enigma, a reserved young man who seemed to be developing a bad attitude toward life. He sometimes wore a pistol in public. His attitude would surely cause trouble if he didn't mend his ways.

"The boy needs Print's strong hand," Uncle

John said. "Print is his idol. He'll take Ham in hand when he gets home."

At nineteen, Jonas was a younger version of Print in appearance, but in temperament, more like his father. Quick to laugh and a reader like Jacob, Uncle John said Jonas was now studying law with Mr. Truly. The young women of the county paid attention to him.

His occasional visits to the farm, when he brought some fresh-baked goodness from Maizie and Louisa, were welcomed. Jacob English sometimes sent a bag of real coffee from his store, which was now thriving.

But what of Print? Would he remember her when he saw her once again?

One early afternoon, Jonas and Julie sat in the swing on the front porch. Julie stared out from beneath the long-skirted elms in the yard to the corn field and beyond, to hills that joined, overlapped, and rolled together. The sky throbbed with clear sunlight and Julie's spirit sang.

She sneaked a sideways peek at Jonas. Was he affected by the afternoon's beauty? He yawned, and she sighed. *Boys! No appreciation for finer things.* They practiced a hymn for church and then Julie tried to bring the conversation around to Print.

"What do you hear from Print and Connery?"

"Not much. They don't write often. Wish I could be with them. A lot more exciting than punching cattle and reading law. If the war lasts another year—"

"Do they have girlfriends to come home to?"

"Heck, Julie, I don't know. As I was saying—"

"It just seems so unfair that Print's dream of building a big cattle ranch was interrupted. He's bound to need a wife to help him, don't you think?"

"Prob'ly. C'mon, let's play with Risky."

Julie found herself alone in the swing watching Risky fetch a stick for Jonas.

Boys my age can't concentrate on an important topic for more than two minutes. That's why I need an older man, like Print.

One day Uncle John handed Julie the reins to drive four miles to the English ranch headquarters. They brought a basket of eggs and two chickens, plucked and ready for roasting. Uncle John left Julie at the ranch house while he visited at the Crossroads store with his friend Jacob.

As Louisa and Maizie talked candidly of Print's strengths and failings, Julie's feelings for him strengthened. He truly was the man of her dreams: a good heart; a hard-worker; loyal and devoted to his family. She could even sympathize with his headstrong ambitions.

He wanted the biggest ranch in Texas and she could help him get it. She would work beside him. Before she left, she, Louisa, and Maizie prayed for Print and Conner and for all the men and their families caught up in war.

If only she could write letters to Print, but it seemed too forward to ask. After all, she couldn't be sure he even remembered her. Or what he would remember. Her cheeks burned at the thought of the rock business.

"I really like Louisa," Julie said to Aunt Betty when they returned home "She's a plain-spoken woman of great kindness and wisdom."

"And she and Maizie are smitten with you, Julie. They enjoy your visits."

"Louisa voiced an unflattering opinion of several young men of the county, including Truman Evans and Cully North. She said old man Evans is still helping himself occasionally to their branded cattle, and Jacob English suspects Tru and Cully are up to worse than that."

Julie felt her cheeks heat. "I probably shouldn't repeat her speculations, but I may as well finish. She said someone robbed the store one night a couple of weeks ago. Not finding money on the premises, they did some damage to the place and stole wheat flour, coffee, and other staples."

"Please don't mention that to Jonas. Louisa wouldn't want the boys to take up the matter. Our sheriff is old and over-worked. Each family must take care of their own property and personal safety."

"We certainly can't count on the brave Home Guard," said Julie.

Uncle John said Texas fared better than other Southern states because prolonged fighting did not take place on its soil, but he admitted that conditions in the state had deteriorated seriously. He said able-bodied men were in service with either the army or the Home Guard, and their families had to endure their absence.

"The drought has made things worse for us. Almost two years without normal rainfall. Newspapers say farms lay abandoned across the state, and unbranded cattle are multiplying and roaming the ranges in ever-increasing numbers."

"Print will be busy when he comes home," Julie said. "He wants to make the English ranch the largest one in Texas."

Uncle John grunted, not exactly a happy sound. "Food is scarce in cities, but we're blessed. Thankfully we managed to bring our garden through the drought, God be praised. And Maizie's garden is better than ours. We can share with our neighbors."

Aunt Betty added, "My hens have never quit laying, not even in the heat of last summer. By trading chickens and eggs for beef from Louisa, both families benefit. We are fortunate, indeed."

Real coffee was unattainable except for small amounts sent from the English store. The parched corn that Aunt Betty ground and brewed was satisfying when mixed with rich cream.

Julie prayed for the war to end and Print to come home safely. Uncle John said the Confederacy was a lost cause, but he feared what surrender would bring to the citizens of Texas. "If only they'd listened to Governor Houston. He saw what the future held for secessionists. Now we're all caught in the net. Under military law, we'll all suffer."

Uncle John entered the house one day just before Christmas, grim-faced and obviously shaken.

"Jacob English has just learned that Print's leg was wounded during a battle near Shreveport. His battery was cut off from the Red River by a large Union force and surrounded."

Julie's heart pounded. Her eyes searched Uncle John's gray ones anxiously. "Is it bad—Print's wound?"

"Let me finish." John Denton took her hand and continued in his deliberate way, telling details that Julie wished he'd cut short.

"Only Print, Conner, and two other Texas cavalrymen were able to get out. Print's men were scouting between the enemy and the river. They spotted a small Union gunboat coming downriver to take up position and bring its large guns to bear against their Louisiana Second Cavalry."

Oh, Uncle John, get to Print's condition.

"Print figured out the boat would have to come near the tall banks of the river at a certain point to avoid shoals, and it wouldn't be able to raise its long guns while it was close to the riverbank. It never takes much to send Print into action, seems to me."

I don't care about that. How badly is he hurt?

"Anyway, it was all those four young hotspurs needed. They waited in hiding until the boat was in position and then, horses and all, they leaped from the river bank onto the boat and captured the thing. The only shot that was fired was the one that wounded Print, who led the way."

Julie held her breath. She noticed Aunt Betty watching her in concern.

"Print has never lacked inventiveness," John continued, "nor backed down from risk. I'll venture to say he thinks the wound in his leg was small price to pay for the good deal they were able to negotiate for their unit."

"John, finish the story. Julie wants to hear about Print's condition."

He nodded. "Print's bunch talked the Yankees into trading the gunboat for a conditional surrender on the premise that their troops would be made part of a prisoner exchange by summer. The whole battery was transported to a military prison in New Orleans, including Conner. Print is supposed to be in a hospital in New Orleans and Con in federal prison."

"A hospital—it must be bad." Julie choked back tears.

"Join me on our knees in prayer for these young men and their family," concluded John.

Julie fell to her knees, but she could not pray. No words formed on her lips or in her mind, just horrified reaction to the echo of Uncle John's words. *Wounded leg...hospital...prison...New Orleans....*

She found it hard to breathe until she glanced at Aunt Betty's stricken face. She had to pull it together. She mustn't become another source of worry for Aunt Betty and Uncle John. She needed to talk to Louisa, that tower of unwavering good sense and faith. She'd know about Print and his chances.

"Uncle John, please go with me to the English ranch. I must talk to Louisa and show my concern, see if there's anything I can do for the family."

"She's right," Aunt Betty intervened. "We'll all go. If I know Louisa, she'll find a way to comfort us, but we must go to her and Jacob, and Maizie and the boys."

It was Hamilton English who came out of the house to invite them in and to take charge of the buggy. He seemed to appreciate the fact that the Dentons had come out of concern for his brothers and his parents. Maybe there was hope for Ham yet.

He was a handsome young man, some inches below the height of Uncle John, but fit from hard work. If only he knew how to smile. His black eyes reminded her so much of Louisa's—and Print's—and his ever-darkening hair was trimmed and clean. Without the pistol he looked like a boy his age should.

Louisa's steady gaze welcomed her friends, and she held out a hand to Julie. Aunt Maizie gave her a long hug. Louisa squeezed Julie's hand as Uncle John voiced thanks for the Lord's vigil over Print and Connery.

"And He is with them right now. My biggest comfort is that both Print and Con know the Lord and where to go when things get rough. Though I'd venture to guess that there are few atheists on a battlefield. War has a way of cutting away all the philosophic nonsense that entertains educated men," Print's mother said.

Julie suddenly found her heart lighter. She recognized the truth of Louisa's words. God was in control and nothing could touch Print except through His loving hands. The Lord could use it all for good.

Born inside Julie at that moment was a conviction: Print would return, and he would find in her the woman meant for him. Just how this would be accomplished, she had no idea; but a plan would come and she would find a way to make it real. War, wounds, prisons, and distance would not prevail. One day she would be the wife of Print English, and only death would separate them.

Chapter 8

The first letter from Connery to Louisa was short and not encouraging. Louisa read his words to Julie for the second time. She couldn't miss a detail.

"Print managed to get a note to me. He says unprecedented numbers of wounded have created a medical crisis in New Orleans. Federal blockades mean a short supply of medications and bandages. The hospital is overcrowded. Soldiers with diseases are separated, but contagion has spread. Print says he'll hold onto his leg, whatever that means. I am fine. Pray."

Faithful people met daily in the chapel for prayer, Julie, Aunt Betty, Louisa, and Maizie among them. Julie prayed for an encouraging letter.

In late January, a letter came, but it was not from Print. It was from a doctor of the New Orleans hospital. A Yankee bullet had broken Print's thigh, he said. Print still had his leg and he was recovering.

Something in the young man's stubborn refusal to be separated from his limb after infection set in touched the doctor's heart. He had moved Print from the overrun, inadequate hospital to his own home in New Orleans. Print was receiving care from the doctor's wife and daughter.

Julie was thrilled by the news for a whole week until a letter came from Print, which Louisa read to the gathering of the two families. Print said he didn't miss the bug-infested bedding of the hospital. His concern was for Con and how he was faring in the military prison, although the doctor's family assured him that conditions there were above average there. Louisa read on.

"I thank God the wound was in my leg. Soft lead bullets leave broken and splintered bones, but if a soldier is shot in the head, chest or stomach, his chances for survival are slim. I know Father would argue that my hard head could turn a bullet, but I believe I'll get through this war with both of my legs still working."

Everyone laughed and Julie urged her to finish.

"I know you're praying," she read. "I think that's why I'm here in this comfortable bed being cared for by two angels."

Louisa smiled. "There—how's that for answered prayer? The Lord provides. Almost a miracle, don't you think, Julie?"

Julie was dismayed to realize that instead of feeling pure relief, her stomach burned. There with Print, and able to tend his needs, was the doctor's daughter—a young woman who was surely beautiful and charming as only southern belles could be. An angel, in Print's words.

Julie expressed words of thankfulness, but they sounded hollow. Louisa's expression said she saw right through Julie and seemed to understand.

A new worry. Not enough to have to fret about

disease and wounds, but now a rival who had every advantage. Julie was so out of sorts on the way home that Uncle John asked if she was not feeling well.

Conner's letter in June said that Print had recovered well enough to be transported to the prison so they were united once more.

Julie's thoughts were jumbled. She should have wished for Print to continue his soft life in the doctor's house, but prison was out of reach of the doctor's daughter.

Shameful. She couldn't look at her face in the mirror.

Conner claimed Print was "thin as a snake," but still the same old Print, and could get around on his crutches without much trouble.

Negotiations were underway, he wrote, for the promised prisoner exchange to take place sometime that summer, so both of them might soon be furloughed and on their way home. Julie could not stop smiling.

Within a month, a compromise was reached and an exchange ordered. Uncle John said all prisoners would have to sign an oath that they would never again bear arms against the Union.

Print, in his letter, said that would be no problem since he was never sure he should have been fighting against his own government.

Jacob and Louisa traveled to Red River Landing where the exchange took place. They could bring their sons home.

The day after Print's arrival, Julie danced around the chicken yard scattering grain and singing to the unimpressed hens.

"Print is home...my life can begin...the happy one I'll share with him."

Good neighbors and good rains throughout the

county welcomed Print and Conner, and Julie could hardly wait to see him. She now held the upper hand over any rival.

Print would be close by and she would find a way to show him she was the woman God intended to be his wife. He had no need for a fluffy Louisiana girl without a notion of country life.

Embarrassed at her willfulness, Julie bowed her head and whispered. "If it is Your will, Lord, and I believe it is, please arrange our marriage." The prayer was sincere, but God might not be opposed to some help.

In following days, her patience was sorely tried. Uncle John visited Print daily, but refused to take Julie along.

"Print wouldn't want you to see him weak and puny. Besides, he convalesces much of the time up at his cabin, clearly needing a dose of lonesome."

It had to be enough to send treats from the kitchen. Aunt Betty said Louisa genuinely loved Julie and could not be insensitive to her feelings for Print unless she was blind.

"You don't even have the grace to be embarrassed," Aunt Betty teased. "May I offer some advice? A man likes to pursue a woman. In my day, our mamas taught us to be contained and a bit unattainable."

"Well and good, Aunt Betty, but Print hardly realizes I'm alive. His last memory of me is as a rock-throwing brat of a girl. I have to do something to let him see how grown-up I am and how perfectly ready I am to accept his proposal of marriage."

"Marriage! Julie, you'll need to get to know the real Print English before you think of marriage. He may not be the dashing figure you remember. War and death can make a man bitter and harden him beyond redemption. Let Uncle John feel him out and remain a woman of mystery for a while longer."

Julie fidgeted, making no promise, until her Aunt Betty added, "Louisa will find a way to mention all your finer points, including your glorious hair and your intelligent eyes—and that pert nose you inherited from your mother. Print will notice your lips for himself the first time he sees you."

Julie smiled and hugged her aunt, but she had not finished.

"You're a beauty and you know it. I've never seen eyes the color of yours. A silvery brown, like printers' ink. You never lack in poise and confidence, so you'll have your pick of the best when the war is over and we get our menfolk back again. Perhaps Print is good enough for you and perhaps he is not. Let's leave that in God's hands."

One morning when he returned from a visit to the English family, Uncle John mentioned that Print had changed, but whether for the better, he said only time could tell.

"He spends time alone at his cabin, working his leg and chopping cedar posts to get his upper body strength back. He's setting aside the crutches most of the time now, but Louisa is concerned about his lack of appetite."

He needs a wife. I could persuade him to eat.

To Julie's disappointment, Print did not come to Sunday worship with his parents and Con and Jonas. Hamilton stayed home with Print.

"Ham follows Print as much as he is allowed. They practice with their pistols every day, even on the Sabbath," Louisa told Aunt Betty with obvious concern.

One morning two weeks later, as the women were getting breakfast on the table, Uncle John said,

"One thing has not changed about Print. He's rarin' to get after unbranded longhorns. Still bent on building that ranch into an empire. He convinced his father they needed more land and was able to buy another four thousand acres."

"Well, John, Print has always been a focused young man. He's never hung out in saloons or lived a wild life that I've heard of. Ambition can be a good thing," Betty Denton said as Julie served the food.

Uncle John's words made one thing clear. Julie would simply have to find a way to break into Print's determined plan. He was not going to be able to ignore her forever. Too much time had been wasted.

Uncle John's tone sounded faintly critical as he continued. "Print has convinced all of the boys to go in with him and they've elected him *caporal*, or boss, of the whole outfit until the time comes to divide it up. He's hired extra cowboys, including old Tuffy Snyder, a friend of Tom Evans, and a new cook, Polly Ramirez. There's too many cowboys now for Louisa and Maizie to feed."

"Do you think it might be a good time for me to visit Print, Uncle John? I've not seen him since his return."

John took time to stir honey and cream into his artificial corn coffee. Julie settled in a chair across from him, willing him to answer.

"Print has big plans right now and I don't think he has time for much else. They're building new pens on that high area north of headquarters. Print has to attend the work in a buggy, but he's there every day—in charge. Determined to make up for lost time. A broken leg won't hold him back."

He took a swallow and added, "They're making plans for a cattle drive by late fall to take advantage of the increase on the ranges."

"Where will they take the cattle?"

"Don't think they've decided yet, with the war still on." Uncle John appeared thoughtful. "The English brand rides the hip of a lot of longhorns already, but with the new cowboys Print aims to double the number of marketable cattle before the drive."

He stared at Julie. "He has ambition. I just pray it doesn't blind him to what else is important."

All Julie heard was a deadline. It was already early August, and Print planned a cattle drive in the fall. That meant eight or ten weeks for her to convince Print to make her his wife before he left. He could not leave the county without a vow in front of a preacher. After all, Louisa had said the family made drives to New Orleans before the war.

What if Print decided to drive the cattle to Louisiana rather than go north? He might come home with a certain southern belle as his wife.

Chapter 9

Julie plotted all day and by evening was ready to bring out her best effort. After devotions, she went into action, her voice filled with enthusiasm.

"Uncle John, why don't you get up a dance at Preacher Sam Cravens' place? We need to celebrate the end of the drought. We can call it a 'rain dance' and get the whole county together, like you said happened before the war. You and Reverend Sam can fiddle and we women will make up a spread of good food. Dance the night away and forget about the war for a few hours."

Uncle John turned to his wife, clearly seeking her opinion. Aunt Betty nodded her agreement, smiling.

"I think that's a wonderful idea, Julie. No one can outdo Sam Cravens at putting together a party. His big cabin holds three rings of dancers at a time. And he likes nothing better than fiddling, unless it's preaching on Sunday morning."

That evening, Uncle John reported that Sam

Cravens needed little prompting to throw a shindig. Whatever grapevine he used, the news spread throughout the county that on the last day of August 1864, San Simon would be dancing.

The Cravens' cabin was north of town, about a mile from the English place. The Methodist Chapel where Sam preached stood about midway between town and the Crossroads settlement where the Cravenses, Englishes, Evanses, Norths, and two other families made their homes.

Ten days until she saw Print English. It would be a night neither of them would forget.

Julie still had a dress to make, but Aunt Betty would have ideas.

The tip of a setting sun was still visible when Julie, Uncle John, and Aunt Betty arrived at the Cravens' comfortable log house. Sited near a creek, it was surrounded by huge, spreading oaks, perhaps the prettiest spot in the county. Buggies and horses were tethered around the barn and along a picket line of ropes between trees.

"I see Jacob and Louisa's rig," called out Uncle John, "and three good horses bearing the Reverse E, so I guess at least three of the English sons are here. Your plan seems to be working, Julie." He chuckled.

Julie winced. She felt, rather than saw, the poke Aunt Betty delivered to his ribs and heard his grunt.

So he saw right through my rain dance scheme, but he won't bring it up again.

Print English would witness her entrance. It had to be Ham who remained at home. At sixteen, boys were still a bit girl-shy, and Ham seemed especially bent on not meeting society's expectations.

After Uncle John handed her down from the buggy, Julie fluffed her glossy hair into its usual abundance around her face. She smoothed the bodice of the perfect russet-colored cotton dress she and Aunt Betty had remade from a plainer one. They had lowered the neckline and added a bit of lace. Mother's cameo necklace hung from a black velvet ribbon.

The rusty hue of the dress and her auburn hair must gleam like polished copper in the fiery sunset. Perhaps Print was standing among the men at the porch, staring in admiration.

As old friends greeted the Dentons, Julie allowed herself a quick scan. Print was not among the few young men who had grown suddenly silent as they gazed at Julie Denton in all her glory. Cully was there and so was the ever-present Tru, but she saw none of the English brothers.

Her hopes dropped when she spotted Ham standing in the door. *Print must have decided to ride in the buggy because of his leg.*

Julie adjusted the basket over her arm, straightened her shoulders and glided into the large front room, then glanced casually about, remembering Aunt Betty's admonition about self-possession. All the furniture had been removed or pushed against the walls, providing a good-sized space for dancing. A long table against the far wall was spread with tempting food.

Julie and Aunt Betty brought out the two rich cakes they had frosted with the very last of the sugar remaining in their larder. Golden fried chicken came from the biggest basket, which had been carried by Uncle John.

She watched Uncle John retreat toward the door. Jacob broke away from a group of men and women to join him. Louisa and Mrs. Cravens crossed the room to greet Julie and Aunt Betty, and near the far end she spotted Conner and Jonas, already surrounded by several girls.

Maizie didn't attend public dances, but where was Print?

Julie finally performed a careful scrutiny of the room. It was Print's horse that was missing. She could hardly wait for Louisa's explanation of his whereabouts, which was not long in coming.

"Print will be along later. He wanted to check out something in one of the pastures while there was still daylight. I warned him about getting sweaty, but he just offered that infuriating chuckle of his and told me not to worry."

It was all right for Louisa to show her exasperation, but Julie tried to hide hers.

Probably some dratted cow.

"Concern seems to be the only emotion I've been allowed to have for Print in the past two years. He's stronger, and beginning to put some meat on his bones—not that he ever carries much. Vows his leg is fit for dancing, so we'll see."

Julie remained aloof from the young women surrounding the English boys and a couple of older ones who stood near the door. She busied herself rearranging the food table and then smiled a welcome to Charlotte Emory as she waved. Charlotte spoke to Conner, who stood proprietarily at her side, and they came over.

Charlotte was utterly disarming in her sweet calico dress with a lace collar, her blonde hair shining. Con was obviously smitten with the lovely girl and her musical voice.

Nothing musical about mine. I always sound so definite. Uncle John does say my laugh is infectious.

Men crowded in from outside. Uncle John and Sam Cravens tuned their fiddles, and Jacob English removed his from the case. Couples took to the floor in a trickle, and Julie was claimed by an elderly widower who still had spryness in his step.

One tune followed another and Julie danced with young and old, including the three English brothers. When Cully appeared at her elbow, she smelled liquor on his breath. Only cool, evasive action could spare her giving him the insult of a refusal to dance.

Julie spun away and called, "I'm right here, Aunt Betty." Hurrying to her aunt's side, she wedged herself in among several older women.

"Is Cully drunk?" asked Mrs. Cravens. "If he starts making trouble, I will personally ask him to leave. That young man is a source of grief to his widowed mother. She knows he's running with a bad bunch, but she's helpless to stop him. He and Tru both come from good enough families, but they're becoming dire news to decent folk in the county."

Julie replied, "No, ma'am, I think he's far from drunk, although I did smell liquor on his breath. That was only a part of my reason for not dancing with him. He has never liked me, and I cannot imagine why he approached me."

"Because you're the most beautiful young woman in the room and he would look better spinning around the floor with you. He's quite a dancer and proud of it," replied Mrs. Cravens.

Julie remained in her protective haven for another half hour. Still Print had not come and Louisa did not seem to have noticed. Julie resorted to inward prayer.

Lord, I don't feel it right to ask you to urge Print to appear. It's a selfish, unimportant request, but I do ask You to help me accept this disappointment. Not to let it lessen my appreciation of the Cravens' generosity and all the work Mrs. Cravens and Aunt Betty put into this night.

Julie was not conscious of closing her eyes, but when she opened them, she realized she was looking directly into the black gaze of Print English, who stood in the doorway scanning the room. For an instant their stares locked and then Print continued his search of the room.

Julie gasped. *Searching for his brothers. He means to drag them away with him to some cow's crisis!*

Chapter 10

The thought of Print leaving galvanized Julie to action. She crossed the floor in his direction, and his dark gaze met and held hers as she neared.

Julie's heart beat fast, but she was determined to confront him before he got away.

What if all her plans had been pipe dreams and there was no spark when she finally faced Print English? What if she found a man as Aunt Betty said men could become after the horrors of war? Embittered, reclusive—one who had nothing left to offer a woman. Julie's senses denied the possibility of any truth in her doubts.

Even more handsome than he was four years ago...expression says he has a fascinating mind...still the man for me...just doesn't know it yet.

Julie didn't offer a smile. She'd display a bit of the mystery Aunt Betty thought so essential to any woman of interest.

Nor did Print speak to relieve the tension. His dark eyes peered directly into hers as they searched his face. A smile began to tug at the corners of his mouth and he raised an inquiring brow.

Julie smiled, pleased to find she was able to sound welcoming and casual as she spoke. "Print, I don't know if you'll remember me, but I'm Julie—"

"—et Booth Denton," he finished. "You were right about the auburn hair, and you sure as tootin' aren't almost sixteen years old now. Mother has told me, and told me again—and perhaps again—about what a beautiful girl you've become. How's your aim these days, Juliet Booth?"

Louisa was right about the infuriating chuckle. Had his voice deepened? It was rich and self-assured, if one ignored the bantering tone, which one could not on this important night. One must answer just as lightly and confidently. He must stop thinking of her as a child he could tease.

"I see your vocabulary hasn't refined," Julie answered with a tiny smile, "and I suppose I'm doomed to remain a girl in your estimation, but you're misguided once again. I am now a woman. A woman who knows what she wants."

There was no mistaking the responsive spark that flashed across his face.

"And what might that be, Miss Juliet Booth Denton? What's in that *woman's* mind of yours?"

Julie did not allow her focus to waver, although she hoped fervently the sudden heat she felt meant that the room was warm, and not that she was blushing.

"I thought perhaps you'd ask me to dance, Print. People call me Julie now, as I never did particularly care for my Booth relatives."

A short laugh escaped lips that curved into a wicked smile. "Well spoken, Julie. You never did suffer fools gladly. And I'd be one to turn down the chance to dance with the most beautiful woman in the room."

Print held out his arms and Julie stepped into them, seeeming weightless as she was whirled off into a waltz that took her breath away. Print studied her with an appraising intensity that would have unsettled her had she not steeled herself to return the scrutiny as unwaveringly as he.

They swept by the fiddlers. Imperceptibly Print tightened his hand at Julie's waist, drawing her closer until she finally rested her head on his shoulder.

Improper. What will Uncle John say?

She could feel his breath in her hair. Print smelled of soap and water and the fresh outdoors. Not too tall and not too short.

Her stomach suddenly clenched. What was she doing? This self-possessed man was just that—a man, years older. He must have experience with women, while she'd had none with any man.

Was she really able to cope with one who held her too tightly and moved her at will into unfamiliar changes in pace and direction with a careless ease that unsteadied her heart?

Don't be foolish. This is what you schemed for.

Print was with her, holding her in his arms, and he no longer thought of her as a red-haired, rock-throwing hoyden. Julie's heart slowed, and she gave herself up to the pleasure of gliding around a dance floor in the arms of a skilled partner. Occasionally she caught an envious glance aimed at her from some other young woman.

Her confidence soared. She was Juliet Booth Denton—a woman of good sense, and surely the match for any man God created. Besides, Print's people and his respect for John and Betty were protections provided by the Lord.

Print would not wish to cause her or her family anxiety. He was bound to act respectfully. *Maybe too respectfully.* She needed immediate progress.

Julie raised her face to his and found him viewing her with an expression that made her heart skip a beat. He did feel something, she was certain.

At last the set ended. Had Uncle John prolonged the music for her? It seemed the tune had lasted longer than usual, yet it was over far too soon.

Before Print could make any comment about leaving, Julie said, "Whew, that was wonderful, but it's too hot in here. Will you take me out for some cooler air?"

He didn't answer, but his hand beneath her elbow guided her out the door. Print turned her to face him in the moonlight. "I think you read my mind, Julie. I was trying to figure a way to get you outside." He stepped slightly aside as he spoke, staring out into the night.

As Print stood at the edge of the porch, moonlight played on each of his strong features: the chiseled planes of his face, his straight nose and full lips. His square chin curved into a clean-shaven jaw, and thick, black hair that fell across his forehead in a single wave.

So handsome—that same dashing figure who came to my rescue.

Print seemed to be enjoying what he could see of Julie as well. He smiled, but there remained a dare in his eyes.

They could melt an old prude at forty paces, but he will try me, as sure as I stand before him.

"Do you have another suggestion, or will you listen to one of mine?"

Julie remarked as coolly as possible, "Of course I'll listen to yours, Print."

He moved to stand behind her, so she couldn't read his face, but she felt his breath in her hair again. He spoke softly, his mouth near her ear.

"What about a walk out to that oak tree?" Print gestured toward a large oak whose branches dipped low to the ground. "My leg's cramping and I think walking may help."

"Now I think you're reading my mind." Julie was pleased to hear the nonchalance in her voice. "A walk should be just right."

Her soul cheered. Under the oak, she might inveigle Print into kissing her. She swallowed hard.

It can't be wrong with the man I intend to marry. Besides, I must make him see that I'm the woman meant for him.

What if he wouldn't comply with her scheme? Print was obviously a man with a will as strong as hers. She'd never be able to lead him around by his nose.

They dipped beneath low-hanging branches into dapples of moonlight. Space from a missing limb allowed the moon to spill its full load of silver upon her and Print, lending an enchantment to the secluded spot.

Perfect. Now if I can just—

As she tried to lean against the tree's broad trunk Print began drawing her slowly to him. Focusing steadily on her, he lowered his mouth to hers. Julie was so surprised she didn't close her eyes, and she realized that neither had he. She stared at him, unable to read his thoughts.

I'm not doing it right. He'll know it's my first.

His kiss suddenly deepened, and Print drew her so tightly against him that Julie startled. He explored her lips thoroughly and then dropped a kiss to close each eye, relaxing his hold. She felt him watching, waiting for her response.

Julie rested for several heartbeats in the circle of his arms. Then she pulled his head down for a kiss that left them both seeking a breath. A still more ardent one followed, and Julie felt the tremors of both their bodies.

With a grip of iron and fingers splayed across her hips, Print roughened his kiss and crushed Julie to him until she squirmed for breath. He lifted his mouth from hers, but did not release her. He watched her through narrowed slits, his lips forming a grim line.

Chapter 11

"Julie," Print growled, "do you know what you're doing? You can't play with me like that. I'm a man—not one of those boys you're used to entertaining on John's porch!"

She shuddered, and Print relaxed his grip. He gave her breathing room, but his gaze did not soften or waver.

Searching my soul.

Julie forced herself to speak as steadily as she could. "I probably don't know what I'm doing to you, Print. I've never allowed any man to touch me. There are no boys, and I'm not playing with you."

His face was chiseled from stone.

"I told you, I know what I want. Since I first saw you, I've known it was you I wanted. I haven't given anyone else a chance."

Still no response, and Print did not relinquish his hold.

"I mean to be your wife, Print English. I love you and I want you to make a man's love to me, but I want it to be after we're married. That's God's sequence and He always gets it right." His hold relaxed a bit. "The kiss was your idea, Print, even if you were reading my mind."

Print released her, putting space between them. He stared at her. Finally, he drew her to him again, more gently. No kiss—he just held her, his hands rubbing deliciously along her back. He buried his face in her hair.

"I'm sorry I did that to you, Julie. You had every right to expect me to remain in control. I shouldn't have handled you the way I did. I'd never harm you or shame you. But you don't play by the rules."

"I don't even know what they are."

He raised her chin, his expression slightly puzzled, and stared at her for seconds, then slowly nodded. "I believe you. You're not like other women I've met. You seem to say whatever's on your heart. You believe it's true because you've already checked it out with God, haven't you?"

It was Julie's turn to be surprised.

Print set her firmly away from him. "But how can you say you're in love with me the second time you see me? My first kiss was meant only to crack that poise of yours. I was the one playing with you, I'm ashamed to admit." He turned away and shook his head. "You don't know me. After you do, you may not want me. I'm not an easy man."

Why do I believe in Print English? She'd barely made his acquaintance; yet he evoked a sense of loyalty and trust in her—feelings that might be unjustified and absolutely untested—but deep within was a certainty that God had put them together. She must convince him.

"Your mother has helped me understand you. You have the qualities I want in a husband. I love you with a woman's love that has nothing to do with how long we've been together."

He rubbed his ear and cleared his throat.

Before he could speak, Julie said, "I know your heart. You're a man of faith and compassion. You were willing to risk a beating or a shooting for a skinny girl who got herself in over her head by throwing a rock. I know your loyalty and devotion to your family, and how hard you're willing to work for your dream."

Julie waited, but Print said nothing. "I'm the woman who will be just as loyal as you and work just as hard to make your dream real. I love you, and I will never look at another man."

He stared at her, his expression still tight. Then he shook his head.

"I can't offer you an easy life. I don't even have time to court you properly. I have to get to those wild cattle now before someone else does. The kind of life I have in mind means a lot of hard work and rough conditions for a long while, until I can get the ranch rolling."

She didn't move an inch, nor did her expression change. She watched him expectantly. He'd have to offer more reasons than tough times.

He squinted, and shook his head again. "I live in a little one-room cabin probably not a lot bigger than the bedroom you grew up in."

Thinks I'm too soft to live his life. Julie ducked her chin. "I don't take up much room." Her voice was small. She raised her face and strengthened her voice. "I understand hard work and sacrifice after nursing my parents until their deaths. Being with you is all that matters to me. I'm someone you can count on, and the last thing in the world I want is a long courtship."

Julie paused and put her hand to Print's face. "I understand the war was a serious interruption and caused you to lose precious years on that timeline you've set for yourself. I want to be your wife now, and help you reach your dream."

He brought her closer. "I'm sorry for reminding you about all you've been through. Mother told me about that hellish time when Bert was murdered and how you stepped up to help your parents."

He stared at her for what seemed to Julie an eternity before he offered a deep, weighted sigh and released her.

"All right. I think I knew my goose was cooked from the moment you began to speak to me. I've got to have you. You've certainly ruined any other woman for me after tonight. I just hope you know what you're getting into."

Julie tried to smile, but not very successfully.

Do I know what I'm getting into?

"You can't yet be twenty-one. Are you really ready to make a decision like this?"

Julie's only answer to his challenge was a big smile. She rubbed the back of her fingers along his smooth cheek.

Print looked bewildered as he caught her hand. "I've always told myself I wouldn't take a wife until I could offer her all the things she wanted, but to hear you talk, you're not going to let that happen."

"No, I won't. Not when we're so right for each other."

"I also said I'd never marry until I found a woman as beautiful and as wonderful as my mother. Don't take this wrong, but you make me think of my mother when you speak."

"That's a compliment. I admire Louisa." *He has to understand.* "We've both been through experiences that would have broken lesser people, and we survived. We're due a bit of happiness with someone we can trust."

She paused to let her words sink in and his expression was gratifyingly thoughtful.

"I trust you with my life and I know I can make you smile a lot more than usual. We'll be so happy." Julie did not try to disguise the love shining from her eyes.

Print pulled her once again into his arms. The single kiss he offered said so much. She had no misgivings about marrying this man.

At last Print raised his mouth from hers. He tipped his head side to side and smiled.

"Ahhh, Julie. I suppose you *are* a woman who knows her mind, and I'm beginning to think you know mine, too. How else could you cause a twenty-six-year-old man to change course the way you have in less than an hour?"

His gaze worshiped her in a way that made her knees wobble.

"I love you, too, Julie. I'll come and ask John for your hand tomorrow."

They left the shelter of the oak side by side. Print said, "I didn't intend to dance this evening. I came to get my brothers on the trail of some cattle crossing our land. I suspect some of the bunch will have our brands, and I think the men driving them will camp down by the river and cross in daylight."

What should she say? She pushed her hair back and gave a hesitant nod. He sounded as if he were thinking aloud.

"I only came to get my brothers," he said again, "and I find myself engaged to a girl I have seen only one other time. Who are you, Juliet Booth Denton?"

"You're going to have so much fun finding out!"

She laughed. “I’m so happy I could fly!”

“And I don’t think I’d be too surprised,” he muttered.

At the steps he took her arm. “Come on. You can help me fetch my brothers. I need to get on the track I was on before I ran into a little red-haired girl who sure as tootin’ doesn’t have the disposition of her upright, scholarly father.”

Touching his lips with her finger, Julie said softly, “Auburn—my hair is auburn.”

He grinned. “It may be late tomorrow before I show up; I don’t know just what we’re going to find down by the river. But I’ll come, and I’ll talk to your aunt and uncle. You’re going to be in the room, too, Julie. I don’t think either one of them will believe me about what happened tonight.”

Julie held back the admonition she wanted to offer about being careful this night—to beg him not to carry a gun. She’d very likely find this her role on more than one occasion after she married Print English.

Chapter 12

Was the ride home with Uncle John to become an inquisition? Never one to shilly-shally, Julie spoke frankly about what happened between her and Print. Uncle John's face was grave, and Aunt Betty's protective arm slipped around Julie's shoulders.

Uncle John drove silently for several minutes, then stopped the buggy. "This is moving way too fast. Your father would never have allowed it. A kiss is not a basis for a marriage, and neither are the feelings that too many kisses stir up." His quiet voice carried a forceful message.

Aunt Betty's hug tightened.

"Print should never have allowed you to push him into promises he has no right to offer or to expect you to return. And push him you did, from the sound of things. A man has only so much control when faced with a woman like you, Julie."

Julie was silent. *I did push things, but so did he.*

Uncle John pressed his lips together and heaved a long sigh. "I'm not going to wait for Print to come to me. In the morning, I'll go talk to him. I don't like the sound of the English brothers going after those cows without the sheriff."

Father would have said the same.

"Julie, you're a precious trust to your aunt and me. God saw fit to allow us to help you direct your life, and no man is going to break that trust until I have assurance that his priorities are straight. Have you told Print you look to God for every decision you make? Is he willing to do the same? I can't be satisfied with less."

Tears sprang to Julie's eyes. "I know how deeply you and Aunt Betty love me. Go, if you must, and ask all the questions you want. I know Print will try to give honest answers. When you've heard him, you'll be relieved." Julie's voice broke, and Aunt Betty drew her close.

"That's enough for now, John. Let's just agree that Julie is a woman who wants God's will above all else in her life. She's young, but so was I when I said yes to your proposal."

"Yes," replied Uncle John, "but I never was the driven man that Print is. I promise to be fair, Julie. He's a conscientious young man, but ambition can cloud the issues."

Uncle John kissed the top of her head. "Don't worry, darling girl. This will work out. You know we can trust the Lord in all things. Let's go home."

Uncle John will see Print is the man God intended for me. He will come to ask for my hand, whatever Uncle John says.

With that thought firmly in her mind, Julie climbed into bed that night and slept.

Sunlight streamed through the window. Julie rose quickly and completed her morning freshening, then returned to her bedside and knelt.

“Please, Father, guide Uncle John as he talks to Print this morning. Help Print to hear the good sense and righteous concern in Uncle John’s words.”

She rose and went to the washstand, peering at her reflection in the mirror. Her cheeks were pink and her eyes sparkled after last night’s dreams.

Print’s kisses...the feelings they bring.

But Uncle John was right to say those feelings were not a basis for a marriage, even if they inspired fine dreams.

I am meant to marry Print. God put us together. He will bless us and we’ll use our hard-won wealth to help people less fortunate. Print will answer Uncle John’s questions and come to claim me today. He said he had to have me.

Julie dressed carefully and arranged her hair. She had no idea what time Print would arrive, but she’d be ready. Together they would convince Uncle John and Aunt Betty.

The grandmother clock struck ten. Horrors! She never slept so late! She hurried to the kitchen and drank a glass of milk, while Aunt Betty busied herself cutting up vegetables for a chicken stew.

Julie’s usual chores seemed unimportant this morning. Even Risky could not tempt her to a game of fetch as they returned from feeding chickens and gathering eggs. She helped Aunt Betty by stirring up a batch of cornbread, all the while listening for Uncle John’s return.

Just before noon, she heard him ride by on his way to the barn. He’d take care of his horse before he came in. Fifteen toe-tapping minutes, spent imagining the worst.

The confrontation at the river went wrong... Print's injured...He refused to talk to Uncle John about his spiritual life...Oh, why did I ever agree to this?

Aunt Betty hummed to herself, and stirred the good-smelling chicken stew simmering on a hook in the fireplace. How could she go on doing routine chores when Julie's future hung in the balance?

Through the door Julie watched Uncle John wash his hands in the basin on the porch. More anxious minutes spent staring at his back. At last he came in. Julie's heart dropped. His brows were drawn together.

She forced herself to remain quiet and allow him to speak in his own time, thirty tongue-biting seconds spent studying his taut face. Uncle John liked to weigh his words, and perhaps in the wait he was in prayer. He took his place at the head of the table. Julie tried a fleeting prayer of her own.

"Bets, let's wait a while before we eat. We three need to talk," Uncle John said.

Aunt Betty poured each a cup of tea. Julie's heart thudded. What would he say?

"I don't have good news," he began. "Last night, Print and his brothers caught up with the cowboys pushing that herd, and it contained branded English cattle. Fred Maher and a couple of his sons were moving them. I've always known Fred to be an honest man. Print admitted he was surprised when Fred said he was hired to move the cattle for Truman Evans."

Tru Evans is always trouble. Oh, Father—

John's measured voice continued, "Print accused Maher of stealing. Ham thought Fred was going for his pistol and outdrew him. Print knocked Ham's pistol aside, but it fired, hitting Conner's shoulder."

Julie gasped. "Is Con all right?"

"Yes, just a graze."

Aunt Betty said, "Thank heavens. Was Fred able to convince Print of the truth?"

Uncle John nodded. "In fact, Print wound up hiring Fred and his sons to help round up enough longhorns to make a drive." Uncle John stirred honey into his cooling tea and waited for Julie's reaction.

She sagged in relief. *From the start I've worried about guns, but Print and I must work it out ourselves.*

"Print and his brothers could not go unarmed to confront possible rustlers, Uncle John. And it was Ham who put a pistol in play. In fact, Print may have averted a killing."

"True. I give him credit for his quick reaction."

Before relief could set in, Uncle John added, "Print's mistake was allowing Hamilton to carry a pistol out there. And Print charged into Fred's camp armed with accusations instead of questions."

Julie shuddered. *He could have been killed. And what of Uncle John's questions about Print's trust in God?*

As if he read her mind, Uncle John said, "I wasn't satisfied with the rest of the matters we discussed."

"What do you mean?" Julie waited, trying to keep anxiety from her face while Uncle John stared into his cup.

Aunt Betty said, "Louisa assured me Print drew closer to God during the war."

"That may be, but I fear Print's reckless behavior could result in tragedy." Uncle John cut his eyes toward Julie. "Love means vulnerability. You saw your father's sanity break under the stress of losing someone he loved."

He can't mean he won't give his blessing. "I'm confident we can find our way together into God's will." Julie's voice quavered.

Aunt Betty said softly, "How can Print resist our beautiful, loving, and honest girl? He'll want to do right by her in all matters, including spiritual ones." Aunt Betty refilled the teacups and continued. "I've heard Louisa's stories about Jacob as a young man. Print's headstrong nature was born in the loins of a man who now is as gentle a companion as Louisa could desire."

Uncle John bowed his head for a long moment. He covered his mouth and shook his head, then reached for Julie's hand. "I won't withhold my blessing if you are certain Print English is the man for you."

He smiled. "You two should have been lawyers instead of Albert. He was good at changing people's minds, but he couldn't make a person like it as you can. I admit, Julie, I planned to speak against the union until these past few minutes."

Julie rose and threw her arms around Uncle John's neck, and Aunt Betty joined in a hug that almost turned over his chair.

The stew and cornbread were served after Julie was called upon to say grace. Uncle John usually reserved that important function as his right, but today his eyes twinkled as he gave Julie the privilege.

Her prayer reflected the thanks that filled her heart, but she hardly tasted a bite of the good stew as she awaited Print's arrival.

Chapter 13

Eight busy days followed: fittings, alterations, and whispered conversations between Uncle John and Aunt Betty. Then a mysterious trip to the English ranch without Julie.

"Surprises are afoot," was all the information Aunt Betty offered. Each day the sun had set before Print arrived at Uncle John's house.

"It's always going to be dark when Print quits chousing longhorns, Julie. And he'll be out the door before the sun comes up," Uncle John warned. "That's the life of an ambitious cattleman. You'd better get used to it."

I can be happy, whatever the schedule.

Aunt Betty and Julie were to spend the night before the wedding in the home of Jacob and Louisa English. "Nearer the chapel," Aunt Betty said. "And you'll have time with Print's father and brothers."

Uncle John drove them out to the ranch, arriving after sunset. Julie could see the gate and road leading up to Print's cabin, but the house she would share with him was a shadow in the gathering dark.

A tingle ran up her arms. *Print's wife. Forever.*

On the porch, he greeted her with a hug and a whisper in her ear. "Hello, sweet wife-to-be. I have some pressing business to finish for us. It's all about tomorrow." He headed out with the other men. Maizie followed.

So much for family time. What are they up to?

Just before they disappeared, Print looked back with his little grin. "Picked you some flowers today." He was gone before she could answer.

The night was a torture. How could anyone sleep? Out of the question, but Aunt Betty snored softly in the bed they shared. Hours dragged by. Julie couldn't toss and turn to relieve her tension.

She hugged her pillow and turned her thoughts to Print. Each day since the Rain Dance, she'd felt more certain of her choice. Even Uncle John was impressed with Print's intelligent conversation. Julie more so with the dark gaze that constantly found hers. Counting her blessings in her man finally sent her to sleep.

The mirror reflected the Julie of her long-held dream. Her mother's wedding dress, lovingly altered by Aunt Betty and Maizie, was a perfect fit. Curls crowned her head beneath a tiara of blue mist flowers. Mother's diamond studs adorned her ears, and Aunt Betty's new lace handkerchief was wrapped around the stems of the bouquet of bee flowers that topped Father's Bible—things old, new, borrowed and blue.

Uncle John's old buggy's brass lamps, polished to gleaming perfection, caught Julie's attention on the ride to the chapel. Aunt Betty's smile was a thin disguise for tears threatening to spill from kind blue eyes. Nothing felt quite real, yet Print was waiting for her at the end of the ride.

Later, Uncle John walked in dignity at her side and lovely Charlotte Emory ahead of them. Frank, home on furlough, stood handsome and erect beside Print as his best man. Julie turned and scanned the congregation. Friends of the two families filled the church.

Jonas and Hamilton appear solemn. Must be wondering what has come over their big brother. Only a week ago he thought only of longhorns.

The two exchanged a look that said they'd never be such easy prey, but Conner watched Charlotte wistfully. He'd soon be declaring for a bride.

Twenty-year-old Juliet Booth Denton and Quentin Printice English were married on Friday, September 9, 1864, in the Crossroads Methodist Chapel.

Fall flowers from the San Simon hills decorated windowsills and filled a large vase on the piano, where Eliza Cravens held sway. Purple gay feathers, verbenas, blue mist, soft green-eyes, and Julie's favorite, golden partridge peas, or bee flowers—Print must have enlisted the whole English clan in picking so many.

Vows were exchanged, and the prayers and liturgy curled around Julie like an embrace. Then they knelt for the final blessing. Print helped her rise and kissed her for all to see. Julie touched the gold band on her finger. His expression warmed her from head to toe.

After a dinner feast at the main house, family and friends gathered on the front porch to wave as Print drove his bride the short distance to the cabin.

It appeared different.

"You've added a porch to the front of our home! There should be a lovely view from there tonight as the moon comes up."

He turned to her with a wicked grin. "We won't be outside tonight. There are certain joys between a man and his wife that should not take place on a front porch."

Julie felt her ears grow warm. She could have cheerfully smacked that little smile off Print's lips if she had not been so in love—and so eager to find out exactly what he meant.

His strong arms lifted her out of the buggy and carried her into the cabin. When her feet touched the floor, he moved to light an oil lamp.

"Look around, Miz English. This is it. I hope you don't take up any more space than you promised. We don't have room for a lot of fancy stuff in here."

Julie's heart beat fast as she inventoried the room. The pleasant aroma of wood rubbed with beeswax permeated the air. A wide-throated stone fireplace, its fire banked, anchored the west wall, and a long table near the kitchen held a barrel with a spigot.

Her small clock stood near the front door. Mother's white china graced open shelves atop a cabinet near the table, which held a vase of showy partridge peas.

In a corner of the sleeping portion of the cabin Julie noted a curtained area, and her mirrored wash stand stood nearby—a particular treasure from her childhood.

White cotton curtains covered the windows. A quilted yellow coverlet spread over a large bed with a massive oak headboard and four turned posts.

"Oh, Print, what a beautiful bed and coverlet!" Julie exclaimed.

"Mother and Father donated their first bed, and Aunt Maizie made the coverlet so we can sleep under a blanket of her love."

"Perfect."

Print watched her closely.

Watching for signs of discontent? Well, he'll be disappointed. I love it.

She walked about, picking up an object here and there. All was in apple-pie order, and somehow Julie knew it always was. Print English was a fastidious man, in dress and habit.

He said, "Open the dresser—top two drawers. The bottom two are mine."

Julie's nightdresses and underclothes were folded neatly to fit within the deep drawers. A framed oval mirror from Aunt Betty's guest room hung above the freshly-waxed dresser. On top lay her ivory comb, brush, and hand mirror.

A tall wardrobe she recognized from Louisa's house held most of Julie's dresses, with a shelf above for hats. Print's clean shirts and pants hung on pegs along one wall. At the end of the lineup were his hat, his sheepskin coat and two of Julie's bonnets.

All the mysterious happenings of the past week suddenly became clear. The whole family had worked hard to make the cabin ready to welcome her.

"It's perfect. You all made a huge effort to make me welcome. You're so thoughtful." Tears rose as she turned to him.

Print's posture stiffened. He crossed the floor to her in two strides and pulled her into his arms. Lifting her mouth to his, he spoke huskily against her lips.

"No way, Julie, are you going to be sad this night. I have ways of making you forget all about anything but me—I mean, us."

Julie couldn't find time to deny that her tears were sad ones. Print's mouth was on hers, hungry, yet tender, kiss after kiss. Uttering a groan, he swept Julie along in his need until she trembled with excitement.

Print gentled his kisses and his embrace, finally raising his mouth. She peeped up at him, allowing her rapture to show. "Oh, Print, don't stop."

He lifted Julie from the floor into his arms and she forced her eyes open. *Why would he stop when things were going so well?*

"Julie, I love you so much."

"I love you, too, Print. I thought we had that all settled. I'm enjoying your kisses and caresses."

"I want this night to be everything you want it to be. Tell me what feels right—and what's too much on this first night of the rest of our lives. We have all the time in the world to get used to each other."

Julie was lost in the black fire of Print's gaze as he stepped toward the big oak bed. "It all feels right. I want everything you do."

She let herself drown in the depths of his eyes and believe each word he said all through that wonderful night. A night she'd treasure forever.

Print woke her with a soft kiss to her neck. Hopefully, he'd repeat it every day for the rest of their lives. He whispered in her ear, "Good morning. I love you, little wife."

They snuggled for a while before Julie said, "Are you as hungry as I am? I'll make breakfast."

Inspecting the food safe, they found a large loaf of bread, a pie, and several jars of preserved fruit and honey. From a bucket hanging in the well, Print brought milk, eggs, butter, and a baked ham.

They ate a leisurely breakfast and Print sat watching Julie putter about, tending their needs.

She stopped beside him for a moment: black hair still tousled from her fingers...shirt untucked... her man. She met his gaze, and felt blood rise to stain her cheeks.

Her man! Sadness would never touch her heart as long as she could gaze into Print's eyes. The ones that glowed such fire last night now brimmed with pride and amusement.

"Juliet Booth, I think I can get used to this attention without much trouble."

Julie placed her hand on Print's cheek and smiled sweetly. "Trouble is what you'll find, Print, if you don't drop the Booth bit. The last Booth man was hanged as a horse thief, but my mother's mother was a Booth and seemed quite proud of them."

Print snorted and drew her onto his lap. He kissed her leisurely then threw up his hands.

"Truce, Julie. No more Booths."

She watched the changing outline of tendons extending from wrists to knuckles as Print rubbed along her arms. His hands were neither too big nor too small. Immaculately clean, with nails neatly trimmed. Strong, capable—those hands made lariats sing through the air and kept lunging longhorns under control. But they had elicited gasps of pleasure from her in gentle love-making last night.

I am so in love with this man I could purr.

She grinned at him and he returned a crooked smile of contentment. He moved her from his lap and rose, cradling her face to offer another kiss.

"How about a ride through the pastures so you can see what I'm all about? Mother said you can have her brown mare as your own." He stopped short. "I borrowed Mother's saddle for you till we can get one made, but I forgot to ask you if you can ride."

"I'm sure I'll manage."

Chapter 14

Print led Julie over to the corrals. She gasped as they approached the mare.

"She's lovely! What's her name?"

"Mother named her Louisiana, but we call her Lou. Here, I'll saddle her for you."

Julie grinned at him and said, "Get out of the way, husband. I'll saddle my own horse!"

She did, with an expertise and speed that had him shaking his head.

"Bert didn't teach me just to fish and chunk rocks. We had our own horses from the time we were big enough to sit a saddle."

"Should have known a feisty red-head could—" Julie narrowed her eyes. "I meant to say, a feisty auburn-haired lady." They laughed together.

Julie added, "When I was a kid I rode astride, and that's what I'll do now if you agree. Uncle John has my side-saddle in his barn, so we won't need to have one made. Have a cross-saddle I can use?"

Print stripped the side-saddle off and put on

the old cross-saddle Ham had used until a couple of years ago.

"Are you going up in that dress, or do we need to go back and put you into some of my pants? I can tie a rope around your waist."

Julie hiked her skirt far up her legs and placed a high-topped shoe into the stirrup. "Pantaloons under my skirts. I thought you might want to ride today. I have a split riding skirt and boots at Aunt Betty's house for ladylike rides." She swung up into the saddle with Print's hand hovering near, just in case.

As they left the barn and corrals, Print watched his bride. Sitting upright in the saddle, skirt and petticoats hitched almost to her knees, Julie exposed shapely calves beneath her modest knee-length pantaloons. The sun kissed her *auburn* hair, firing it into a gleaming russet cascade down the back of her open-collared dress. She held the reins with confidence and Lou seemed to trot in pride.

Print suddenly felt taller and stronger than usual, and pulled in a deep breath. Julie was a rare woman.

"Lou's a single-foot," Print explained, "meaning she puts only one foot on the ground in each step of her gait."

"I understand. Means she has a four-beat gait. Makes for a smooth ride. I imagine she can cover the ground in a hurry."

His heart swelled. Julie was young and gave hints that the headstrong, not-quite-sixteen-year-old girl still lived inside, but she was all his.

The woman I waited for.

He smiled at her, thinking of the dance.

Never had a chance—even if I'd wanted to hold onto my bachelor ways.

Her face glowing with excitement, Julie was soon ready to kick up the pace. She turned a mischievous smile in his direction and dug her heels into Lou. They were off, Print in hot pursuit. When Lou sensed Print's mount at her heels, she increased her stride until they were practically soaring.

It felt good to be out with his wife, galloping under a sky where clouds piled up like pillows. After several minutes, Julie pulled back on the reins, slowing Lou to a canter.

"She's wonderful. Lou is just the girl for me."

Print grinned. "I think I'll keep the one in the saddle."

After they had ridden a mile from the cabin, he suddenly reined up and motioned for Julie to do the same.

"Don't move."

The brush rustled and a dun-colored longhorn cow pushed around a juniper shrub. She stopped, head in the air, staring intently in their direction. She didn't move, and neither did Print or Julie.

"Look at the ground under that small cedar bush in the tall grass and tell me what you see," he whispered.

At first, Julie obviously saw nothing, her face a blank, but as she continued to stare at the spot, a smile formed. "A calf. It's barely visible—almost the same color as the ground, and lying flat with its chin on the ground. How enchanting."

"Enchanting—I'll have to teach that word to Zeke, the new cowboy I hired." Print chuckled.

"So tiny. Does it belong to that cow?"

"Maybe the calf is hers. Her own is certainly there, but so are several others, likely hiding in the grass. She may be the nanny of that one, watching a nursery while other mothers go to water. She'll go when they return. Each cow recognizes the bawl of her own calf and can pick it out of a hundred others."

Julie had not moved.

Print continued softly, "In longhorns, the protective instinct of the female is especially strong. The only help a bull gives in rearing the calf may be hooking off a predator. Cows keep their calves hidden until they're strong enough to run."

"Can we go closer? I want to see the baby."

"Better not. We don't want to spook her. She'll charge in an instant if she thinks we're a danger. Let's ease out of here."

"I understand how she must feel. I would never let anything hurt *my* baby." She stopped and her ears turned pink.

Oh, darling, babies there will be, but I want you all to myself for a while.

Farther into the ride, in a shallow stream, they allowed the horses to drink. A mockingbird flew from a brushy shrub and perched on a nearby cedar's dead limb. His head cocked to the side, then he rose straight up, did a flip in the air, and flashed his white wing tips.

"Protecting his nest," Print said. "I saw one put Tige, old cow dog, to flight one day on the range. Not easy to intimidate that dog, but the mockingbird dived and pecked till Tige turned tail."

Julie smiled until a noise caught her attention. "What is that sound?"

"You'll see." Print turned his horse away from the water and Julie followed.

A tawny brindle bull emerged from the cover of a cedar thicket to descend the gentle slope on the far side of the creek.

Print's voice was soft. "He's probably six or seven years old, and at the top of his game. We'll stay here so you can see what the old boy does. He's talking to himself."

What a spectacle. The animal advanced, his head swaying with the weight of thick, lengthy horns. Hoarse and deep, almost like distant thunder, the mumbling talk went "uh-huh-uh-huh-uh-huh," as he repeated six deep and deliberate notes, the last one a descending, jerky rumble. The bull halted and raised his head in a high, defiant bellow that startled both of them.

Print whispered, "He's bull-o'-the-woods around here and that bawl now and then reminds everyone."

Julie shivered, still watching the creature.

"Telling us he knows we're here, but he's coming on anyway," said Print. "We rely on the wind to teach us about a coming rain shower or a skunk that's become a neighbor, but that old boy relies on his sense of smell for life itself. He's constantly testing the air for information."

Julie was clearly transfixed by the latent strength of the animal's body. His powerful neck showed a great bulge just behind the head. A big dewlap, a long flap of skin, hung centered beneath his lower jaw. Powerfully muscled foreparts and lithe flanks warned the bull could move swiftly and with force—in any direction he chose, and against any obstacle.

"You remember the old-timer Frank mentioned at the wedding dinner? Several years ago Tuffy was working close to two fighting bulls, and not watching them. Suddenly one broke away and rammed into his horse. Killed the animal and crippled Tuffy for life."

Julie gasped. "Oh, Print!"

"Ask any old-time range man to name the quickest animal he's ever known. He won't say a cutting horse, a wildcat, or a striking rattlesnake. He'll say an angered longhorn bull."

Julie was silent.

Processing the information. She'll have to learn to deal with the risks cattlemen take for granted.

"We'd better go," Print said.

Exhilarating, riding beside my husband while he explains his sometimes-dangerous work. Print is smart and experienced. He can handle the danger.

It had started as a lovely ride, but in less than a mile they topped a rise leading down to another branch of the creek. Print surveyed the surrounding land, and his mood changed. He began searching the ground and frowning.

What's bothering him?

Print remained silent, riding slowly and purposefully, studying the ground.

Julie stayed close, filled with questions. At last, she could stand it no longer. "Are you going to tell me what's wrong, spoiling our time together?"

Print barely glanced at her. "These are wagon tracks. There shouldn't be any out here."

He seemed to forget she was by his side. They followed the track into the brush. Print stopped near the creek and stared down into the water.

Julie's gaze followed his. Mossy, brown rocks jutted up in the middle of the stream, causing small ripples in the sluggish flow. Here and there quieter pools beckoned. It was an inviting spot and Julie made plans to return. Perhaps she'd bring a book to read, or her paints.

She turned to Print, ready to tell him of her plan, but he was not seeing the beauty of the place. His face was tense and resolute, his gaze narrowed.

Splashing out to a large rock, he heaved it onto its side. There, still caught by the rim of the boulder, were several cowhides.

"They weighted them, to keep them out of sight. These belonged to four of our cattle. Nobody needs that many at one time to feed his family. Someone is selling the meat, and I have an idea who it is."

"What will you do?" asked Julie.

"Nothing, right now," Print replied, much to Julie's relief; but the day was spoiled.

They turned back toward home. Her heart thudded leadenly. Print's face was forbidding. He sat stiff and silent in the saddle.

Had he forgotten she was beside him? Surely he would open up after they were home, but something told her a door had closed between them.

He can't close me out this way. I need to know what he's planning. Uncle John says Print has a temper. Says he's unpredictable when he's angry. I must be careful not to let my own temper get out of hand.

Uncle John customarily shared his worries with Aunt Betty. She'd seen them together, wrestling problems down to size. He obviously valued her input and she trusted his judgment—the way it should be between a man and his wife. God's Word was clear. Husband and wife were united. They turned to Him for decisions. Print was leaving her out.

Julie squared her shoulders. *Used to his bachelor ways. Those days are over. He may resent my intrusion, but I have a duty to speak.*

Soon the cabin was in sight. It nestled under the brow of the hill—their sanctuary against troubles of the world. Julie treasured her role as Print's trusting wife, but there were truths to be spoken, and she must find words to fulfill her wifely responsibility.

Chapter 15

At the cabin Print helped Julie dismount and took the reins of both horses, ready to lead them to the barn, but she caught his hand.

"Let's sit in the porch chairs. We need to talk. I pray that my words won't upset you, but they could. We don't need hard words inside our home—ever."

Print frowned and met her gaze with a challenge in his, but he looped the reins over the rail and took the chair beside hers. No smile touched his lips and his voice was toneless. "What's on your mind?"

"I respect your God-given authority as my husband. I want that to be clear. But I, too, have a responsibility."

He rubbed at his ear, his expression wary.

She struggled with her own resentment, but anger would not serve her. Careful to keep accusation from her tone, she said, "The two of us are on my mind. Either we're a team or we're not. If we don't share what bothers us, we'll never become a couple. I need to know exactly what you plan to do about the poached cattle."

Print's eyes narrowed and his jaw tightened.

Can't stop just because he doesn't like it. He must understand.

"You see, darling, I believe we need to talk to one another and to the Lord about everything. Two people as strong-willed as we are will never find real union unless we do."

Print's face showed no sign of agreement or encouragement. His gaze was appraising.

Julie waited through a sentence prayer before she continued. "God says a man and his wife become one flesh—and that means more than just making love. It means we become one person together joined in the Lord."

Print tipped his head to the side. He took her hand. "You may be more woman than I bargained for, but I know you're right about this. I've seen Mother and Father wrestling with tough decisions, hands joined and heads bowed." He rubbed his jaw and took a deep breath. "I didn't want to worry you."

"If it's something I need be concerned about, I want it to be with you—not by myself, wondering what's going on inside you. Trust me, I'm no shrinking violet."

He said nothing. What was he thinking?

"I'm a strong woman with a good head on her shoulders, taught by intelligent, godly women and men to face truth."

Print's mouth turned up at the corners, and Julie sagged with relief.

"God cares about all our problems, and He has lasting solutions if we'll turn to Him," she added.

Print's smile disappeared. "How will God tell me to handle a thief who's stealing my living? Your Uncle John obviously thought I was wrong in the way I handled Fred Maher, but I don't know any way but to put a stop to it!"

Julie was now certain Uncle John's pauses before speaking were prayers. She waited. At last words came to her. She said softly, "Uncle John was upset only because you gave Fred no opportunity to explain."

His brow furrowed. Julie reached for his hand. "What would you have done in Fred's place, if you knew you hadn't stolen anything? What if someone came riding into your camp and called you a thief?"

Print's frown softened. He mumbled, "Probably wouldn't have handled it as well as Fred did. He reached into his shirt, and Ham thought he was going for a gun. I could see he wasn't, and diverted Ham's aim. Fred pulled out papers of sale signed by Tru Evans. Of course, they weren't genuine."

"Your quick reaction probably saved Fred's life. You said Ham's aim is accurate."

"One of the best."

Now or never. "There's something else I must say. I'll be failing you as your wife if I don't." She paused and searched Print's face. It had tightened.

"Uncle John is worried about Ham carrying a pistol at his age. He fears Ham doesn't have the judgment to go along with his skill. I must agree."

Print's eyes narrowed. "Julie, every man in this country is going to have to know how to defend himself when this war is over and the riff-raff move in. War doesn't end when they put away the rifles and cannons. Military overseers will move in and corruption will run wild. Ham is young, but he's adventuresome and cocky. If I don't teach him how to defend himself, he won't live to see the day he marries and has a family."

"Will you promise me you won't teach him just

to shoot, but that his gun is a last resort? Take him with you to confront the man who stole your beef. Make Ham leave his gun at home. Let him see it can be settled without gunplay."

"Am I allowed to carry?" His tone was sarcastic.

Julie's heart was in her throat. "There's a legal way to stop this poaching. Turn it over to the courts. Swear out complaints against thieves. But remember, it takes evidence, not just a hunch." A long silence. She held her breath.

"Print?" It was a question and a plea for understanding.

A twinkle of mischief lit his expression. "Spoken like a lawyer's daughter. Well, I'm ready to find out things about my lawyer's daughter other than how smart she is. I'll put up the horses and come back to you." He reached out and cupped her chin. "You make sense, Julie, and I won't forget this sermon on the porch."

Thank you, Father, for Christian parents. They set the example.

She anticipated going to church tomorrow with Print. Her first outing as Print's wife and an official member of the English family. Also a chance to be with Uncle John and Aunt Betty.

"I want to get things off on the right foot," he had said earlier. "Sundays will be God's day every week for the two of us."

I pray he'll learn to view every day as God's. Those longhorns pull him away from everything but his dream.

"Good morning, little wife." Print nuzzled Julie's ear. "Up and at 'em. The sun will soon be up. Can't be burning daylight."

Monday. The first day of the work week.

Julie staggered out of bed and washed as he dressed. “I’ll make breakfast and dress afterward.”

Print added logs to the fire. “Make that coffee strong enough to trot a mouse on.”

Ugh. Hot mud. How can he drink it? Julie finished breakfast and set it before Print.

He hastily blessed the food. “Busy day,” he said, and not another word until he finished eating. “It’ll be the usual. Up at the pens most of the day. I’ll see you before dark. If you need anything, ring the bell on the porch. Maizie’ll hear it. Ears like a cat.”

“What would you like for dinner, Print?”

“I’ll bring a round of beef from the well. Fried steak would be good.”

After he brought the meat, Julie went with him to the door, and he bent to give her a brief kiss.

Already thinking cows. She left the door open to watch him hurry down to the corrals. In the early light, she could see his horse, saddled and waiting. He loped away with his brothers.

Julie washed, dressed, and made the bed, fluffing the pillows and smoothing Aunt Maizie’s coverlet. At last it was perfect. As water heated for the dishes, she dusted furniture surfaces. Then she swept the front porch and washed and dried the china.

Too early to start dinner. How would she spend the rest of the morning? *Make a cake and take some down to Louisa and Maizie.*

Later, Maizie said, “Steak for dinner?”

“How did you know?”

“I figgered you asked him. If you ask, it’ll always be fried steak. If you want to cook something else, don’t ask. I’ll put up some biscuits for you and you can bake them just before you eat. Print likes bootheels. They're strong enough to sop the cream gravy."

Julie watched carefully as Maizie stirred up the bootheels. Maizie baked three of them and Louisa and Julie slathered them with butter.

"They smell heavenly," Julie said before the first bite.

Maizie's buttermilk bootheels were not as thick or fluffy as Aunt Betty's sweet milk biscuits, but they had a tangy taste that reminded Julie of yeast bread. "Buttermilk and baking soda don't make fluffy biscuits, Julie, but they stick to cowboys' ribs."

Julie returned to the cabin after lunch with the biscuit dough. She floured a table top and rolled it out, cutting biscuits into perfect rounds with a teacup, then topping each with a dab of butter and covered them with a damp tea towel. Next, she turned to preparations for dinner—supper, Print called it.

The first big meal I've cooked from scratch by myself. It has to be perfect.

She had fried steak with Aunt Betty, but never on her own. It was tricky to get the flour coating to adhere. Using Aunt Betty's method, Julie soaked the beef slices in cold water with just a pinch of baking soda. Then she seasoned the meat and coated it with flour. Milk made too thick of a coating for Uncle John's tastes.

Lard melted in the big, iron spider skillet. Its short legs kept it from direct heat, but the meat needed constant watching. Couldn't let it burn.

When the steak was done, Julie peeled potatoes and sliced them into lightly salted water in a small kettle. They'd have to wait. Steak could be kept warm, but potatoes needed to be mashed just before eating. Plenty of cream and butter would make them smooth.

Light faded from the sky into dusk as Julie stood on the porch. She heard rather than saw the men ride in.

Inside, she spread the coals to set the spider oven of biscuits near the edge. She put the potatoes on the lowest swivel arm of the fireplace crane. The steak waited higher up, near a small kettle of gravy. Then she went back to the porch to wait for her kiss and squeeze.

"I'm dirty and I don't smell good. You may not want to touch me till I've showered."

"Now, please." She had second thoughts when his beard sanded her cheeks. He was sweaty and hairy and his shoulders sagged.

"Feel like I've been rode hard and put away wet," he said as if he were describing his horse.

"You're exhausted. I imagine you're hungry, as well. Shower while I get dinner on the table."

Print emerged from the shower wrapped in a disreputable old robe but smelling better and appearing somewhat revived. He dressed, then shaved at Julie's wash stand while she piled food on his plate and set it on the table. She poured his cup of mud. Even the smell of it set her teeth on edge.

Print sat down and sniffed. "Smells good."

She turned away to get the biscuits. Now was the time to prove her mettle. Julie understood the importance of stick-to-your ribs food for a cowboy. When she turned back, Print's plate was pushed back, and his head rested on the table.

"Too white-eyed tired to think about eating right now," he mumbled.

I worked for hours. It'll ruin if he doesn't eat soon.

Julie returned the food to its pans to stay warm. She stirred more milk into the gravy and potatoes and sat across from Print at the table, drumming her fingers.

I suppose every rancher's wife faces this. He asks for a complicated meal and then is too tired to eat it. But there'll be enough for leftovers tomorrow evening. Steak and biscuit sandwiches, fried potato cakes, and sliced tomatoes.

A fifteen-minute nap restored him, and Print dug in. "Sinkers are the only righteous sop for fried steak and cream gravy. Are these Maizie's?"

Through gritted teeth, Julie answered. "Yes."

"Well your steak's as good as hers. I bet your biscuits will be, too. I'll help with the dishes, and we can sit on the porch."

Julie nodded. "You can have apple cake later. Right now, I want some words from you."

Print lifted her up and swung her around. "And I want more than words from you, dear wife." They laughed together.

Chapter 16

For a month, Maizie watched the initiation of Julie into rancher's wife. Early on a weekday morning as she cleared away breakfast, she said to Louisa, "We can both relate to the tragedy in Julie's past. That sweet thing has become my pet. After all, she chose to place herself beside another of my pets."

"She loves and appreciates you, too, Maizie."

"She trusts me, and that's a powerful bond. Julie's waiting for me at the corrals. I'm off to help her with that dogie calf Jonas said Print brought in."

When Maizie arrived, toting a big basket of necessities, Julie was sitting next to Print on the corral fence. She pointed to a small black-and-white bull calf standing on wobbly legs.

"That mud-plastered creature doesn't seem long for this world."

"I found its mother dead in a bog hole," Print said. "Less than a week old and too weak to run. Probably saved from coyotes by other cattle. I knew where to find two soft hearts to give him a chance."

"I'm glad you did. And thankful Maizie knows how to save him."

"Adiós, ladies. Good luck." Print kissed Julie's cheek and rode away.

"First thing," Maizie said, "we need to pour a bottle of warm milk down this orphan's throat."

When he finished guzzling the bottle, she and Julie gave him a bath at the horse trough and wrapped him in one of Maizie's old quilts.

"Hand-raisin' a calf is no end of trouble, Julie. I'll keep him fed tonight and we'll get one of the boys to bring us a thrifty cow with a young calf tomorrow. She can take on this dogie. Even that won't be an easy proposition, but Jonas is another soft heart. He'll help us."

Julie carried the basket as they walked down to Maizie's cabin, the dogie in Maizie's arms. She said, "Aunt Maizie, how do I get Print to talk to me about important things?"

"Let me think just how to put this, darlin'. It can save you a lot of grief if you can get your head around the idea. Print's a cowman, and you gotta understand, they're always kinda' alone even when they're with someone they love. He'll take some special handlin', but he's worth your effort."

Julie smiled. "I know that, Aunt Maizie. Why didn't you marry?"

"I never found a man I thought tol'able, what with all the trouble and sweet talk it seems to take to keep one happy; but I think you'll never be sorry you took on Print. He's a man, Julie—a real man, as only God can make them. And I'm glad he found you. You're good for him."

The next day Jonas drove a not-too-wild cow with her female calf into the pen. By tying the cow's head close to a fence post and hobbling her hind legs,

Jonas and Maizie forced her to let the orphan suckle. She wouldn't give up more than a cup of milk at the first suckling with the strange calf.

"We'll have to supplement feedings today, but by tomorrow, she'll take him. We'll keep her own calf away from her. The cow and calf will bawl themselves hoarse, but the dogie'll get good feedings tomorrow. She has plenty of milk to feed two calves."

"Cruel, but necessary, I suppose," said Julie.

"It takes some persuasion to get a new mama for a dogie. We can't talk cow lingo, so we hafta' use force to convince a stubborn old cow of her Christian duty. Just look at that little creepmouse go," said Maizie as the calf wiggled his tail and guzzled. "He'll soon be gettin' more than his share and be able to take care of himself."

"Come to the house with me, Aunt Maizie. I sprinkled down a batch of laundry. We can talk while I iron."

After half an hour of watching a perspiring Julie wielding heavy sad irons on Print's wrinkled work clothing, Maizie asked, "How do you manage the washing?"

"Print builds the fire and fills the wash tubs before he leaves on Monday mornings. 'Course, there's still rubbing the clothes with lye soap and scrubbing them on the washboard. Some of the stains are stubborn."

"And rinsing and wringing and hanging them out to dry." Maizie watched Julie's face. "And moppin' the kitchen floor and front porch with some of the soapy water, as we all do on wash day."

Julie nodded. "Print is going to lower the clothes line. I have to stand on tiptoe." She set the iron back on the stove. "It is a job. Then I iron several days a week. I can't do it all at one time." She shrugged. "All part of housekeeping."

Maizie stomped back down the hill to Louisa. "There's no sense in that young'un having to cook every day. Lordy mercy! She has way more than she needs to do with those filthy clothes Print piles up. We need to take this in hand."

"We invite them often, and would gladly prepare all their meals. The additional mouth of one small woman is no burden, but we have to allow Julie to become the one Print turns to for his needs. I don't want to have to fight you to keep you from going up there to take over."

"You're right, Louisa, but it's hard for me to stay out of it."

Louisa mused, "Print's new cook, Polly, has a wife and a grown daughter. Jacob says they can use the work. You and I can still make the lye soap, but we can hire Polly's women to do the laundry for Julie and for us. Let her concentrate on shaping Print into the man God intends him to be. I'll run the idea by Jacob tonight."

A few days later, as Julie did the breakfast dishes, she evaluated her new life for the umpteenth time. The high spot of every day was the time just after dinner. On fine evenings, after Print finished his bookkeeping, he and Julie sat on the porch for the precious hour he devoted to her before he fell into bed. Julie felt certain Jacob had insisted Print save the time for his wife.

She made the most of it and listened to every word, so attentive to his descriptions of the work that his face showed he enjoyed their talks. What began as a duty in Print's mind became the high point of each day for both of them.

Print's other must for every evening was to kneel with Julie on the bedside rug for prayer. One night he fell asleep on his knees, and she had a terrible time rousing him enough to get him into bed. He found motivation and strength for his other pursuits with Julie, but sometimes his lovemaking came after a long nap.

Still I drink him in. He's my man and this is the life he led before we married. I promised to be a loyal and worthy mate, but I must be cautious about asking for changes.

Print's plan was important, but Julie couldn't suppress a few disloyal words. She stretched out the dishcloth and stared out the kitchen window. "Where is all this leading? Is it money and power-lust driving Print? Or is it a genuine belief that he's destined to own every long-horned cow and calf in the county, and all the acreage he can buy? There, I got it out of my system. I need to trust him."

One night in mid-October, not long after Print and Julie had fallen into bed, she whispered, "Are you still awake?"

"Mmmm...I'm almost asleep. What is it?"

"It won't take a minute. I want to ask you something."

"All right, sweetheart."

"Was that Louisiana girl beautiful?" Julie propped up on an elbow, watching his face in the moonlight pouring in through the front window.

"What?" Print drawled. "What Louisiana girl?"

"That doctor's daughter—the one you said was an angel. Was she beautiful?"

"Well, she was a handsome lady, but Dr. Keller has to be seventy, and his unmarried daughter in her forties. Her hair is graying. But she's an angel, all right—an angel of mercy. She and her mother took good care of me." His eyes were still closed.

"Print English! Why in the world didn't you describe her in that letter to your mother?"

He stared up at her. "Why? What difference did it make?"

"I was worried sick that a lovely Southern belle was there with you, tending to your every need and soothing your brow. You should have made it clear just who she was."

Print's lips smothered a grin.

"To think I rushed around getting up that dance before you could leave on a cattle drive. I was afraid you might take those steers to New Orleans, as you did before the war, and come home with a fluffy wife."

His infuriating chuckle was louder than usual. "You mean that whole Rain Dance was part of your scheme to marry me? I think that's one of the funniest things I ever heard! And all because I called a sweet lady an angel."

"Well, I had to do something. You hadn't even seen me since your return. Probably still thought of me as a red-haired, rock-throwing brat!"

Print's expression sobered. "I see what you mean. That night at the dance changed things for me. I no longer think of you that way."

He grinned and sat up. "Come here, you auburn-haired, rock-throwing brat and let me show you just how I do think of you."

"You horrid man! I don't believe I will."

"Yes, you will. You will," Print answered lazily, chuckling again as he reached for her. Julie giggled.

The next morning as Print stepped off the porch into the tiniest crack of dawn, Julie thought she heard him still laughing.

One night on the porch, after Zeke left, Julie asked Print about the ranch hand's story. He came fairly often, and occasionally brought an older cowboy, Tuffy, with him. Print had hired Zeke about the same time he hired Tuffy and the camp cook, Polly, prior to the wedding.

"Is Zeke from this part of the country? He sounds more southern."

"Father knew Lon Haskell, Zeke's dad, in Louisiana. Impressed by him. Sent him a letter when I decided to hire a right-hand man, and Lon sent Zeke."

"I like him," said Julie. "He's very kind to me."

Print nodded. "He rides for the brand. Zeke's loyalty belongs to the man who hires him. He's intelligent and has a skill with cattle born of long experience. But his aptitude for horses is God-given."

Julie smiled. "I heard your father say any horse that bucks Zeke off will have to shed his skin with him."

"He can curry the kinks out of anything you can throw a saddle on." Then Print offered his highest praise: "He's a good man."

Julie understood all she needed to know about Zeke in those words. She enjoyed his company when he could be persuaded to visit with them on the porch. That evening they had talked of the coming cattle drive. It was apparent Zeke was not in favor of rushing it.

"I can't set store by your plan to drive cattle across the state line right now. Too dangerous, what with the war all around us."

Print said slowly, "Might be something in what you say."

"By early spring I can set up a deal with Smith, McCandless and Carson," Zeke said. "They're honest cattle buyers. We can drive our herd to the Red and they'll meet us. The odds are better for an Indian Territory delivery. Cuts down on the risk of losing the herd to the military or rustlers. They're harassin' both armies."

Print was silent for a long minute. "It's shorter. Won't be away from home as long."

Julie wanted to shout *hurray*. The new timeline should relieve some of the pressure, and Print might be able to relax his wild urgency about gathering cattle. Perhaps she could enjoy more time with him—her kind of time, when his mind was not focused on longhorns.

The next day, Zeke knocked on the door with a pail of milk in his hand.

"Thank you, Zeke. Have time for a cup of coffee?"

"Allow as how I might," Zeke said. "Mr. Print is shoeing a horse. But I'll sit on the porch. Too dirty to come inside."

No use arguing with the man. Julie joined him, two cups in hand. Hers held hot tea and Zeke's, some of Print's hot mud.

"I appreciate all you do for us—for me."

"You belong to the brand," he said. "It's my place to watch over you, just like I do Mr. Print."

"You're easy to talk to, Zeke. I'll feel safe asking you anything I don't want to ask Print. When I have a question for Print, I want it to be an intelligent one. I need to become a knowledgeable rancher's wife."

Zeke smiled. "You will, Miz Julie."

"And it makes me feel good to hear about my man from someone who understands him. I can tell you my fears, because I know you'll never give even a hint of them to Print."

"I promise you this, Miz Julie. I'll watch over Mr. Print and back his play, whatever it is."

"That's a comfort, Zeke. Dealing with some of the men in this county is as dangerous as working with wild cattle. Guns could be involved. Print is impressed with your ability to handle a pistol. I'm impressed with your quiet wisdom."

Chapter 17

Several days later, Julie was enjoying a particularly beautiful sunset on the porch. She thought Print was also, but he turned to her and said, "Even with the recent large-scale raids, I count seven thousand branded Reverse E cattle. There'll be eight thousand by spring. Not all will be marketable, of course, but I figure I can drive at least three thousand four-to-eight-year-olds. Pretty easy job with my crew of cowboys and Tuffy Snyder. Tuffy won't be worth much, but he'll want to go."

Julie smothered a sigh and thought back to her first day on the ranch, when she'd seen the pretty creek. Her dream of resting on its grassy banks to read or paint—or enjoy a picnic with Print—remained unfulfilled. She was beginning to understand more clearly Louisa's love-hate relationship with cattle.

The needs of those cows took up too much of her husband's time, but she must choose her words wisely. After all, she'd made a promise to Print to help him reach his dream.

I've learned a lot about the ranch.

Smaller sales than the one now planned had been the norm but the numbers had steadily grown. Each year a new crop of calves was born, and wild cows and calves were added to the herd. Grown bulls couldn't not be branded, but they followed the cows.

Most of the men remaining in the county were either too old or too young for the army, but some were recent immigrants from Mexico—experienced vaqueros, who stayed off the army rolls. Print had hired two of them. They, with Zeke and Tuffy, Fred Maher and his two sons, Polly, and Print and his brothers, made a force of twelve relentless men bent on gathering, branding, and castrating young longhorn bull calves.

Cows, of course, were also branded, but Print said they were exempt from a drive if their calves were too young or if they were good breeders.

Julie mused, "Tuffy is aptly named. He's a tough old bird, but I like him. His wind-bitten face is a cobweb of lines, and his voice seems to crawl over slivers of glass, but he has a certain charm."

Print laughed. "Cobwebs, glass, and charm. Hardly seem to fit together, but I know what you mean. He and Zeke have become close friends."

Crippled in the range incident Print had related on their first ride, Tuffy still found a job with Print because Frank had mentioned the old cowboy's need. Frank's kind heart and Print's generosity provided for the old fellow.

Tuffy also enjoyed part-time work with the Sanders spread. He was a good go-between for the two big ranches, both fighting determined rustlers.

"In the old days," Print said, "Tuffy could uncork a bronc with the best of them. Now he's pretty much up the spout."

Julie laughed. "Some evenings you come in pretty far up the spout yourself."

He allowed a smile. "On a drive, Tuffy might make a fair cook's helper if he can lower himself from cowboy status. Not an easy deal for a man who's spent his life on a horse."

And you're one of them. If I didn't insist on the buggy, you'd have me ride a horse to church.

The next morning after Print swallowed his breakfast—obviously not tasting a bite—he rose to leave and Julie, as always, went to the doorway with him for her squeeze and kiss. As Print finished the unfocused kiss, his mind clearly on the work ahead, Julie held his face between her hands.

"Are you happy living with me?"

"What? Julie, why do you have to ask me that?"

"It's just a question."

"Come here," he said, leading her back to the table. He sat and pulled her onto his lap. Leaning her back on his arm atop the table, he studied her.

"I guess you can say I'm happy living with you—if you can stretch happy till it breaks."

His hand rubbed her cheek. "I've drunk you in like fine wine. You've filled me up, all the cracks and crevices, and you're healing the chinks in my hide."

Tears sprang to her eyes, but he hadn't finished.

"I know you're happy living with me, because I hear you humming, and then you look at me the way you do. I guess I haven't learned to show you how I feel, but I will."

Julie rose, swiped away a tear, and said, "It was just a question, but I'm glad I asked it. Now you better get out of here before Zeke comes to see why I'm burning your daylight. He'll know it's my doing."

Print laughed as he made his way out the door. "I'll show you my appreciation tonight."

It was Julie's turn to laugh.

One crisp November morning, Print readied for a trip to town.

"I'll go along," Julie said, "and check on the dress goods I ordered from Mr. Bowden."

Print swung by Sheriff Longworth's office first to check on the complaints against Tru Evans and his father Tom. Julie waited in the buggy.

As he crawled in beside her, Print said, "After seeing Tru's signature on the papers Fred Maher gave me, the sheriff thinks we have a good court case. Old man Evans is no doubt selling some of our beef in that butcher shop he opened after he left the Home Guard. But it's hard to prove rustling without catching thieves in the act."

"I hate to think of the grief we're causing Frank by placing his father in line for a prison term," Julie said.

"When he comes home, he'll understand. Frank won't be worried about Tru. He's never agreed with his brother's bumming around with Cully. Since it's Tru's name on the bogus bill of sale, maybe old Tom won't have to answer."

Print drove just up the street to Bowden's store. Before they could get out of the buggy, Cully stood up from the edge of the nearby saloon porch where he'd been sitting with Tru. He started walking toward Julie's side of the buggy.

Julie turned to Print, watching for his reaction. He sat relaxed, but his face was taut and tension had seeped into his shoulders.

Cully didn't speak. Julie's quick glance showed

his gaze locked on her. She turned away.

As usual, Print wore his pistol. *Please, Father, don't let this confrontation between two strong-willed men end in disaster.*

When Cully was about ten feet from the buggy, Print growled, "That's far enough, Cully. Don't come closer to my wife."

Cully's words were slurred by the drinks he'd had. "Maybe most of the land north of town belongs to you, Mr. high-and-mighty *Prince* English, but the streets of San Simon don't. I can walk where I want."

He continued to advance slowly until Julie could detect the liquor fumes emanating from him.

In an instant Print stood and leaned over her. He sent the buggy whip slashing across the bridge of Cully's nose. Hurling himself to a position between his enemy and Julie, Print confronted danger. Cully backed away cursing. His hand clutched a red welt rising across his face.

Print's eyes were slits. His hand near his gun, he said, "It's your call, Cully. You're pretty drunk and I'm not, but unshuck your pistol if you want to. I don't have time for funning around."

Tru had remained in his chair on the saloon porch throughout the exchange, never moving a muscle that Julie could see. Now he said, "Don't believe I'd accept the invitation if I'z you, Cully. You're sure to get the little end of the horn. Bowden's in the door, holding a shotgun."

Cully glanced toward the store and then back to Print, glaring pure hatred. He pulled his shoulders back and dropped his hands to his side. His fingers twitched. But he didn't pull his pistol.

Print turned on his heel and returned to the buggy, directing a nod toward Mr. Bowden, whose shotgun was still leveled at Cully.

After driving a few hundred feet, Print pulled over to the side of the street. He turned to Julie.

"Zeke says Cully has become as savage as a meat axe and loco to boot, and he may be right. That was certainly a crazy thing he did back there. That man has become a danger to women."

Julie only nodded. She couldn't squeeze a sound past the knot of fear that had formed in her throat. Tremors coursed through her body. *It could have ended horribly.*

"He was undressing you with his eyes right in front of me, and Tru seems to egg him on. Don't go near Cully, and never let him catch you alone."

Her voice was anxious. "Was I somehow at fault, Print? Did I do something to encourage Cully to come at me?"

"Of course not. Cully's becoming a sick and twisted man without any help from either of us."

"He probably hasn't forgotten that day I threw the rock. How I wish I could take back that incident."

Print smiled and then became serious again. "You may not agree with how I handled him, but a man has to take a stand. We can sit on the porch and talk if you want to, but I'll tell you now, I'll do the same thing tomorrow, and a thousand tomorrows after that, if the situation arises."

Julie laid her hand on her husband's arm. "I trust your judgment, and I never doubt your loving concern for me."

She did trust him. He might never confide his innermost secrets; there were parts of him—perhaps more than other people—that were unknowable. As Maizie had said, a cowboy was always a bit alone.

She added, her voice shaky, "I just pray it doesn't make you vulnerable to men who would use it to destroy you."

A sob burst from her and Print's arm was instantly around her. She quavered. "I'm thankful I didn't have to face Cully alone."

"Never do that," said Print. "Don't even think of it."

Chapter 18

The next morning, Print told his brothers and Zeke about the encounter with Cully.

Hamilton's face was indignant. "That wasn't enough, Print. Cully insulted your wife, and Julie deserves better. She's one of the sweetest, best women I know besides Mother. She can't handle the likes of Cully, and a buggy whip's not going to scare him off."

"I'll take care of Julie, little brother."

"I know Cully and Tru have started breaking in uninvited on those *bailes*, the dances in Gallo. Whooping it up, insulting everyone, and dancing drunk. Teresa says the girls are afraid of them, especially of Cully."

Gallo was a tiny settlement where Polly and three related families lived. Teresa was Polly's niece. She and Ham had become close friends.

"I might start going to some of those dances," Hamilton continued. "If I'm around when Cully insults Julie or Teresa or any other woman, I'll show him he has the wrong pig by the tail. I won't just hit him with a buggy whip—I'll give him a taste of my pistol."

"Pull in your horns, Ham. I'll take that sidearm away from you if I hear any more talk like that," Print warned.

Hamilton snorted and walked away. Print shook his head. He needed to spend more time with Ham. The boy had some hot-headed notions. Mother might be right about letting him carry that pistol.

On the other hand, not to have one was just as dangerous. At least if someone saw the gun, they might think twice about taking Ham on.

Julie and Print sat on the porch after dinner on an unseasonably warm evening in early December. As the sun sank lower, the light of day bled away into the dusky colors that come before a velvety night.

Print asked the question she'd been dreading. "How was your day?"

Julie squirmed. "There was a small problem. It was the fault of that dogie calf, Print. He needs to stay in the corrals."

"What did he do?" Print watched her closely.

"He kept coming up on the porch trying to get at my basket of pansies. I shooed him away at least three times this morning and once in the afternoon. Please see that he stays penned."

"Julie..."

"Oh, all right. I may as well tell you. I finished my chores and had some time before I needed to start supper, so I decided to heat some water for a good soak in the tub. I crawled in the bath and relaxed until the water began to cool. Just as I was crawling out, I heard a noise on the porch again."

She stopped and searched Print's face. He seemed prepared to receive the story with the grave attention it deserved. She needed reassurance and it should be her husband who gave it to her.

"So, I just wrapped my old blue towel around me and flung open the door—there's never anyone around the house in the early afternoon. I shook the towel at the calf and said, 'Shoo!'"

She slumped lower into her chair. "He shooed all right—and so did Zeke, who must have come onto the porch to corral the pest. I've never seen that man move so fast. He was almost out of sight before I got the door closed."

Print's expression was serious, and he shook his head.

I've caused embarrassment for my husband.

"What will Zeke think of me? I'm so mortified about the whole thing, Print."

He reached over and took her hand, his face still grave. "Julie, I think Zeke will stay shooed. He won't need a second warning."

"Print English! I can see you're about to burst from want of laughing. I'm serious—what should I do about Zeke?"

"You need to come here and get thoroughly kissed by your husband, and then we can both laugh till we drop. You can bet Zeke is doing some hooting every time he thinks of it, not that he'll ever mention it to a soul."

He pulled Julie into his arms and both of them dissolved into mirth.

The next day Louisa received a surprise visit from Betty. After the amenities were done, and the cups of tea were poured, Betty said, "Julie doesn't know I'm here. She's determined to fulfill her role as Print's supportive wife, but John and I are concerned the work may be too much for her. She appeared worn out at church on Sunday."

"I agree, and Maizie frets over the same thing. It's easy enough to get some help for Julie. But Print's obsession with his cattle is at the root of the problem. It will take more prayer and thought. Julie sees him slaving day after day and feels the need to work as hard as he does."

"Exactly," said Betty. "She doesn't want to disappoint him."

"I've been hesitant to interfere, but Jacob and I have been discussing this for some time. We're ready to use our resources in changing the direction our oldest son is taking."

"I knew I could count on you, Louisa. Print is a fine young man, but Julie says he's reluctant to talk to her about important matters. Especially his worries. He must imagine he's protecting her. You and I both know a marriage is built on trust."

"I give you my word that I will do what I can."

"And I will pray," said Betty as she left.

The next day, Louisa mentioned a health problem to Julie. "Perhaps you and Print can eat breakfast with us for a while. Then you can help me around the house."

Julie said, "I'll help all I can, Louisa. I can easily find time."

Oh, yes, darlin'. And when would that be? Between trips to the clothesline and ironing board or frying steak?

"I'm so grateful to God for giving me three mothers to replace the one who is now with Him."

Louisa reached for Julie's hand and said, "Jacob has suggested hiring Polly's wife to help us with laundry. Polly's daughter, Apolonia, also needs a job and he's wondering if you'll accept her help. The family can use the extra money, and I think Print will like the idea. He mentions how hard you work."

And I can use the breakfast table as a counseling session. Have to be careful to use humor to remove any sting from my words, but I can ask questions and point out changes that might be helpful.

As they took a tea break one morning a week later, Julie said to Louisa, "I see the intent behind some of your questions; you're concerned about Print's obsession with his work. Maybe my strict adherence to the bargain I thought I made with him isn't helping."

"Didn't realize I was so transparent." Louisa smiled briefly. "Let's give Print this. He's a respectful son. Still sensitive to any disappointment we might feel in the way he conducts his life."

"Oh, I agree Louisa. Of course, he should be. You two are wise and caring. I feel the same."

"Jacob is beginning a gentle campaign. He'll find ways to help Print evaluate what he's doing to fulfill his vows to you. You're a gift of God to our headstrong son."

Tears rose in the eyes of both. They hugged.

Julie and Print were on the porch a week later. He sat rigid in his chair, arms crossed over his chest. Something was on his mind.

After a long silence, he said, "Some things Father mentioned have set me thinking. Do you believe my dream of an empire is wrong?"

Is he beginning to question his burning ambition? The days of relentlessly driving himself, his brothers, and his cowboys?

"Not wrong, Print. But what is your reason for needing more and more? What will be enough? And how will great wealth help us be happier?"

She bit her lip and bowed her head for a moment before she said, "Will it make you more confident before God that you're on the right track?"

A long moment of silence. "Never thought of it like that. Especially the part about God. So, you think God has an opinion about how many cattle I gather?"

"His interest is your motive. Why you're building an empire."

"Father mentioned it takes me away from the time I have with you. I do treasure you, Julie. I still remember your question about if I was happy."

"I know you love me, Print. I have absolutely no doubts."

"It was selfish of me to let you work as hard as I did. I should have been the one to suggest getting help for you with the laundry."

"None of that matters to me, Print. What I need from you is more of this kind of conversation—when you tell me about what concerns you."

"A man is supposed to protect his wife. There are things you don't need to know. This is a rough country and things happen that I never want you to hear."

"You mean, don't worry my pretty head? I'm not some delicate—"

He wagged his finger. "No rocks."

She smiled. "I hope you see that protection is not all I need from you. I need you to trust me to handle anything you say. It's easy to imagine the worst when you don't tell me the facts."

He sighed, and his mouth turned down. "Hey, enough of this. Come sit in my lap, my auburn-haired beauty." He wiggled his brows and twirled an imaginary mustache.

"Oh, Print. We need to talk about this. But at least it's a start. I do love you, you aggravating man."

That night Print lay awake, thinking. He'd have to try harder. Julie listened each time he talked of his dream, but he needed to hear hers. They hadn't even talked of children.

Maybe he could pray with her about business decisions. Should be an easy way to make her feel his trust. But there was no way he could tell her about his worries.

She couldn't know of the knot in his stomach every time he heard another story about that bunch down in The Bend. Like the murder of the old storekeeper just across the county line last week. She'd never sleep again.

Wrong. Julie would sleep. The thought became a certainty.

Julie had a lack of anxiety he'd never known. How he could obtain it, he had no idea. But he meant to find out. Father said he needed to talk to other godly men, like the Sanders brothers.

They were successful ranchers, committed to relying on Christian principles in their operations. They talked with Print about their cow camps and how they managed their affairs, and had begun planning how they could make the spring drive a truly massive one. Both of their big outfits would pool their resources with his, offering a safer and more profitable alternative. If they'd heard that plan from God, He must be a pretty good business man.

Suddenly his thoughts sobered. His chest ached. *I believe in the sacrifice of Christ, but have I missed its deeper implications?* He'd never thought about the fact that God "wanted sons, not grandsons," until John had pointed it out last Sunday over dinner.

I've been God's grandson since birth. Even during the war when I prayed, I felt God heard me only because of the worthiness of my parents. The idea of coming closer to God was frustrating. How did it really work?

"He'll always be a cowboy," Julie reflected to Aunt Betty two days later. "According to Maizie, they're a breed apart from other men. My father enjoyed discussion and opposing viewpoints. I can't imagine Print becoming as open as Father, but I believe he's trying to let me in. We pray together about business decisions now."

"It's a start," said Aunt Betty.

Julie smiled. "I'm thankful you took my side when Uncle John had doubts about Print. I love that man so much."

"This has been my prayer for years: I pray that I can accept the things God asks John to give me—not ask for what I think I need. I ask God to help me appreciate him the way he is. To help me remain a praying wife, and to allow God to make changes in my husband. Not to say I won't take him to task now and again."

They laughed together.

"I'm going to pray your prayer every day, too, Aunt Betty. I think I've been too focused on my disappointments. I need to accept Print and allow God to guide him."

Won't be easy for a lawyer's daughter with decided opinions of her own.

The Dentons were obviously growing fonder of

Print. The frantic days of his "fall frenzy," as Uncle John called it, were giving way to a more considerate husband.

"Print's learning what I learned a long time ago," Uncle John said. "Never give your animals more attention than you do your wife unless you like sleeping in the barn. Print is beginning to put the needs of his wife above the needs of ignorant cows."

John Denton's opinions always went straight to the bone, but Julie saw he was wise enough to pull back with Print. He treated Print as the son he never had. During Sunday meals with the Dentons, Julie watched the two men laugh together, both of them sharing a sharp wit and a view of the world a tad off-center.

Uncle John talked matter-of-factly about how he stretched out his decisions before his wife and his God. Print said he could see advantages of a life directed by the Lord instead of going it alone. But he rubbed his ear the way he did when he was undecided.

Chapter 19

One night a week later, Julie and Print sat at the table sipping cocoa. The fire had burned low, but lent a cozy warmth to the cabin.

He nodded drowsily. "Ready for bed?"

Julie murmured, "Mmm-hmm." She was tired and slept almost immediately, but in a couple of hours, Print whispered, "Are you awake?"

She answered sleepily and turned toward him, in the habit of meeting her husband's need, but he did not reach out for her.

"I have a question."

He stood and opened the curtain, allowing the moon's white light to flood the bed. Print had something on his mind. She fluffed her pillow and leaned against the headboard, waiting. He climbed back into bed and propped on an elbow.

"How do you know when you're in God's will?"

She sucked in a quick breath. The question was so unexpected. Had she heard him rightly? "Do you mean me, personally?"

"Yes. How do you know when you're doing what God wants of you?"

This moment might be one of the most important in her life. Her heartbeat quickened. *Tell the truth, no matter how foolish it sounds.* "I hear music."

His eyebrows shot up, and Julie hurried on. "Not notes or singing, but it feels like music—a rhythm inside. I'm not sure whether I'm hearing or feeling. Maybe it's a song God sings in my spirit."

"Do you hear that music right now?"

"Always, when I'm with you."

From his expression, the comment almost sidetracked everything, but he managed to stay on the subject.

"Is there anything else that helps you know when you're doing the will of God?"

How do I put this? "I feel at peace. If I obey His Word, I don't have to worry about the results. Wisdom is built in."

Print moved closer, cupped her chin in his hand, and stared at her. "And what happens when you deliberately disobey or when you make a mistake?"

"The two are different, at least in the way they affect me. When I make a mess of something—sin inadvertently as Sam Cravens says on Sundays—I tell God I know I did something wrong, even when I'm not exactly sure what it is."

He released her. "And what happens to the music and your feeling of peace?"

"Not really gone, but they're distant." Julie hurried on before she lost him. "I ask Him to help me get back on track." Her mind raced. "We all sin, Print. Uncle John says God wants persistence, rather than perfection."

Print grunted. "Good to know. So, when you're back on track?"

How was he taking this? His expression gave no clue, but he was still asking questions. Julie winged a prayer for the right words. “When I’m back on the right path, the music becomes distinct and so does the peace—His peace, I’ve learned. I relax in the fact that God is in control, even when things go wrong.”

A puzzled frown furrowed Print’s brow.

“I wish I had better words.”

“What if you deliberately sin?”

“The music stops. I feel separated from God. Unable to stand myself until I can hear it again. I have to have the music, Print. It’s what I live on—like food and air. I don’t think my body works well without it.”

Print kissed her fingertips, but said nothing.

She touched his cheek. “Is this making any sense to you, darling?”

“Maybe. Go on.”

“After Bert and my parents died, I lost God’s peace. I was angry with Him. But He stayed with me, protecting me with His ‘cloak of mercy,’ as Uncle John called it—even though I said hateful and unbelieving things. Maybe I was testing God to see if I could make Him stop loving me the way I felt I had stopped loving Him.”

“It’s hard to think of you mad at God.”

“I was very angry, but He kept showing me His love in the people around me, and in His creation and His word. Gently God called me back until I could no longer resist. I came back, sobbing and grateful. He never lets us go, once we are His.”

Print pulled her to him. “I’m not ever going to let you go, either, even if you get really mad at me.” He rubbed her back. After a long silence, he said, “Do you think I should hear music?” His voice sounded a bit weak.

She laughed. "Oh, Print, I've no idea how God is telling you when you're in His will. I imagine He does it differently in each person because He made each one of us so distinct from another. Does that sound right?"

Print didn't answer, but lay back, staring at the ceiling. Julie relaxed into her pillow, praying that her words had brought him closer to God. He took her hand and sighed.

A few days later, Conner and Hamilton were riding a southern range in a brushy pasture. Some distance from headquarters, Conner spotted four men driving cattle. "I don't recognize those cowboys or their horses," he said.

"I'll bet that beef is wearing Reverse E brands," Hamilton declared.

"We need to turn back and get help. Print's told us more than once not to go it alone."

"*I'm* going after them, with or without you," Hamilton growled, spurring his horse.

His head is as hard as Print's. Conner managed to catch up, and they followed the cattle. "That big brindle cow at the back of the herd may be one of ours. Let's see if we can get close enough to make certain," Conner said.

The brothers followed until the animals reached a deep creek, where they began milling around. The four cowboys driving them were too preoccupied to notice Conner and Hamilton moving slowly through the brush. Finally, the brothers rode close enough to get a clear view of the brands.

"Most of them have the Reverse E," Hamilton said. He pulled his rifle from the scabbard. Without warning, he broke cover and fired. His shot hit one of the cowboys at the rear of the herd. The rustler fell from his saddle.

Conner whipped out his own gun. The fat was in the fire.

The two men in the creek surrounded by panicked cattle couldn't bring their guns into play. The third man pulled his rifle and began firing back at Hamilton from his rearing horse.

When Conner's shots came too close, the thief housed his rifle. He pulled his wounded companion up onto his own mount. The two forded the creek, not far behind the others who had turned tail to run.

Hamilton spurred in hot pursuit, but Conner rammed his horse into Hamilton's, knocking his brother to the ground. Conner jumped on top of him, keeping a firm grip on the arm that clawed for a pistol.

"Ham, it's me. Don't make me hit you. It's over." Hamilton quit struggling and both stood up. Retrieving his hat and knocking the dust from his clothes without meeting Conner's gaze, Hamilton remounted. The two gathered the cattle and drove them back to a range near the work pens. Hamilton's face was set and he said not a single word, even at the barn. He cared for his horse and started toward the ranch house as Print listened to Conner's story.

"Come back here, Ham. We need to talk."

"I don't want to hear it. I saved our cattle. I'll patrol alone from here on."

"If you can shake Zeke off your tail, you might. I'm putting him in charge of you on future range patrols."

"Zeke will be better than a tattle-tale."

Conner stared after Hamilton's departing figure. The near disaster was irrefutable proof of his lack of judgment.

Print said, "Let him go for now. I'll have a tough talk with him. Both of you could have been killed, outnumbered as you were."

On a frosty January morning a week later, the cabin smelled of wood smoke, frying bacon, and rich coffee. As Julie poured his morning mud, Print said, "Ben Truly is ready to record the deed in a new land deal. I want your signature on it. Can you go to town with me?"

"Oh, yes, and maybe we can spend some time with Uncle John and Aunt Betty."

"Dress warmly. We'll take Lou and the buggy."

Julie waited on the porch for Print to bring the buggy. The smell of winter tinged with smoke filled her lungs. It felt good to be alive, and she offered a prayer of thanks for her life with Print.

He often allowed Julie to take the reins, while he watched his wife and her mare with a satisfied grin. But this morning Print didn't move from the driver's seat. Julie took his outstretched hand and he pulled her up beside him. He seemed in a hurry to be off.

She peeked at his face. *In full-fledged business mode.*

She tried to set aside her disappointment and enjoy the crisp loveliness of the day. Like jewel boxes, huge live oaks displayed their evergreen leaves, glistening like tiny diamonds in the early morning sun. A few high clouds streaked the sky. But the morning's beauty was diminished by the speeding buggy. It fairly flew along the lane.

She blurted, "You're pushing Lou too hard."

"Please don't tell me how to drive a buggy, Julie." His voice was infuriatingly calm.

She glared at him, but his full attention was on driving. She gritted her teeth to keep her tongue in check. Aggravating how handsome she still found him, even when she was annoyed.

She concentrated on the pleasure of watching her mare. Lou moved swiftly and smoothly. Such a joy to own. She never failed to come a-running each time Julie approached.

Print offered a brief comment or two, but none of the banter she enjoyed. *Thinking cows again.* Remembering her prayer about allowing God to shape him, Julie didn't try to pull him out of his business reverie. Or was she sulking?

They soon reached town and drove directly to the attorney's office in the single stone building on San Simon's main street. Print helped her from the buggy and tied Lou to the hitching post as Julie straightened her hat. They then made their way up the stairs to the office of Ben Truly.

Acting as he often did on Print's behalf, Ben had bought the new property in a sheriff's sale. Print acquired small pieces of land adjoining his own acreage whenever the opportunity arose. As Julie placed her name on the document, she had second thoughts. How had the loss affected the elderly man who'd been forced to forfeit the property when he could no longer pay taxes?

She remembered Uncle John's words. "Good will is not a ready commodity when a determined man is involved. Human nature being what it is, envy and lack of communication can build enmities between men who might otherwise be friends."

Her husband didn't bother explaining himself to other men, and he had slight patience with anyone trying to learn more of what he considered his business. To some Print might appear arrogant.

Occasionally even to his wife.

Building a communicating marriage had to be done prayerfully and wisely. Other tactics failed miserably with her man. Print had improved, but he still kept things from her. Didn't want to worry her. Maizie had let slip that business about Ham and the rustlers.

After she'd signed the deed, Print and Ben began discussing war news, and Julie said, "I'll wait downstairs."

Outside, she removed her canvas jacket, put it in the buggy, and stood in the welcome winter sunshine. The day had warmed considerably. A loud voice caught her attention.

Three men had emerged from the saloon next door. One pointed toward her, and an elderly man, who'd obviously taken too much drink, staggered in her direction.

"Miz English! 'M Jed Early. Need t' talk t' ya."

Julie stepped back toward the office door, but the elderly man hurried forward to cut her off. He stumbled and fell against her. When she reached out to steady him, he grabbed her upper arm and uttered an oath, trying to get himself upright.

The old man offered no real threat. Julie regarded the two men who remained outside the saloon, watching intently.

They put him up to this.

A thud of boots sounded on the inside stairway, and Print burst from the door. He must have spotted her from a window. His face twisted, he reached for his pistol and raised it, ready to crash the weapon onto Early, who still clung to her arm.

Julie thrust the unstable man away and stepped to the side, but she was still too close. The gun was already in descent. As the elderly man floundered away, she found herself facing a maniac with a gun, which would clearly connect with some part of her anatomy.

Somehow Print was able to control the action, and the pistol spun into the dirt. Only his hand hit her shoulder, but the impact sent Julie reeling to the hard earth. She fought to catch her breath.

The inflexible face staring down at her was almost unrecognizable—one whose nostrils flared. Print grabbed her extended hand, and pulled her up.

"Get in the buggy."

Julie refused to flinch from his infuriated gaze. He relaxed his grip, but not his expression, as he watched the old man reeling back toward the saloon.

Julie yanked her hand away. She dusted off her skirt and on wobbly knees climbed into the buggy, ignoring the offered hand. Print swooped up the fallen pistol and joined her with a glare. She bowed her head.

Reins tight in hand, staring straight ahead, Print lashed Lou away from the corner. They sped away toward the edge of town, the visit to Uncle John and Aunt Betty clearly a casualty of the encounter. The buggy didn't slow for the two miles it took to reach the creek crossing. At last, Print stopped, allowing Lou to lower her head and drink from the shallow water at her feet.

Here it comes. Julie lowered her head and touched her forehead with a shaking hand.

"Julie," Print growled in a voice far worse than the one he had used under the oak, "Don't ever do that again! Don't *ever* get between me and another man! Do you hear me?"

She remained motionless.

"Look at me! Never do that again! *Never get between another man and me!*" he shouted.

She swallowed the wave of rising resentment. Someone had to remain reasonable. Using the last drop of her restraint, Julie raised her head and managed to sound almost normal when she spoke.

"Thank you for coming to my aid, but I was in no danger. Can't this wait until we reach the porch?"

Print's struggle for control still contorted his face. "You could have been badly hurt trying to save that worthless old drunk!"

"I wasn't trying to save him. I was trying to save myself and you. You could have killed him, or at the very least, been guilty of a serious assault."

Print's expression was mulish.

"Two men tried to use him to cause you harm. You had no way of knowing that as you came to my aid, but I did."

Print's breathing was coming under control, but anger still blazed on his face. "What are you talking about? That old man is the one whose land I bought this morning. You were an easy target to get to me."

"I realize that, but I had to do something. You were out of control."

He stared at her for a moment. "You could have been seriously injured—if not by him, by me!" His voice shook.

Julie saw fear and vulnerability replace the anger in his expression.

"The last thing I'd ever want to do is harm you." Print's trembling hand covered his mouth for a moment.

"The two men I saw set up the skirmish, Print. They wanted you to kill old man Early."

His troubled expression showed his anguish. He appeared beyond speech.

"Two men I didn't recognize came out of the saloon with Early. One of them pointed at me and said something to him. They were obviously working him up into a confrontation, counting on your temper to play into their hands. They would have been innocent witnesses to assault or murder, depending how hard you hit that drunken old fellow."

Print shook his head. "Julie—"

"I wasn't in danger from Early. He was too far gone. His hand was on my arm only because he fell against me and tried to right himself. You had no idea that was the case because you couldn't see what had happened."

Print's intent contemplation softened a bit.

At least he's thinking rationally again.

Lou had quenched her thirst and buried her muzzle, blowing in the water in sensuous enjoyment. Print shook the reins and uttered his *chirk*, the clicking noise that set Lou back on the journey home. There were no more words between them.

Julie didn't trust herself to speak. Her injured shoulder throbbed, and anger flared as the image of Print's furious face filled her thoughts. How could she live with a man whose temper could veer so dangerously out of control?

Chapter 20

At the cabin, Print lifted Julie from the buggy and strode ahead of her to take his usual chair on the porch. Julie followed. Neither spoke. His face was tight, but he was once again the man she knew as husband—a man of reason. That other one, the out-of-control maniac who had reached for a pistol as his first line of defense, was gone.

Father, please help me and help him. What can we do?

She treasured Print's respect. He didn't view her as a helpless, clinging female. He believed in her as a woman who knew what she wanted and why. She liked thinking for herself and enjoyed her certain amount of independence. Print trusted her good judgment and she didn't want to risk losing his faith in her.

Her defense of Mr. Early may have jeopardized all that and driven a wedge between them. But Print's flash of temper had compelled her to take action. It was her wifely duty to intervene. And she had suffered as a result. Could she make him understand?

In an almost normal voice, he said, "Let me see your arm."

"It's nothing. Poor old man Early just steadied himself against me."

"Let...me...see...your...arm."

Reluctantly, Julie offered her right arm to Print. He unbuttoned her cuff. Faint purple fingerprints were forming midway up her arm, where the old man had gripped it.

Print grunted. He stood and leaned over to unbutton the top of her dress. He pushed it away to see the damage he'd caused to her right shoulder. The red, swollen area would soon turn blue. A groan escaped his lips.

Print bent his head and brushed the damaged shoulder with his lips. "Julie," he breathed.

Sweeping her up from the chair into his arms, he entered the cabin and set her down, but he did not release her from his arms. She could feel his breath and his kisses in her hair; then she felt his tears.

She raised her face to his and tried to wipe away the moisture from his face, but he stilled her hand, making no effort to hide the fact that he was crying. Was she the first to witness Print's manly tears, or had they wet the face of a fallen friend in battle?

He crushed her to him, his voice broken. "What are we going to do? How can I keep you safe in this forsaken country? Even I hurt you, and I love you more than I love myself. I can't live without you, Julie. You're my music. I don't have any music from God except you."

Julie held him and placed her face against his chest, then kissed his neck, the only part she could reach. His embrace tightened.

"God put us together, and He will keep us safe.

There's never any other security in this life. But you cannot believe that I am all you have to live for. You cannot give me first place. I must not be God in your life. He created you for His purposes and I'm here beside you to help. I'm just a part of it."

Print said nothing before he released her. When he spoke, his face mirrored his inner anguish. "I lost control. I never meant to harm you, but I did, and I don't know what to do about it."

"I'm all right." Her brow furrowed. "Bruises heal themselves, but temperaments do not. You need some godly wisdom to help you deal with your anger. I cannot live with that."

Print's expression was haunted. "Don't leave me, Julie."

She relaxed her frown and gazed deeply into his eyes. "Get help, from Sam Cravens or your father." Her voice was firm. "I never want to face your black temper again."

He stared back at her and finally shook his head. "You won't."

Print left the cabin and did not return before she went to bed. Julie banked the fire, readied for bed, and left a lamp burning on the kitchen table. When he came in, she pretended to be asleep. She didn't feel ready to talk more, even after hours of prayer.

Print lay beside Julie, boiling with the overload of activity in his mind. Strangely, despite his tumbling thoughts, he felt almost peaceful.

How wonderful to be lying beside this woman in their bed. What he had with Julie was to be savored and enjoyed. He would never again jeopardize it in anger. Sleep tried to claim him, but he fought it. He wanted more minutes of lying beside her, cherishing the gift of his wife. He stroked her head gently, but she didn't stir.

Wise, Julie. I don't think you're asleep, but enough has been said for a while.

The next morning, he woke her with his usual kiss. "I love you. I was so wrong. I wanted to tell you last night."

"I was awake when you came in."

"I thought so." He got up on an elbow and peered down at her. "I told Father about the trouble with old man Early and what my temper cost you. He had much to say, and we prayed about it." He pulled her closer. "It will never happen again."

"I forgive you."

About a week later, Print came in one evening looking so disturbed Julie prolonged her embrace.

"What's wrong?"

He took her hand and led her to the table, where Julie took a chair. Holding her hand more tightly, Print mumbled, "They found Teresa."

Julie stiffened. She didn't want to hear this. Judging from Print's expressiont, it couldn't be good news.

Teresa Galindo was Polly's niece—Apolonia's cousin—and she was an absolute treasure of a girl. Only fifteen, but so filled with a love for life and for God. She had disappeared from outside her home three days ago and a large search party had formed.

"What do you mean, they found her? She isn't—"

"Teresa's dead, and she was murdered."

Julie sobbed and lowered her head. Who in this world would want to harm such a sweet child?

She looked up. "How—"

"Don't ask details; they'll only upset you more. She was found in the brush south of town, near the Wyatt pens—a long way from her home in Gallo."

Print stroked her hand. "Her funeral is tomorrow. We're all going, including most of the hands, as a show of support to Polly and the other families. We'll leave a skeleton crew here to keep an eye on things."

Julie rounded the table's corner as Print opened his arms and pulled her onto his lap. She cried bitterly against his chest. Finally, she raised her head and wiped her cheeks. He kissed her before she stood.

"I need to finish dinner."

"Let it wait for a while. I'm not hungry." He stood with her, and his face darkened before he growled, "Those thieves and murderers from The Bend are out of control. I didn't tell you two riders were found east of here ten days ago, probably murdered for their horses and saddles. I feel certain the same bunch are responsible for Teresa, too."

Print pulled Julie closer, and kissed her again and again, obviously worried about her safety in the midst of strengthening evil. Her thoughts were haunted by grief for Teresa and her family, and worry for Ham and Print.

The day after the funeral, Print announced to Julie that he would move Zeke from the bunk house into a cabin of his own on the hill, midway between their cabin and the one Conner was building less than a quarter-mile away.

"A man and his sons from Gallo say they can get Zeke's little structure up in under a week. From his porch he'll have a clear view of all the houses."

“Zeke will be a good sentinel,” Julie said.

Print held back the latest bad news Zeke brought about two men he called his “lickspittle kin from Parker County.” Lawton and Dalton “Doll” Dillard were twin cousins of Zeke’s mother with reputations as hired killers.

“I saw ’em in the saloon with Tru Evans and Cully North,” Zeke had said. “If the money’s right, I’ve never known ’em to turn down a job, no matter how brutal.”

The Dillards would pose a problem. Tru and Cully were up to some really bad medicine if they decided to bring in hired guns like the Dillard brothers.

“I’ll fix their flints anytime you say. Jus’ give the word.”

“We can’t go looking for trouble.”

“We ain’t gonna haf’ta, Mr. Print. It’ll find us soon enough with them two around.”

The other news Print held from Julie was about the knots of men who were talking after Teresa’s funeral of forming a band of Regulators—vigilantes ready to take the law into their hands. A vigilance committee was a very risky solution. It could become a mob. Mobs wrote dark and mysterious stories, filling even their own members with fear, and the innocent sometimes suffered.

Father had said, “They draw up by-laws to guide them, and they become judge and jury. Offenders may be given an opportunity to leave, but the committee might arrive with a rope.”

“A rope may be what they need in San Simon County,” said Print, thinking of Teresa.

“Violence breeds violence, son. In the end everyone loses, and the fact that the men we’re talking about are decent and honest won’t save them.”

Print said nothing, thinking of his armed cowboys. His father had reluctantly added his support to the decision to become a gun outfit.

"It's a dicey business," Jacob said, "but present conditions are just the sort to provide support for vigilantes. Looking back over the past year, I can count eight murders in San Simon and two adjacent counties, the most recent being Teresa."

The talk with Jacob angered Print, but it alarmed him even more. No one was safe from an assassin's bullet in the right circumstances. And Julie was alone in the cabin all day while he worked. She would have to practice with him, shooting pistols and rifles. He brought a sawed-off shotgun to stand by the door of the cabin, next to her clock.

After dinner the next evening, Julie went to practice with Print. A gentle breeze carried the promise of a frosty night. A few clouds had gathered in the west, and God had flung another glorious sunset across the Texas sky. The sun, sinking behind the clouds, was a fiery ball, painting the horizon with brilliant reds, corals, and purples. Father had always said such a sunset was God talking to his children, reminding them of His power and beauty.

If only they were out for a horseback ride and small talk. Print could tell her more of his plans for the coming cattle drive, and she could drink in his eagerness. She had learned several interesting facts from Zeke that she could turn into good questions.

Anything that brought them closer was worth the effort. But guns? He knew how she felt about them. Yet, here they were.

After they dismounted, Julie said, her face set and her lips barely moving, "My aim with a pistol or rifle is as accurate as it is with a rock. Bert made sure. But I'm reluctant to touch them. Especially that shotgun."

Print's voice held no acknowledgment of her lack of enthusiasm. "No need to raise it to your shoulder. It might knock you down. All you need to do is brace it atop your hip, cock th hammers, and fire from the waist. The shot will scatter and do the job."

Setting her resentment aside, Julie fired at a dozen targets, proving her aim with the pistol and the rifle.

"Good eye. You're a natural." He put the shotgun into her hands.

"Too heavy. I don't think I can hold it steady."

He settled the gun into its proper place on her hip. "Your stance is the same, one foot forward. Brace the side of the stock against your body."

"Cock the hammers, then pull the triggers, one at a time?" Julie looked doubtful.

"Yes. In actual use, you probably won't need a second shot."

Her first shot destroyed a prickly pear ten feet away. The noise was deafening. "How far will it shoot?"

"Farther than that, but a close target is best."

She fired the other trigger. Cactus pulp again flew into the air. "I detest this thing."

"But it's going to remain by the door," Print said firmly. "You're alone while I'm working. But when we're away on the cattle drive, you must never be at the cabin alone. Take advantage of a good vacation and spend the days dividing your time between the Dentons and my parents."

She rolled her eyes, but said, "I hear you." She couldn't allow him to become obsessive about imagined threats to her while he was on the drive.

He needed to be aware and focused every minute. Moving three thousand cantankerous longhorns presented far greater dangers than she would face in the midst of their protective families.

She dreaded the thought of the cattle drive. Weeks without Print. What would she do with her time? She should be turning the soil for her vegetable garden, but Print had said to let it go this year.

Her life would be on hold while he was away. He wouldn't have time to think of her. She imagined him on horseback for long daylight hours and sleeping with one eye open every night. Longhorns were always ready for a scrap, he said. Even the cows were all pluck and vinegar, but the herd instinct made it possible to gather and drive them.

Print knew the cattle and their ways. He wouldn't be in unusual danger from them, but the same could not be said of weather, conditions of the trail, and greedy brush-poppers waiting for an opportunity to profit. For the first time, Julie acknowledged that a pistol belonged on the hip of her cowboy.

I'm just thankful I'll never have to use one for anything but practice.

Chapter 21

On an evening in early March, Julie and Print sat on the porch. She wore the fluffy shawl Bert had given her on the last Christmas he'd been in her life.

It warmed her shoulders like his hug.

If only he could have met Print. They'd have been such friends. She dismissed her wistful thoughts to listen to Print's words.

"Spring grasses should be just long enough for grazing," he said, staring into the distance. "Feels like I can already see and smell the trail. Spring drives are my favorites. Not a whole lot left to be done before our departure date of April 3."

Not far off. It's too cool out here, but I'm not going to give up a minute with him.

Perhaps not much was left to be done, but Print was back in full frenzy, spending even longer hours in the saddle or at the pens. Julie stifled a heartfelt sigh.

"We've almost finished road-branding the steers for the drive," he said.

Those dratted animals. He was clearly ticking items off a list in his head, but it was her duty to show interest.

"What is a road brand?"

"It marks them as a part of a trail herd. The Sanders' cowboys will use the same brand since the cattle all go to one buyer, and will be driven as a single herd after we cross the Red."

Julie shuddered. Bert had died in that wild country near the Red River. "Zeke said moving the cattle across is the most dangerous part of the drive."

"The river is always unpredictable. If it's low, there's quicksand, and if it's high, some may drown. But we've done it several times in the past." He studied her face. "Not to worry, sweet wife."

"At least you won't have to face hostiles in Indian Territory since you'll sell the cattle just on the other side. But what about Confederate patrols on this side?"

"We have plenty of armed cowboys. Ready to go in? I'm tired."

The transformation back to obsessive cattleman became so thorough that a couple of nights later, Print did not return to the cabin until after midnight. He'd been caring for one of his favorite mares following a difficult breach foal. He loved his horses.

Julie heard him on the porch and unbolted the door. "What are you doing out here?" she asked as he unrolled his disreputable bedroll.

"I've got to be away from here in less than three hours. No point in my coming in. Besides, I can't even think about that cold shower. I'll be fine in my flea trap on the porch. You could bring me a pillow, though."

Julie came out with two pillows and a feather coverlet.

"Move over, cowboy. I'm coming in."

"That's plain foolish. This porch is hard and it's cold out here."

Preparations to crawl into the makeshift bed didn't cease.

"I don't smell good."

Julie stretched the coverlet over Print's form and turned back a corner.

"It's going to be close quarters in here. I'm trying to warn you. You know what usually happens when you crowd up to me."

She snuggled right up to her hairy brute. "Maybe some of the joys between a man and his wife can be shared on a front porch, after all."

Julie awoke sometime later in Print's arms. He'd had less than the three hours planned for his rest, but didn't seem to mind. He carried her into the house, still in her smelly cocoon. He grinned down at her in the earliest light of a coming dawn and tried to place her on the floor near the fireplace and its banked embers.

Julie put her arms around his neck. "It sure doesn't take long to spend a night with you."

Print's laughter sounded a bit like God's music in her ears.

Apolonia and I can wash that disgraceful bedroll and put a few patches on it. I can't let my husband sleep like a tramp.

Two weeks later, a warm Sunday afternoon brought the perfect time for a ride through the pasture to Julie's favorite spot, The Ring of Oaks, a pond surrounded by spreading trees.

Her spirit sang in the fresh beauty and aromas surrounding them. The green expanse of springtime pastures, and the immense arc of sky like pale blue glass overhead made her feel small. Squirrels chased each other between the trees and a curious cottontail rabbit peeked from behind a patch of tall grass.

They spread a blanket and Print folded the edge over her legs. "Don't want you to take cold."

"Not cold at all. My canvas jacket is warm. I've been dying to talk to you about the frolic. Louisa says the Sanders brothers like the idea—a barbeque and dance to celebrate the coming drive."

"Father says most of the county will turn out to support us. The drive is important to locals. Men will earn gold, not scrip."

"Do we know how much beef to provide?"

Print laughed. "Not to worry. Mother and Maizie will ramrod the affair, but there'll be plenty for you to do. Polly and his son will be on hand to do the barbequing and my brothers and I can spare time to help with the heavy lifting—setting tables and all."

Julie murmured her gratitude. They both grew quiet, watching the light fade from the sky.

"Frank is home," Print finally said. "This time permanently. His captain told him not to bother to return after furlough. Southern forces are close to surrender."

"That's strange. Seems like he'd be needed more than ever."

"Frank said he wasn't the only one furloughed. I suppose his captain is a realist. Realizes the hopelessness of further battles." Print was silent again, then added, "Frank can join us at the frolic."

Julie smiled. "Glad he's home safe. I'll enjoy getting to know him better."

Print shook his head, and his brow furrowed. "He's not himself. I'm worried about how the war has affected him."

"You said he was always moody."

"But something's different. We were like brothers in the old days. Now he's closed me out."

"War changes people as it changes the land. But you came home whole and such a fine man. I prayed for you often. I'll double my prayers for Frank."

Print raised her fingers to his lips and kissed them.

On a spring-like evening in mid-March the stage was set. Julie and Print and the rest of the English clan welcomed people arriving in droves. Impromptu tables made of boards spanning saw horses groaned under pounds of barbecued beef and smoked hams supplied by the two ranch hosts; innumerable fried chickens brought by Aunt Betty and other lady guests; bowls of potato salad and beans; sliced onions and pickles; desserts of prized jams and jellies to spread on sourdough biscuits; and cakes and pies.

But the real attention-getter was Aunt Maizie's stack of three apple pies, one atop the other, to be sliced through like a layer cake.

Lanterns hung from trees, and fiddles sawed their cheery sounds. Voices sounded the excitement of the evening. The aroma of smoke and food tantalized Julie. She was ready to fill a plate. Later, she sat on the ground beside her husband and leaned against Print's strong shoulder.

"Tired?" she asked.

"Just going to hold your hand," Print said. "Don't have the energy to dance right now."

"Frank seems to be on the floor for every set."

As if he'd heard her mention his name, Frank smiled at them over the head of his latest partner and Julie added, "He's giving all the girls a whirl. Do you suppose he's thinking about settling down? He's two years older than you."

Print barked a short laugh. "Spoken like a true married woman. Don't be trying to fix him up. He says he's waiting till he can offer his woman an easy life—the way I planned, until my dreams were shot down—uh, I mean completed, by you."

Julie raised her head. Print's innocent gaze was on the dancers, but a tiny grin tugged at his mouth. "What? What are you thinking, Print English? And don't bother to pretend it's uplifting. That grin gives you away."

He laughed. "I can't help thinking about the last time I saw you at a dance. There I was minding my own business, entertaining serious thoughts about fulfilling my dream, when I was confronted by a rock-throwing, red-haired vixen from my past, who lured me into slavery."

Julie scoffed, "It seems to me you stood your ground that night. Trying to intimidate me with your worldly airs and manhandling me around the dance floor, before tricking me into a rendezvous under an oak tree. All because I didn't fall at your feet the way most females did."

He growled. "Don't rile me."

"Seriously, Print, what did you think when I approached you that night? What was your first impression?"

His eyes still on the dancers, Print said. "I thought you were beautiful, but I was actually a bit miffed at you."

Julie stared at him. "Why in the world? You hadn't seen me or spoken to me in years. Surely you weren't still holding a grudge about that rock?"

"No, I liked the rock business—thought Cully had it coming. The problem was that Jonas told me how he'd been trying to gain your interest, coming by with goodies from Mother and Maizie. Talking to you at preaching, singing with you. He said he hung around, but you gave him no encouragement—treated him like a brother."

Julie gasped.

"That kind of ticked me off. After all, you and Jonas are not far apart in age and he's a handsome, upright young man. There was no reason for you to ignore him."

"But I was in love with you. I did think of him as a brother."

"Yes, but I didn't know that. I thought you were probably a bit uppity—you know, vain and stuck-up. So, when you came sailing across that room to me, I decided I'd take some of the starch out of your petticoats."

"Really." Julie's voice was tight. "And what did you think when I asked you to take me outside?"

"I thought, *Cuidado—watch out. She'll try to add you to that stringer of teen-age fish she keeps. Planning to be lovely and unattainable in the moonlight and soon have an older man panting after her.* So, I thought, *Okay, Julie. Let's go outside.*"

The cheek of this man—and I thought I was in control.

"I decided I'd maneuver you under that oak tree and give you a few real kisses that would scare the bejeebers out of you and send you skittering back to your front porch. But you took me completely by surprise. I mean you turned the tables in a way I never expected."

Her smile was complacent. "You were dealing with a woman who knew what she wanted." They both dissolved into laughter.

Happiness surrounded them that evening—the

joyous voices of people relieved to have something to take their minds away from worries of war and the actions of unpredictable men gathered in The Bend.

Julie watched Frank's face after he joined them. He told a couple of humorous stories about himself and other soldiers, but his expression belied amusement. Had the horrors of war embittered him?

He needed a godly wife—one who could warm the chill he held inside. But Print said he mistrusted women. He'd declared for a girl before he was twenty years of age, and been disappointed when she chose another man.

"Frank hasn't courted a decent woman since," Print once told her. "He has a jealous streak. One encounter led to gunplay when he'd been drinking. The other man was wounded. An understanding jury gave Frank a second chance when he volunteered for army service."

Julie had in mind the perfect mate for Frank, but she'd have to be careful. Men could be cantankerous if they thought they were being managed, especially in matters of the heart. Print must suspect nothing of her plan.

"One of the best evenings in memory," Louisa said as she and Jacob joined the group. "Here's a piece of Aunt Maizie's stacked apple pies, Frank. She saved it for you since you were busy dancing."

"Thanks." Frank reached for the plate. "I'm not sharing this bit of heaven."

Louisa touched Print's arm. "Son, look at your cowboys. A good bunch of men, but I know you esteem Zeke above all of them."

Zeke and Tuffy sat on a stone wall, laughing.

Print said, "Zeke takes care of all of us, but Julie and I are his pets. He's more like another brother than my cow hand."

"What about me? I thought that was my job." A silence fell, and Frank added, "For Pete's sake. I was only kidding."

"You'll always be my brother. No one can share in what we have. Years together."

Frank nodded. "We've had some times." Louisa patted his shoulder.

A few minutes after ten o'clock, Zeke took his leave.

"Going on patrol," Print said. "Every night he makes the rounds before he goes to bed. God pity an intruder if Zeke finds him."

Frank pulled out a big gold watch.

"May I see it?" Julie asked. In the lantern light an inscription was barely visible. "What does it say?" She held out the watch.

Frank put the watch back into his pocket. "An inscription to my grandfather. Been with me since I was nine years old." He thanked his hosts and hostesses, then said, "I'd better be leaving, too. Mother's feeling really bad."

Julie gave him a hug. Handsome Frank and his loyalty to Print over so many years. She'd continue her prayers and her scheming. After all, God had agreed with her about Print, and that was working well.

Print and Julie said their goodnights a few minutes later and walked the quarter mile to the cabin, hand-in-hand.

"You all did a good job, Julie. Everyone had a great time tonight."

"Your family has many friends who came to wish you well with the drive. I'll be glad when it's finished and you're home again." For a couple of weeks, she'd been thinking she might have some very welcome news for him when he returned.

They entered the cabin. Julie put her arms around Print and he bent his head. Suddenly he snapped to attention. “Hear that?” All thoughts of happiness fled when Zeke’s voice called from the bottom of the hill.

“Come quick, Mr. Print, and don’t bring Miz Julie.”

“I’ll be back as soon as I can. Bolt this door and keep the shotgun beside you.”

It was almost half an hour before Julie heard the shots—four of them with short pauses between. They came from the direction of the corrals. Julie drew the curtain aside, trying to see out into the night. In the light of lanterns held by several men, figures moved around the corral area, but not in urgency.

Another two hours passed before Print came in, finding the door on latch. He moved quietly, in case Julie was in bed. Print prayed that would be so, and he wouldn’t have to tell her before morning. He eased into a chair and took off his boots.

At the other end, Julie was asleep, head on the table; the shotgun beside her outstretched hand. Gently he picked her up and eased toward the bed.

Don’t wake, sweet baby.

Her arms went around his neck. “You’re safe.”

“It’s under control. Tell you about it in the morning. I love you, little one.”

“I’d rather hear it tonight.”

Print’s heart sank. He took a deep breath and sat on the bed, Julie in his lap. He stroked her hair. “It’s the horses. Somebody got at them with knives and we had to put down four of them.”

Julie went rigid. “Not Lou. Please, tell me Lou is all right.”

She read the answer in his eyes. Sagging against him, she refused to cry. They held one another, finally slipping into bed fully clothed, holding onto each other like children.

Chapter 22

Just at dawn after the raid, Print woke, hoping the noise he heard was Zeke returning from the mission he'd set for himself hours before. He'd adamantly refused to take Print with him.

"You'd get in the way. It's a one-man job. They're my kin with a grudge against me." Zeke whistled for his horse, which came running from the pasture, undamaged.

He saddled up and mounted, but Print caught the bridle. "Zeke—"

"No use giving orders, Mr. Print. I make no promises."

He won't worry about legalities. Has his own ideas about justice. But what can I do?

Still searching for a way to stop him, Print had watched Zeke ride into the night, a sense of failure nagging him.

Now he lay sleepless in bed, offering what felt like futile prayers, trying not to disturb Julie.

She says trust, but how can I trust when I can't

see? God wouldn't want to be part of Zeke's plan.

Print rose and dressed, careful not to disturb Julie, and made his way to the barn. When a voice called from inside, "I'm here," a huge breath escaped Print's chest.

Zeke emerged, carrying a lantern. "I dealt with them cutters. Don't think anyone'll ever find 'em." His voice was matter-of-fact.

Print winced. He didn't want details. The implication of the quiet words caused his hands to shake. How could he prevent more violence? He tried to turn away, but Zeke stood waiting. "Was there something else?"

"Course, it was Law and Doll did the cuttin', just as I said. They still had the bloody knives on 'em. I brought them knives so you can see for yourself. I knew it was my cussed kin before I caught up with 'em. They were holed up in that abandoned ranch house down in The Bend—jus' them two."

Only two. Print offered a silent prayer of thanks. *What am I thinking? We're talking about two dead men.*

"First off, I did Doll. No reason on God's green earth to spare him, but I talked a while with Law. Thought I might let him go if he come out with some good answers. He never was as bad as Doll. Admitted right off to the cuttin's, and said Tru and Cully put up the money for the job. He said Cully told 'em not to miss your stallion and the little brown mare."

"Zeke, you leave Cully and Tru to me."

Zeke's stare was flat. No promise in those dark eyes.

"He said somethin' else, Mr. Print. He said someone is givin' orders to Cully and Tru. Law swore he didn't know who the other man is, but this other gouger has always run things, according to Tru. Law said this head honcho has a lot of info on us."

"Go on."

"I believed him 'cuz Tru and Cully all'uz seem to know exactly where our cowboys are. Same thing with the Sanders outfit. Someone knows an awful lot about ranch bid'ness in this county and is usin' it to pull off some heavy stuff."

"Can't be Tom Evans—his brain is pickled. Buck Evans is smart enough, but he's taken a good wife and seems to have settled down. Frank may know who else Tru is running with besides Cully."

Zeke continued. "Your job to figger out who and why. Mine to stop it."

"Hold it, Zeke. There's not to be any more—"

"Law said there's more'n thirty men in this outlaw ring. Most of 'em deserters, like we thought, but one or two of 'em are well-known bad men."

"One of them must be giving orders. Did he give any names?"

"Nope. But said these outfits are in 'most every part of the state and pass cattle and horses between 'em. It's a reg'lar business."

Print shook his head and turned away, thinking Zeke had finished his say, but he touched Print's arm.

"That ain't the whole story, Mr. Print. Law up and tol' me, on his own, that Cully was the one who took that young girl, Polly's niece."

Print stared at Zeke.

"Law said Cully came bringin' her down there to that shack where him and Doll and Tru were all holed up. Said Cully misused that child every way a man can. Took her into another room, but her screams were so loud, Doll said he could still hear 'em. Went on till Cully finally tired of her."

Print's empty stomach heaved.

"Law said Cully came in and told the other men they could have a go at her. Law an' Tru didn't want no part of it. Doll used her, but refused to kill her, like Cully told him to."

That sweet teenager at the hands of those men. Dear God, I can't—

"So," Zeke's relentless tale continued, "Law said Cully carried that pitiful kid outside an' laid her in the dirt. He put a mesquite limb across her throat an' then stood on the ends, astraddle her, starin' down into her face as she died."

An oath slipped out. Rare these days. And it didn't help. *Never does.*

"I never seen Law sorry for anything he ever done, Mr. Print, but he looked sick about that. But the fact is, he didn't try to do nothin' about it, so I finished him, too."

What can I say? I can't fire Zeke. Not when he thinks he's doing his job, riding for the brand. I should have found a way to stop him.

Print's next thought was of Ham. "Don't tell this to anyone else. Not Tuffy. Especially not Ham. I don't want Ham brooding on the story and taking action of his own."

Zeke's lips flattened. "Didn't plan on telling anybody else."

"I need a horse."

Print saddled the unfamiliar pasture horse Zeke brought, missing his own well-trained mount of several years. He rode over to the Crossroads store, where he knew his father would be making an early start, and repeated Zeke's tale.

Jacob appeared as sick as Print felt. "I'll go with you to the sheriff."

"I don't think we should try to take this up until we're back from the drive. I need to be here when the news breaks. They'll retaliate when we arrest Tru and Cully, and we'll need our full force against that bunch. They'll be after me. Don't think they'll do anything for a while. Not with the story out."

"I'm not sure, Print. I see what you mean, but this is a crime that must not go unpunished."

"Zeke says both Tru and Cully have left the county. I want us to think this through, especially with that vigilante business circulating."

Jacob nodded slowly. "You're right."

"Don't tell the women, Father. Maizie might let it slip to Julie."

"She needs to know, son. She needs to know how dangerous they are."

"It's my decision. Julie will never hear the real story of Teresa's death."

His father finally nodded, then said, "I wonder what Frank will do when he finds out about the involvement of his brother and cousin in this brutal affair?

"Probably shoot them himself," said Print. "Only hope they don't kill him first when he takes them on. I'll talk to him. He needs to be warned."

Later that afternoon, Frank said he'd heard nothing of Tru and Cully in several days. "Hard to believe about my own kin. We have to stop them, but I promise not to confront them by myself. It can wait till you get back." He shook his head. "It'll kill mother. You know I'd be with you on the drive if she weren't so sick. Even Buck's no help. Has to see after his own family."

"You're where you belong. She has only you. We'll take on Cully and Tru when I get back. Drop in on Julie when you can to see if she needs anything."

"You know you can count on me."

Print went back to frenzy mode, finishing last-minute requirements for putting into a motion a herd of thousands of Texas longhorns.

Always at the back of Print's mind was Zeke's story. The mutilation of the horses had been brutal: tongues cut out, a foot cut off, leg tendons severed. But the story of Teresa's death haunted Print. He had to keep it from Julie. She had treasured Teresa as she did Apalonia.

Apalonia. Have to warn Polly without telling him the whole story. He'd go after Cully bare-handed.

When Print warned him about the danger from Cully, Polly said, "My second oldest son will take care of the women. José is strong and unafraid—and good with a pistol."

His sons gathered around him the night before the drive was to depart, Jacob said to Print, "You're more than ready for this one. You know the country and the location of watering holes. You're a good weather forecaster, and you know those cattle better than I ever will. You can calculate the best travel time, where to cross rivers, and how to let them graze without losing time."

Conner said, "He better, or we're sunk."

The brothers laughed together without Print. How much confidence did they really have in him leading this all-important drive? Years of war had eaten up the family's savings and they needed this one. Payment in gold.

Father added, "I know you'll continue our tradition of no work on Sunday. The Sanders brothers agree. The Sabbath is still the Sabbath, wherever you are. Let the men see you read your Bible and hear you pray."

As a new sunrise lightened the sky, Print and his cowboys were in the saddle. The cattle were a sight to behold, and the Sanders herd was not yet with them. The two herds would stay a distance apart to allow better grazing until they reached the banks of the Red River.

Print and Zeke were leading the way for three thousand longhorns on a trail to Indian Territory. Men's livelihoods and his family's prosperity rested in Print's hands.

A heavy responsibility without Father beside me, but I'll finish the job the way he taught me.

It felt strange to bow his head and lead the prayer Father had always voiced before they left. Julie kept a brave front. Print bent for one last kiss before he turned his back on home, his face toward the Red. Atop the first rise, he turned in the saddle. Julie raised her hand in a last farewell. He waved his hat in big swoops and so did Zeke.

I already miss her.

The cattle ranged in age from four to eight years old and averaged a weight of eight hundred pounds by his estimate. No scrubs among them.

Zeke drawled, "Spring's showin' her full face. Mesquite trees in new leaf."

"Julie would tell you it's a fresh green that seems to bleed into the blue of the horizon. She'd love to paint the pink phlox and bluebonnets sprinkling every hill and ravine. Now me, I'm appreciating prickly pear blooms, fresh spring grass, and tallow weeds. A cattleman's paradise."

Zeke's smile was content. "Air smells good, too."

The animals were soon strung out more than a mile. Cattle seemed to find their own places in the order of things. Print had to allow the herd to form its own rhythm and establish its leaders, as well as spacing and pace. No matter how wild the longhorns, it usually didn't take more than a few days to create a herd that moved itself. But it took a while for them to learn to eat on the move. It was the job of his cowboys to prod them.

The lead steers, larger than the rest, found their places up front by mid-day.

"Prob'ly ten-year-olds," Zeke observed.

One was a brown with wide-spread horns that twisted straight out, and the other a white, with tips that crumpled in. Their response to one another was remarkable. Their heads swayed beneath the burden, but they insisted on walking side by side.

Print said, "By the end of the day they'll have established their rhythm dance. Those horns will rarely click in contact with each other."

"One of God's mysteries," Zeke said.

Zeke's God is the One of the Old Testament. I've got to stay on top of him. Can't have any more illegal violence.

Wish Julie was beside me, sharing the scents and sounds of the day. One day I'll take her along on a drive.

Julie was a treasure. Prickling the edges of his mind was her saying he must put God ahead of her. How? God was distant—his friend, but not his heart, the way Julie was. Her prayers sounded like she was speaking to Uncle John sitting right there with her.

The way she talked, if you put God at the head of your affairs, nothing was off limits. You had to ask permission to get about your own business. And that foolishness about music—it made no sense, however charming it sounded coming from her.

John's words echoed in his head until Print pushed them from his mind. *God doesn't have grandsons.*

As long as he could keep Julie and not God as his waking thought, he felt comfortable with the relationship between him and his Maker. It seemed to be working pretty well and Print felt better and better about his spiritual progress.

Julie said it was God's place to keep her safe while he was away—God and His helpers—Print's parents, Frank, and the Dentons. He'd take over when he got home.

Chapter 23

"I'm letting the men chouse the herd, driving them farther and faster than we'll do later on," Print said to Zeke late in the evening of the first day on the trail.

"Good idea, Mr. Print. Discourage their urge to turn back. Figger we'll be coverin' at least ten miles. Good for untried cattle."

On the bedding ground that night, Print cautioned his men, "Let 'em have all the room they want. You'll be on the move all night circling cattle, so we don't care how big a bed they need. Don't want to heat them up and make them run. Extra guards tonight. Don't like the look of that sky in the west."

As he eased his gelding back toward the campsite, he called softly, "Sing to 'em, fellas, and keep 'em happy this first night out."

He had arranged groups of six night guards to take shifts of four hours each, reminding them this was one of the most critical duties. No one could afford to fall asleep in the saddle. Only he and Tuffy were exempt. Print sighed. Tuffy had pleaded that he had one more cattle drive in him, but he couldn't be trusted with night duty.

The voices of riders crooning to the herd sounded a bit like lullabies to cranky babies. It took almost nothing to spook the nervous creatures and a stampede was bad business. Broken bones or limps were standard after cowboys dealt with stampeding animals.

Polly was prepared to act as doctor, as well as cook, with his stash of medical supplies. He appeared ready to run a tight ship, taking firm control of the chuckwagon and its precious cargo of food, medicines, bedrolls, extra saddles, and other necessities. Said he planned to pick up any fresh vegetables available at farms or stores along the way. "A good cook is second only to a good trail boss," Father always said, and Print had to agree. Polly would be their doctor, dentist, barber, and banker on the trip.

A distant roll of thunder brought a grunt from Zeke. "Sure hope that cloud don't have us in mind. I 'magine some interesting tales have died with men who never had a chance to tell 'em after a stampede."

"Mmm-hmm. Don't you know."

After an hour Print was satisfied the storm would stay in the west and settled down for a night on the trail. His head on his saddle, he listened to tired talk from returning night guards, and gazed into a black sky filled with a million stars.

He usually put himself to sleep planning his next drive and how to invest his profits, but his cowboys' thoughts would be different. They dreamed of trail's end and how they'd spend their hard-earned dollars. The few single men might want a bath, a shave, a woman, and a seat at a poker table. Then they'd be broke, and ready to ride again.

But the married men would be using their earnings for their families. Gold was hard to come by, especially since the war started.

"Ham was already asleep when I checked. How's he doing?"

Zeke answered, "Doin' a good job as second wrangler. Kept the string together all day, and moved 'em at the right pace."

"He'd rather be up front, but a cowboy starts at the back of the herd, even if the *caporal* of the drive is his big brother."

"I tole him, Mr. Print. His job is jes' as important as mine. Can't keep movin' without spare horses."

Each man had four horses on this short drive instead of the usual six or eight. Print would decide when a change of mount was needed. *Glad I can count on Ham to have them ready.*

As trail boss, Print had chosen the horses for the drive and set the rules. Each cowboy kept his night horse saddled and tied nearby as he slept—the surest-sighted and clearest-footed ones available. They were fleet runners, essential during a stampede. A big flat-bellied horse was usually a sturdy swimmer when fording creeks and rivers. Some were cutting horses used when herds mingled together and had to be separated. It was up to Print to know which animals were needed and when. He felt confident of his choices.

"Night, Zeke."

Print heard the chink of pinto beans hitting a kettle as Alfonso, Polly's oldest son, culled small stones that made their way into the mix. The pintos would simmer over the fire all night in a cast-iron Dutch oven while another pot soaked in water. Beans were always ready for anyone who wanted them.

Polly was setting up sourdough biscuits for a

breakfast which would come at first light. The flour had cost Print dearly, but it was important to have a good second day treat as a change from the usual corn tortillas of the bunkhouse.

Print settled into his usual reverie before sleep claimed him. Before Julie, it had been the lure of the trail that filled his dreams. Its ever-changing monotony and its images were burned into his memory: saddling up in the dark, the aroma of campfire coffee, watching the sun send its first fiery shaft into a new day, bawling cattle, sandy bedrolls and smelly clothes, rain showers and rainbows melting down a canyon, the sweet smell of air washed clean. And always the limitless sky stretched overhead. One day he'd ask Julie to put it all into a poem.

Cully's face loomed. Something had to be done about Cully and Tru and that bunch of hide-peelers down in The Bend. Maybe he'd find answers during days on the trail. If he was lucky those two would never come back, but they'd go on inflicting pain wherever they were.

Maybe Frank had handled it already. How had Tru turned out like he did when both his brothers were good men?

Hope Frank sticks to his promise to wait for me to confront them. Should have said more to him, but he was too worried to discuss anything. After all, it's his brother and cousin causing all the grief.

"A river is a sometime friend, Julie, but tonight it's a destructive enemy. Large trees become battering rams in the torrent. No one caught in the deeper water will have a chance. I'm thankful we got to the Menefees when we did." Uncle John spoke as he and

Jacob drank coffee and ate sandwiches, preparing to make another trip to town for refugees from the raging San Simon River.

"At an estimated depth of forty feet now, and still rising. Water covers most of the streets around the courthouse, inundating businesses and nearby houses," said Jacob.

Julie, Aunt Betty, Louisa, and Maizie busied themselves with the first load of displaced persons brought by their men folk. Aunt Betty fried chicken while Maizie scrambled eggs and Julie sliced ham and bread. The Menefee family of seven had been saved, but their house—and everything in it—was a probable loss to the flood.

Even if it didn't wash away, Julie dreaded to think of the cleanup. Shoveling mud left by filthy water, and cleaning out vermin and rot. And Mr. Menefee was away fighting in the war.

One of the young Menefee boys worried about the family dog, and an older girl fretted about her pet goat, Pearl.

"We didn't have any warning, Miz Julie. I went to bed and the next thing I knew Ma was shaking me awake. We had to wade in water up to our knees inside the house. I don't think we could'a made it to Mr. Denton's wagon without his rope."

"God used Uncle John to protect you, darling. What is your name?"

"Janie. I'm ten. Me and Ma had to see to the safety of the little 'uns, and I didn't have time to go for Pearl. The baby needs Pearl's milk. With Father gone to war, we've had a hard time of it, and now this."

"Goats are notoriously capable animals. Pearl is surely safe somewhere," Julie comforted. "And the good people of this county will help your family."

Pearl would have to fend for herself. Finding dry garments and serving food were Julie's primary concerns. She refused to think of animal lives that would be sacrificed and much needed crops that would be washed away, when human lives were at stake. She whispered a prayer for the victims and their rescuers.

Within the next hour, a man and woman were brought in. They had a harrowing tale to tell. "Our house was near the river and its first rolling rise swamped us," he said. "Armpit deep in water while my wife stood on a table, I kicked out a window. We made it out as the house collapsed. We climbed onto the roof and rode the torrent for several minutes. When the roof started breaking up, we were saved by the branches of a huge pecan tree."

"God was surely with you," Maizie said, offering more hot coffee and filling children's cups with cocoa.

"We found refuge in the tree—along with three or four bull snakes, a raccoon with its young, and a young bobcat," the exhausted woman said. "None of us was too worried about our neighbors in that tree. I guess we felt a bond in staying above water."

Print had been gone for six days. Julie whispered to Louisa, "I pray conditions on the trail are not as dangerous as the ones here. Every stream must be on the rise in these torrential rains. And they still have to face the Red River. If it's on the rise—"

Maizie looked up from flouring chicken. "Don't borrow trouble, baby."

Aunt Betty urged Uncle John and Jacob to rest a bit before they went out again.

"No time. At least four houses have washed away—the fate of some occupants still unknown," John replied.

Julie studied his tired and worried face as

she fed the Menefee baby a bottle of milk, while Mrs. Menefee dressed the children in dry clothes. Julie smiled down at the baby boy as he guzzled down the warm milk. His tiny fingers sought to circle the bottle around hers, and his brow furrowed in concentration.

I can't wait to be holding our own child.

"Thank God for your large and sturdy house on high ground. And your generosity to refugees," Mrs. Menefee said, her voice tight.

"We're all in this together. Jacob and Louisa brought crates of supplies from their store. Lots of good beef and flour. We'll see everyone in the county come together to dig out from the flood," Aunt Betty assured her.

In the following two weeks, contaminated water supplies claimed two more lives and the threat of cholera lingered. Neighbor checked on neighbor. Already-scant supplies of food were stretched to cover unexpected needs of destitute families.

Julie rejoiced with Janie Menefee when Pearl was found, and she cried with relatives at burial services of recovered bodies. She comforted herself thinking of Print and the surprise awaiting him.

Two days ago, Louisa had asked, "How far along are you, Julie?"

She must have showed her stupefaction. She'd given no hint of the amazing possibility. "How can you see anything?"

Louisa laughed. "My Indian ways. I can tell by your eyes. I'd say about eight weeks, but you'd know better than I."

Aunt Maizie hooted. "You're never off more than a week."

Julie hugged both women, rejoicing in their wide grins.

"I think you're about right. I didn't tell Print before he left because I wasn't sure, and I didn't want him worrying about me when he had three thousand worries in front of him every day. I can hardly wait to see his face when I do."

Louisa said, "A child has a way of bringing a man closer to his woman. I think part of it is his joy at the confirmation of his manhood. Every man must worry about just how much of a man he is until he has done his share to place that first baby in his wife's arms."

She took Julie's hand. "Every life is a miracle, but the miracle of seeing your own first child is an experience that will take you by surprise—although I found it the same at the birth of each of our four."

Louisa as mother and now as grandmother to her child—and Aunt Maizie as a bonus. Aunt Betty, Uncle John, and wise Jacob English. What a privileged child hers would be, surrounded by so much love, as she had been through all her life. She could hardly wait for Print's return—his arms around her and the joy on his face when she told him about the baby.

Her unconscious smile faded as Julie pinched her bottom lip. *Parents! Responsibilities. Worries.* Sobering thoughts.

She was so inexperienced with babies, and Print held onto an obsession that still occupied first place in his hopes and dreams. Could he subjugate his ambition of a longhorn empire to form an unbreakable bond with a scrap of wailing humanity? One who needed constant attention and care? Could he accept the fact that there would soon be someone in their lives more precious than they were to themselves and to each other? One whose loss could shatter them—perhaps irreparably?

Of course he could, as happily as Julie. They would discover for themselves the maturity required of each of them. God was about to enlarge their world, and the baby would only deepen their devotion to one another and to the life they were building. God had seen her through the nightmare with Bert and her parents. He would be with them every day; and they had the wisdom of Jacob and Louisa.

The real gift of godly parents. They loved us in God's way. And now it's our turn. Print will be a wonderful father.

Chapter 24

Inspired by the cleanup after the flood and the fine spring weather, Julie decided to do her own. *Nineteen days Print's been gone. Our home has to be perfect for his return, when I tell him about the baby.*

"Uncle John, I want to drive out to the cabin today. Maizie and I will give it a good cleaning."

"Nesting urge," said Uncle John. "You can drop me at the store to visit with Jacob and Louisa while you women stir up dust. It's less than a mile to the home place through the pasture. You can pick me up when you finish. Don't get out on the road by yourself. Stay on the pasture road."

But arriving at Maizie's cabin, Julie found the usually perky Aunt Maizie in bed with a cold. "Wait another day or two, Julie, and I can help you make that cabin shine."

"Must be today. I can do it alone; won't take long. I'll be back to fix our lunch. You stay in bed." Julie hefted a kettle onto the fireplace crane, poured water, and sprinkled seasonings into it. "I brought two chickens. They can simmer while I clean house. Chicken soup never fails to help a cold."

Julie drove up the hill and parked the buggy on the north side of the house. Sitting for a long moment she breathed in the spring air, damp with the promise of life renewed by the rains.

A nag of guilt reared its head. Print would never think to ask if she'd gone alone. This wasn't an intentional disregard, but still...

She climbed the steps, then peered around the place and down the hill.

I'm not alone. Apalonia and her mother were setting up their wash tubs. José was with them. *Unusual.* He'd never helped them before.

Just a shout away. Surely Print couldn't object. After all, she'd only said she heard his warning—no promise involved, though he'd believed she would follow his demand.

She was alone every day while he worked. This was no different. Inside, she bolted the door.

Julie slipped into house-cleaning mode like a stone into a pool. It felt good to be hard at work after days of pampering in the houses of Louisa and Aunt Betty. The time with Print's family and the Dentons had been precious; still, it felt like an interruption to her real life with Print.

Life lacked color and importance without him. Even the coming surrender of the Confederacy at Appomattox Courthouse—a monumental event in the country's history—failed to truly matter. Julie waited for Print. The delightful secret she carried would be especially joyous when shared with him.

She stripped away bed linens and curtains and raised the windows to allow fresh spring air to chase away any lingering mustiness. The kitchen floor was almost dry.

Julie peered under the bed and pushed the wet mop to trap an elusive dust bunny she'd missed with the broom. Not much left to be done. Then she'd go down to the big house to finish the chicken noodle soup for Aunt Maizie.

I'll get our sheets and curtains down to Apalonia soon so they can finish.

"Hallo, the house." The voice sounded close.

Julie crept to the window and stood to one side where she had a view without being seen. Frank sat out front on his roan horse.

Relief flooded her, but also a tinge of guilt. Did he know about the half-promise she'd made to Print? Julie unbolted the door and stepped onto the porch.

"Hello, Frank, what brings you out so early?"

"I saw John at the store and he said you were heading out this way. Decided I'd better come up here and check on you. Where's Maizie?"

"Down with a cold." Julie smiled at him. Frank had been to the Denton and English places several times to see if he could do anything for Julie and to report on the worsening condition of his mother.

"Anything I can do to help? Mother would tell you I've become pretty good with a broom."

"I'm almost finished. Kind of you to come by. I seem to have all kinds of watchdogs."

"Well, you know Print. I got my orders before he left and I wouldn't want to be found derelict in duty by that man. Shouldn't he be getting back sometime this week or next?"

Julie confirmed the timeline with another smile. Frank was a handsome, good-hearted man. He'd make some woman a fine husband before long if she had her way.

"How's your mother?" She'd taken food to the house on several occasions in the company of either

Uncle John or Jacob. Frank was usually the one at Mrs. Evans' bedside, instead of her husband.

"About the same, I think. She enjoyed the baked apples you brought the other day. We all did. I like apples any way you serve 'em." Frank studied his watch and said, "I suppose if everything's okay here, I better be moving on."

"I'm cooking chicken soup for Maizie. No trouble to stir up a batch of dumplings for your mother; I know she likes them. I'll get José to bring them later. He's down at the wash house." Frank offered a smile and trotted away.

Julie brought out the pillows and put them in porch chairs for sun and fresh air to work their magic. *I'll bring out the bedside rug before I go to the trouble of locking up. Apalonia will put it back before she leaves.*

Julie hung the mat to air, and watched the laundresses moving back and forth between wash kettle and clothesline as José added wood to the fire. Although they were too far away to make out features, the light was so clear she could visualize their faces.

She stood for a few moments, basking in the warm sun and enjoying the light breeze. How God had blessed her! She thought back to those terrible months after Bert died and her parents had given up in despair.

If only they'd held on, Lord. You would have brought them joy again. But I'm thankful they're at peace with You.

Julie came back around the front of the house, and focused in the direction of the gate. Frank must have cleared it minutes ago. There was a rider, though, moving at a trot toward the cabin.

Frowning, she remained rooted to the spot, until

the apprehension knotting her stomach solidified into sickening certainty. There was no mistaking that figure—Cully North on his big gray horse.

"Thank you, God!" Julie cried. "What if I'd still been around the side of the house when he rode up?"

She could never run the quarter mile down the hill to the ranch house before he caught her on that horse. No use to go back into the cabin and bolt the door and windows. Her buggy stood in plain sight.

Why, oh, why had she broken her implied promise not to be alone? She had deliberately taken things into her own hands. In essence, lied. So clear now that it was too late.

He was still some distance away. Julie made her way inside. Her hand shook as she hung her bonnet on a peg and reached for the hated sawed-off shotgun standing next to her grandmother's clock. As she cocked one of the hammers, it made a loud click. She stared at the gun.

What am I doing? Her chest seemed to collapse. She struggled for a breath. The sight of Cully seemed to have pulled the pin that held her together.

I must remain calm.

Print thought him a danger to women, but Cully had offered her nothing worse than sarcasm and a few threats when she threw the rock. With God's protection, she need not be afraid. So why the shotgun in her hand?

Lord, please forgive my deception. Guide me. Help me to be wise in dealing with him and not give way to panic. I cannot use this gun against a human being. But our baby...

She positioned herself in the doorway, balancing the shotgun in her right hand. Her long skirt concealed it as she watched Cully cover the remaining ground.

He pulled up directly in front of her, the gray gelding almost straddling the bottom step. A smile played at the corners of his mouth. Pushing his hat back, he pulled off his gloves, tucking them into his gun belt.

Dust covered his clothes and boots, but the belt and scabbard appeared well-oiled, as if they received lavish care. He turned to the distant figures of the washerwomen and then back to Julie. He touched the brim of his hat in a gesture of respect, belied by an insolent grin, then scratched at a roughly bearded chin with a dirty thumbnail.

"Mornin', Miz English. You're a fine figger of a woman standin' on that porch. Don't think I've seen better."

Julie swallowed her distaste and stood straighter. *No fear or uncertainty. It's what he wants.*

"Thank you, Cully. What brings you out this way?"

In no hurry to answer, Cully's examination roamed up and down her body before it shifted again to the distant laundresses. José was no longer in sight.

Julie tightened her knees to stop their tremors. She had to appear in control.

Cully's voice was nonchalant. "Well, ole' Tru came out to see about his sick mama, so I thought I'd ride over here and see if I could do my own good deed for the day."

Forcing herself not to flinch from his squint, she said, "How's that, Cully? What do you think you can do for me?"

He continued his insulting inspection.

He's enjoying this.

Finally, he replied. "I know ole' Print's been gone for some weeks now, Miz English. I thought to myself, 'Cully, that purty li'l wife of his may have some things that need takin' care of.' You know, things only a *man* can handle."

He turned in the saddle and hooked a long leg around its horn. Scratching again at his beard, he drawled, "Print may know more about cows than 'most any feller in this county, but I've never been sure how much he understands about women. Now, I do, Miz English. I know exactly what a woman likes. Yes'm, I always know, and I figger there must be somethin' you need right now."

He paused for another gander down the hill. "Anything at all, Miz English. Don't matter how rough it is. I like it rough—so, just ask away." His grin bared strong, yellowed teeth in his stubbled face. Cully's pale gray eyes devoured her, his expression carrying a worrying hint of insanity.

The floor beneath her feet suddenly felt unstable. Julie's gut bunched, and an unpleasant taste rose at the back of her throat. *Print is right—he's dangerous.* The weight of the shotgun felt good in her hand.

She answered levelly, "I'd have to think about it, Cully."

He didn't move, the grin in place. Julie stood as if considering his offer.

Too close—he can launch himself off that horse and be on me in an instant.

"Well, one thing is certain. You're of no use whatever as long as you're sitting on that horse."

Cully didn't seem to know whether to be pleased with her response or disappointed that his intimidation met with failure and a cool challenge of her own. His smile wavered, then returned full force.

"Guess I can fix that for sure," he said with a laugh, sliding off the horse and leading it to the hitching rail a few feet from the steps.

Reins in his hand, he stood glowering at Julie. No smile now. His expression had hardened and reflected pure hatred. For a few long moments he watched, never moving a muscle. Then he looped the reins carelessly around the rail. His glance flickered down the hill before he turned to give Julie his full attention.

Cully's tongue brushed across his bottom lip. "Mmm-hmm, a fi-i-ne figger of a woman. I find a way with a woman. Sometimes she don't know what she wants, but I do. Yes'm, Miz English, we'll work this out together, and I don't even expect thanks. My pleasure to oblige a fine woman like you."

As if he had all the time in the world, Cully strolled toward the porch and Julie, until he was directly in front of her, his focus always on her face. He stopped, a foot from the bottom of three steps.

"Ya' know, Miz English, I've been owin' you for a long time."

"You owe me nothing, Cully. I was wrong to invite you to stay. You should leave. Go now."

"Now that's not right, Miz English. I can't go without payin' my debt. I owe you plenty, and I owe ole' Print a helluva lot more. I can pay ya both at one time. Yes'm, let's just think of today as payday."

Julie stood unmoving. As his right boot touched the bottom step, she took a single pace forward and raised the shotgun to her hip.

I can't let him hurt our baby.

"Drop your weapon on the ground, Cully. What you're thinking is wrong. Just go. Don't make me shoot."

Fear blazed for a moment on his face. Then he clawed for his pistol. He managed to draw it from the scabbard before Julie pulled the trigger. The full blast struck him in the chest and propelled him backward.

His gun hand stretched above his head. The firearm twitched in his grip.

Julie came unsteadily down the steps and placed her foot on the weapon, staring down into the gray eyes until they glazed over.

She felt nothing. Completely devoid of emotion—even revulsion for the damnable thing she'd done. Julie stood, knowing she would see no response from Cully. He was dead and she had killed him. Murdered him, she acknowledged.

Just before she climbed the steps, she glimpsed Apalonia and her brother running in her direction. She didn't wait for them, but entered the cabin. Taking three new shells from the opened box on a pantry shelf, she slipped two into the lovely black velveteen drawstring purse Aunt Betty had given her at Christmas, that holiest of seasons.

A profane use of a beloved offering. She loaded the gun's empty chamber with the other one and made her way onto the porch.

Apalonia and José stood rooted, gawping down at Cully. Julie brushed past their shock and horror, saying, "Go to the store and tell Jacob and Louisa and Uncle John that I killed Cully North and am on my way to Sheriff Longworth's office."

In a daze, she drove the miles to town and entered the office, carrying the shotgun with her. Only when she reached her destination did she wonder why she hadn't gone to get Uncle John first.

Julie registered every detail of the scene. Her ears were ringing. The light seemed so bright. At his desk, Sheriff Longworth's gray head bent over some circular, a cup of coffee at hand.

His head came up and his eyes widened. "Miz English, what in the world are you doing with that shotgun? Are you all right?"

He rose hurriedly, but before he made it around the desk, Julie spoke. Her voice sounded as empty as she felt. "Sheriff Longworth, I have just killed Cully North out at our cabin."

She pitched forward into blackness.

Chapter 25

My head's muzzy and my vision is blurry.

Julie blinked. The dim light was not a distant sun but a lamp in her former bedroom in Uncle John's house. Why was she here? She was supposed to be with Jacob and Louisa these last days before Print came home.

Ice filled her veins. Every stark detail of what happened at the cabin played in her brain—the shotgun; Cully's dead gray squint at the sky; and the buggy ride to Sheriff Longworth's office. She closed her eyes.

"Julie, dear, Print will be here soon. The men should be on the way home and Deputy Amos rode out to meet them. He'll bring Print back ahead of the others. Dr. Samuels says the baby and you are both unharmed, praise be. You're a very brave girl."

The voice belonged to Aunt Betty. Through her lashes, Julie could see an anxious face bent over her. Nearby were Uncle John and Jacob and Louisa, all of them watching her with concern.

"John, take my place while I warm the broth. Julie needs nourishment. It's been almost two days." Louisa rose and went with Betty to the kitchen.

Uncle John's strong arms lifted Julie while Jacob fortified the headboard with pillows. He placed her upright in the bed and held her face.

"Julie girl, you did what you had to do. I don't want you wasting time thinking about right and wrong or what might have been. You did what you had to." Uncle John patted her shoulder.

She shook her head. None of it mattered anymore. She was too tired to wrestle with the thing.

Prayer was useless. As she drove the buggy to the sheriff's office, she'd tried again and again. But no words came. God's Spirit had left her. She had grieved Him beyond endurance with her willful decision to murder a man, even if it was Cully. None of it would have happened if she'd listened to Print as she had half-way promised.

I murdered a child of God. I murdered him when he didn't yet know the solace of God's love. I can never be forgiven.

Aunt Betty returned with the broth. Julie tried to avoid the spoon, but Aunt Betty wouldn't retreat. "Julie, you must take nourishment. If not for yourself, do it for the baby."

The baby! Cully would have hurt the baby!

She allowed her aunt to spoon some of the chicken broth into her mouth and swallowed. Julie tasted nothing, but she didn't resist as Aunt Betty kept carefully spooning the wholesome broth. At last she finished, and Julie spoke for the first time.

"Is it all right for me to sleep again?"

Although both women surely knew Julie would not sleep, Aunt Betty nodded. Julie turned her head away.

The hall clock ticked and Louisa's chair rocked gently as the hours passed. Her four anxious parents had renewed their vigil and their silent prayers. No one spoke, pretending that Julie slept.

"When will Print get here? Julie needs him," John finally whispered impatiently. "Where is he?"

Sometime before dawn Julie heard the thud of boots and a jingle of spurs across the boards of the porch. Jacob arose from his chair, but Print was already standing in the bedroom doorway, staring at Julie.

She raised her arms a moment before he strode across the floor and clasped her to him.

"My brave girl. Ah, Julie, darling." He examined her and turned to look askance at Uncle John.

"Dr. Samuels says she's all right," John said softly, but his voice held another message.

No. I'll never be right again. I murdered a man.

Uncle John and Aunt Betty left the room quietly. Louisa kissed Print's cheek as Jacob clasped his shoulder. They tip-toed out, closing the door behind them.

Print lifted Julie into his lap, crooning to her and rocking her in his arms. She clung to him, his strength her balm. Print was here, loving her.

In the midst of her consolation, reality intruded. She had to find words. He must know. She could read loving concern written on his face.

My husband—he deserves to know.

Julie forced herself to utter the damning truth. "Print, I murdered Cully North. I deliberately killed him. He hadn't harmed me. Didn't even leave his horse until I dared him. It all happened because I broke my promise to you."

Print continued to hold Julie for a long moment. Then he turned on the bed and carefully leaned against Julie's pillows, taking her back with him, her head on his chest.

Maybe it'll be easier if she doesn't have to look at me.

"Tell me, Julie. I want you to tell me everything you can remember—get it all out."

She seemed to remember every word and action, but her voice, flat and toneless, belied the horror in her words. It matched her dull stare as she sat up.

"That's how it happened. I seemed compelled to get him in front of my gun. I set him up. There's no other way to view it."

Print sat up and placed Julie against the pillows to face him. He stroked her hair back, kissing her forehead. Placing his hands on either side of her face, he searched her troubled eyes.

"Julie, you don't murder a rattlesnake. You see him coiled, ready to sink his venom into you. Just before he strikes, you exterminate him. You did not murder Cully. It was self-defense."

"It was the baby, Print. I knew he'd hurt our baby if I let him near me. But it was wrong, because the music is gone. It won't come back. The music is gone."

Julie began sobbing as if her heart had shattered. Print held her until his shirt front was soaked with her tears. This was not the time to speak of the baby she mentioned—that time would come, but not now. He shed a few tears with her as they held one another.

At last Print lifted Julie's chin. "My brave girl," he said again. She moved his hand to the side of her face and rubbed her cheek against it, her gaze sliding away from his.

"Julie, I have a story to tell you, and it's one I should've told you before I left. You begged me to keep you in the picture, but I took it upon myself to withhold from you. I thought I was protecting you." His tone was bitter. "Perhaps if you'd known, you wouldn't have faced the danger you found out there at the cabin."

Julie's expression held no particular interest. Print kissed her hair and thought about what he'd say next.

"It was Cully who killed Teresa, Julie."

Print told Julie the story Lawton had confessed to Zeke, omitting only the most horrific details.

"Julie, Cully meant to do the same to you. He meant to use you in every vile way he could find and then when you begged him long enough, he may have killed you quickly, or he may have begun all over again."

Julie shook her head.

Print said, "Listen to me. When he finished with you, he would've gone and set up an ambush with those men he runs with. He'd have waited for me and my brothers because he'd have known we'd come—no matter what, we would come. You not only saved a new English soul, darling, you saved several less-worthy ones. Thank you, precious one, for your courage."

Her gaze held Print's so long that he wondered if he had done right by telling her.

"You didn't trust me enough to tell me and I can't blame you. I'm not trustworthy. I broke my promise to you."

"No, sweetheart. *I* was wrong—so wrong. I wanted to protect you, and I almost got you killed."

Her face was expressionless.

"That thing that compelled you, as you put it,

was a mother's instinct to protect her young. That's what told you to get Cully in front of your gun, however you had to. That instinct did not kick in until you gave Cully time to have his say and show his hand."

"It was horrible." She covered her face with trembling hands.

"You may not have recognized any real danger in Cully, but the instinct did. It told you to act, and act quickly. You didn't fire until he went for his gun."

Print gently pulled her hands from her face. "God gave you that instinct, Julie. He puts it in all mothers—even in cows. A mother is the only protection a baby has for a long time, since most males seem to be so unreliable. It had to have been the Lord who threw Cully's timing off so he didn't catch you unaware. God's hand is all over this, Julie. He brought you safely through because He's not finished with you. God has big plans for you—for us. A baby."

"Print, please take me home. I never feel right anywhere else. Perhaps, there with you, I can get a grip on myself."

"We're going, Julie, and I won't leave you and our baby for a minute."

Print kept his word. He and Julie set out for the ranch the next morning. He stayed beside her. The ranch became an armed camp. His pistol hung just above Julie's shotgun.

Zeke and Print's brothers gathered on the porch. As Julie pretended to sleep, Print joined them. The men looked as tired as Print felt after the long ride home last night and his sleepless concern for Julie.

"Trouble's coming," he told his troops, "and

we've got to be on our taps. Can't tell when or where they'll strike, but they'll come."

Zeke nodded. "Them hide-peelers won't let Cully's killing go unanswered."

Print warned, "Their response will come as a concerted attack to take out as many brothers bearing the name English as possible."

It was like watching a storm build. He could feel the charge in the atmosphere and see changes taking place everywhere. Jacob and Louisa did not go to the store, and promised they wouldn't until it was over. For the first time in years, Print realized he wasn't thinking about his longhorns.

Conner, Jonas, Hamilton, and Zeke fanned out to their appointed duties. Patrols were ceaseless as armed men rode in pairs to check perimeters and see to the needs of animals.

A caged tiger that first day, Print paced and watched for an opportunity to act, but it never came. No threatening wind arose to warn him of the power within a black cloud building somewhere outside the cabin. The threat was invisible, and all the deadlier. Somewhere forces gathered against him, but he didn't know where or when they would strike.

Sheriff Longworth rode out to the cabin. Citing the fact that Cully had drawn his pistol before Julie fired, he said she was sure to be exonerated of blame.

No matter. Cully's friends would place the load of responsibility squarely on Print. They couldn't ignore the death of their cohort and the challenge to their growing power.

Print caught sight of Julie as the sheriff left. She sat tense and withdrawn. He had to do better. He couldn't worry her like this. He needed a plan.

That night, Julie's restless movements told him her wakefulness matched his own. He explored ideas of how to help her.

His words the next day were ineffective. They sat at the table over cooling cups of coffee. Julie's was untouched, even though he had weakened it with plenty of cream.

"Want to hear about the drive?"

"If you like." She dropped her head as he spoke. Did she hear anything he said?

Later: "Maizie brought lunch."

"I'm not hungry, but I'll eat." She took a few desultory bites.

They sat on the porch. The wind sighed through the small mott of oaks in the side yard. It felt like a winter day to Print, though it was still bright spring. A chill loomed inside as he watched Julie's blank features.

He pointed out everything and anything he thought might be of interest, but there was little response. No, she didn't feel up to a ride through the pastures. She drank the milk he brought and nibbled at a ginger cookie.

The third day, he thought of reading to her. He picked up her Bible and read from the scriptures. Julie relaxed a bit. He read and he read and he read. Sometimes they were propped on the bed, with Julie's head on his chest, listening. At times they sat at the table and sometimes on the porch. Where they were didn't seem to matter to Julie.

Occasionally she raised her face to his, watching and listening for something, but Print had no clue what she expected. He wasn't sure how much of the ancient scripture she apprehended, but the words sank into his soul. Words of a plan born in the mind of God before the creation of His people, all people. He read of God's unwavering determination to bless them all. He read of how God knew about him—

Print—while he was yet in his mother's womb.

"God has a purpose for each soul he creates," Print whispered to Julie as they rested on the bed. "He set men free, in that incomprehensible love of His, to follow God's plan or to go their own ways. Have I been going my own way, Julie?"

She didn't answer.

Reading the story from the beginning to the crucifixion clarified the message. He had never before read continuously in the scriptures for so long. He thought of Julie's words about praying for understanding. That was the job of the Holy Spirit, she'd said, to help people comprehend God's words. As Print read, he prayed.

Apolonia or Maizie arrived regularly with meals, and Print pretended to enjoy the food to encourage Julie to eat.

"For the sake of the baby. Please." Another bite. No sparkle danced in her eyes—no life. She'd become a silent wraith. Print prayed desperately and willed Julie to return to him.

Should I shake her—shock her? Anything to get a response. Carry her away on my horse to the spot she loves, the Ring of Oaks?

He shook his head. Where she was didn't matter to Julie. As long as he was with her, she continued to go through the motions—a faltering echo of the life that had once filled her.

On the fourth day he continued his reading. The words were Julie's lifeline. They kept her present, whether she understood them or not. She still searched his face for whatever it was she expected to find there. He tried smiles and amusing stories, but she showed impatience to get back to the reading.

Print prayed for the Holy Spirit to come to him and offer him guidance in this dilemma. He needed wisdom beyond his. What could he do to help her? What if Julie remained in the dark place forever?

Chapter 26

On the fifth day as he read, a thought came to Print, but he pushed it away.

Frightening. It didn't arrive like the ideas and physical urges he knew—ones which sprang to the front of his decisive mind—clearly the thing to do, and demanding immediate action. It was a whisper somewhere deep inside him.

It continued throughout the day, a few words at a time.

Make love to your wife. Trust her. Comfort her with your vulnerability, your willingness to risk her refusal. Be weak for her. Show her how much you need her. You two are one and neither is allowed to withdraw from the union.

He couldn't act on insubstantial wisps of words. What if Julie misunderstood? What if she thought he was being insensitive to her trauma, thinking only of his physical need? He fought with himself until late evening and Julie watched even more intently, appearing to sense the conflict within him.

He watched her restless hands, fingers twisting buttons or picking at her sleeves. Dark rings smudged the skin beneath her vacant eyes. Her hair clung dankly to her bowed head.

Julie, where are you? What is going on in your mind? How can I reach you? Should I follow the whisper?

Common sense finally prevailed, and rightly so. He could not risk losing her trust. Even this poor imitation Julie was better than none at all. All she needed was time.

He heated water in the fireplace, then drew back the curtain that screened her small body bath in the corner, poured, and tested the water. He reached out to help her unbutton her dress when a bolt shot through him.

He pulled Julie into his arms, continuing to undress her, as he rained kisses over her mouth and eyes, anywhere he could reach. He moaned in supplication, willing her to understand that he would never take advantage of her, this shadow mate. Each kiss carried with it a plea.

"Accept me; let me help you. Let God save us both. I love you. I need you. Come back to me. Don't turn me away in disgust, although I can understand how you might. Julie, Julie."

She hung in his arms, limp, her eyes wide, staring. Suddenly her mouth came alive under his. Her arms pulled him into an embrace that fused his body to hers. She clawed at the buttons on his shirt and pulled at his clothing, saying his name again and again. He wanted to shout for joy—until a new uncertainty seized him.

Does she really want me to make love to her or is she mocking me, trying to make me comprehend the selfishness of my insistence?

Print continued to obey the whispered command. Sweeping her into his arms, he lifted her to the bed, beginning the ritual they had developed between them in the earliest weeks of their marriage.

Julie sobbed and his confidence shattered. He tried to retreat, but she pulled him to her.

She whispered, “Don’t stop. Make love to me. Take me out of this prison.”

At the end he found he was crying and she with him, but Julie’s eyes shone with more than tears. They held the real Julie-glow again, those same silvery-brown eyes that challenged him the day she was trying to act seventeen.

“Print, I can hear the music! Can you hear it?”

It wasn’t music he sensed, or heard. It felt more like he had forgotten how to breathe and was floundering—until God filled his lungs minutes ago. The rhythm increased.

“I feel it.”

She put her lips to his ear and whispered, “You must have convinced God of my repentance through your prayers—the ones I could never put together.”

“No, Julie. It wasn’t your sin separating you from God. It was mine. My unwillingness to surrender control. It feels like I’d locked my soul into a box that I’ve finally allowed God to open.”

Maybe one day he could explain it to her, or perhaps on some level she understood as she’d searched his face these past days. Perhaps she’d hunted for awareness on his part. Finding answers could come later. At this moment, Print’s chest swelled with gratitude. It rendered him weak and helpless as he stared into the face of God.

The next morning as Julie sat reading her

Bible, she gasped in new awareness. Scripture was so clear! God's Word assured her of His unmerited grace forever. The realization triggered a response: it had not been Print's sin separating her from the music. It had been her own.

She had refused to accept the power of God's forgiveness the moment she confessed. Instead she'd allowed herself to sink into an abyss of self-loathing and condemnation. *Because I believed myself above such an act. Pure pride on my part.*

Somehow Cully's murder had seemed different—inexcusable. She despised guns and thought she'd never be persuaded to use one. If God had pardoned her—and that was His promise—she must forgive herself.

I'm not special—just another sinner, like all others. How arrogant of me to think my sin was beyond the scope of God's power!

Jesus had hung on that cross and absolved his murderers. Her foot tapped the floor in time with the unmistakable rhythm inside her. She was forgiven! She couldn't wait to share her discovery with Print! He mustn't be allowed to blame himself.

But even rejoicing in her freedom from guilt could not erase the thought of Cully lying dead in the dirt. She had taken a human life, and would bear that knowledge forever. The Lord forgave, but the consequences remained. Her duty was to not allow that knowledge to keep her from moving forward with Him.

Men's voices came through the open door to the porch. It was the sixth day after Print's return from the drive, and he was talking to Zeke and Conner.

After congratulations were voiced about her recovery, she heard Conner say, "Polly's boy came this morning with a story he picked up somewhere.

He said there was a gathering of men in the Maddox saloon yesterday. Tru and his bunch—some of them strangers in town. He said Sheriff Longworth dropped in on the meeting, but could find no reason to break it up. No proof that anything was afoot—just a lot of drinking."

Her heart turned to stone. *Those men hate me and blame Print. I've put everyone in danger.*

Zeke added, "That's not all, Mr. Print. Those two old Ziegler brothers, the ones with that small outfit down toward The Bend—they told me they saw that bunch on their way back. Said a gate in hell had opened up, and the devils looked ready to go to war."

"We will be, too." Print sounded confident.

"I think whatever's afoot won't be long in comin' now," Zeke said. "The Zieglers figger there's thirty or forty men down there now."

Julie gasped. *Forty men! Oh, Father...*

"How do you two think we should handle this?" Print asked. "I don't want to put the women at risk."

Zeke said, "Been thinkin' about it, Mr. Print. Maybe we should all hole up at the pens, away from the houses, and wait for 'em there. We can fort up in the work cabin."

Conner said, "Good idea. It's a stout structure."

"Act like we're jes' gettin' on with things, but we can let word slip that all you brothers are goin' to be spending' nights up there, close to the work. I can talk too much this evenin' in Maddox's saloon, like I'm braggin' how nothin' scares you off. Bid'ness as usual."

Print said, "Maddox is either Tru's flunky or he wants to stay in good with him."

"Father will want to be with us," Conner said. "Mother and Maizie and Julie can't stay out here. They'll have to go to town."

Oh, Print. Not separated again.

"They can stay with the Dentons," said Print. "John and Sheriff Longworth and others will keep an eye on them. Besides, I can't see Tru being willing to kill women, no matter how much he hates me, or even Julie over Cully's death. Tru never was the sick twist that Cully became."

A plan was in motion. Print was back in his element, leading men. A thrill coursed through her as he said, "This will take some prayer and some planning. I've got to think about it and talk it over with Julie. Give me the rest of the day."

Print came back inside, and his eyes immediately sought her face. "Are you all right?"

She searched for a light note. She couldn't show her worry. Even her discovery from scripture must wait. "What are you up to now?"

He grinned, then took her hand, his face sobering. "As it happens, I *am* up to something. I need you to be at your best as I tell you about it." His brow furrowed. "There's a situation brewing, and it's going to demand the very best from each one in this family, women included."

"I heard what you said to the others."

"Pray with me. We need God's wisdom before we put legs on any plan."

Her heart lifted. Print was willing to follow God in this. Had she, when she killed Cully? Everyone seemed to think so. Her stomach knotted as she remembered, but no bitter bile of self-condemnation choked her.

Print said, "It's frightening to think men hate us enough to want to end the life we're building."

"I know, but we can't be afraid to stand against evil. Father always taught me that we must put on the armor of God and stand."

"Evil won't win. God has already protected you from this bunch once with no help at all from me. And this time He has Zeke, me and my brothers, and a bunch of armed cowboys, who've had enough of being pushed around."

Julie smiled. "I'm sure He is properly grateful."

"We're in a bad box. We can't go after them. That would be murder, not self-defense."

Her brow furrowed and Print's expression was contrite—as if he wanted to bite his tongue. He quickly added, "Father said a grand jury failed to indict Tru for killing old man Crawford last week. He thinks a string of indictments against some of the others, including Tom Evans, will come to nothing. People are afraid to stand up to Tru's bunch, but we can't take the law into our hands."

"That's true,. If I had it to do again perhaps—"

"Julie, don't. That's finished."

"You're right. It's a new day. God has forgiven me." *Now I must claim my forgiveness each time the thought arises. Later I can share my discovery. Print needs this truth for himself.*

Print said, "We'll have to wait for them to come to us. We'll be ready." He rose and pulled Julie into his arms. "You've made it clear to me that God is our only security. Your wisdom and faith will keep you in God's hand. I married a red-headed warrior of God."

"Auburn," Julie whispered to her cowboy.

The third evening of the work at the pens, Print, his brothers, Frank, and Zeke sat around a small campfire.

Zeke said, "The news has been passed around the county that the English brothers are working at the pens."

They rested inside a narrow yard fenced by poles and rawhide to keep cattle from fouling the ground near the cabin. Armed cowboys surrounded them.

Print felt the tension in his chest and imagined each man felt the same.

Frank held out his plate. "Some more of your cornbread and that good stew of beef, potatoes, and *chiles,* Polly. Then I'll have to go."

Light was beginning to fade from the sky and large flocks of starlings wheeled in changing patterns as they returned to their roosts.

Frank stood and studied his watch for a moment. His face was grim. "Tru showed up last night. I ran him off. Told him to leave the house for good. I can't stomach the sight of him, even if he is my brother. He must have known Cully's intentions the day he went to Julie."

"I'm sorry, Frank. No way is it your fault."

"I couldn't hurt him. It would have killed Mother. He and another thug are headed for Mexico." Frank swallowed hard. "If Dad will stay with Mother, I can come back tonight. Y'all need all the help you can get here."

"We're all right. Stay with your mother. You're the only one she can count on."

Jacob and Zeke waved to Frank from the porch. He hesitated, then trotted off, shaking his head. Polly cleared away and began getting things ready for breakfast.

Good that time at the pens isn't wasted. Enough real work takes place each day for me to feel the tug of tired muscles, but— Print's jaw hardened and his chin jutted. *Come on. Let's get it over with.*

Two men were posted to headquarters, although the women had been sent to town with John. *Don't need fires destroying the houses or barns.* One of the guards was Tuffy. No use in a firefight, but he wanted to help however he could.

Print marshaled his troops carefully this evening in the established routine: two guards on the eastern trail that led from the reservoir up to the pens. A hundred yards to the west, Zeke would take his regular watch alone. The most likely approach was the southern one, through a walnut grove near the cabin. Print and his brothers would take turns covering the woods. Guards rotated on a three-hour basis, except Zeke. He never left his spot, but Polly went after midnight to allow him a nap.

Print said, "Con, you'll take first watch in the woods tonight. Ham, second watch, alone tonight if you think you can handle it."

Ham glared up from his perch on the porch. "When are you going to quit doubting me?" He flexed his fists, obviously spoiling for a fight.

"No heroics, Ham. If you hear anything, start firing and the rest of us will be up and at 'em."

Ham went back to oiling his rifle. Conner reached over and took the gun. "Clean as a whistle."

Ham grabbed it. "I know my job."

Print said, "You may want to stretch out for a while and have a nap. I'll wake you at ten, Ham. The rest of us won't be far behind you turning in. This waiting is as tiring to me as a hard day's work."

Chapter 27

Sometime after midnight, Print awakened. Tired of the smell of unwashed bodies and manure-laden boots, he'd stretched his bedroll out on the east end of the porch, seeking cooler and fresher air. He wasn't sure what awakened him. Then he heard it—the bray of the jack they'd penned with some mares.

He picked up his firearm and made his way, crouching, off the end of the porch to the cover of a thick juniper bush. He listened, allowing his eyes to adjust, wondering why Ham had not responded to the jack's warning bray. He heard the rattle of a bridle and the sound of a booted foot hit the ground outside the fence.

From the shadows, Print whispered, "Ham?" No reply. He was ready to call again, when a blast from a shotgun lit the yard. Shot rattled on the porch where his bedroll lay. He glimpsed the figure of a man near the edge of the walnut trees.

Print levered and triggered three shots from his Henry and heard an outcry. Then pandemonium reigned. Guns protruded from windows and around the edge of the now-open doorway. An eardrum-breaking din from shotguns, rifles, and pistols echoed outside the yard and inside the cabin.

Print darted across the porch and made a swift rolling break into the doorway. Just before he reached its safety, the sharp bite of buckshot struck his left hip, numbing his leg. Hands dragged him inside. Everyone, including Print, began a withering return of fire aimed in the directions of brief belches of flame from the perimeters of the yard.

Guns fired from all directions as Print's night guards reached the scene, pinning the raiders between two sources of defense. Print recognized the sound of Ham's long gun firing with the others. It was the noise of the battlefield. Men could be dying.

Why does it have to be like this? Why can't we get along together?"

The game began getting too hot for the attackers, with Print's cowboys in front of them and behind them. A withdrawal began, but the nightriders apparently found it hard to get away from the constant barrage of the English brothers and their cowboys.

Rustlers began mounting their horses, keeping to the brush, and moving away to the north back end of the log structure—the only direction open to them. That side of the cabin had only a few high-placed rifle slots, and no one inside yet tried to man them.

Hamilton came from the walnut grove, carrying his now-empty firearm. His head hung. His voice was hoarse. "I must've fallen asleep. How bad are you hurt?"

Zeke stared at Ham and shook his head.

Print said, "Quiet down and load your piece. They may regroup for another try at us."

Jacob put his arm around Ham's shoulders.

"Print's right, son. There's no time for guilt and recriminations. We're not safe yet. They won't give up so easily." He moved over to Print's side. "Let me see your wound."

"No time for that. Con, can you see out the slots in the back?"

"They're lighting torches," Conner called and fired through an opening. Three thuds sounded on the roof. "They're trying to burn us out!"

Print said, "We can't stay in here. Maybe we can get behind that big wagon in the yard. Turn it on its side and take cover. Ham, you and Jonas will have to help me move."

Bullets whistled around them as several cowboys struggled to turn the heavy wagon on its side. Hamilton and Jonas hefted Print between them and dragged him to safety. Zeke and Conner remained unscathed as they stood at both ends of the porch to cover the retreat. Their firearms talked loud and clear and rustlers hit the dirt to get out of the way. One was not so fortunate and fell hard.

Print called, "Anybody hurt?"

"I have a crease above my elbow," Polly said. "But it won't keep me from shooting."

Flames lit the night sky as fire licked at shingles. Masked raiders poured around both sides of the cabin, firing, but the heavy double oak bottom of the wagon offered a good shield, and defenders returned an effective fire. Print's cowboys outside the fence poured shots into the night.

Another attacker went down, and then another. The nightriders began to retreat. Hamilton peeked around the edge of the wagon toward the west side of the cabin and uttered an oath. Before anyone could react, he jumped from behind the wagon.

"Tru!" he called, and began firing.

Print lunged after him, but his wounded leg gave way, causing him to stumble. He failed to get in front of Ham and bring him to the ground. Print was trying to bring his Henry into play when he saw Ham's body jerk twice and crumple.

Print struggled to one knee. A masked nightrider crouched beside Tru, his shape concealed in an open slicker. Tru, who wore no disguise, turned to retreat. But his masked companion remained. His rifle swung in Print's direction.

A pistol beside Print began barking. Zeke pulled Print to his feet, continuing to fire as Print swung his own gun into play. Tru's departing figure was visible along with that of his masked companion, who got off another shot before he ran. They fled toward the back of the burning building.

By the time Zeke got Ham behind the wagon, the yard was clear of attackers. The night held only the sound of horses pounding away into the night. Zeke tore away Ham's shirt to examine his wounds, Jacob beside him. Print watched anxiously.

Zeke raised his eyes and shook his head. "Grievous wounds, Mr. Print. We gotta get him some real help."

Jacob said, "Let's get this wagon back on its wheels. We'll fill the bottom with hay and use it for an ambulance. Keep us surrounded. That bunch may be waiting in the brush."

Zeke and three others lifted Print and Hamilton inside, allowing Ham's head to rest in Jacob's lap. The group struck out for headquarters. When Print and his fighting men reached the big house, a lamp burned in the front room and Louisa stood on the porch. Zeke said he'd bring the doctor.

"I knew it would be tonight. That's why we're here instead of in town," Louisa said, as she and

Julie followed the cowboys carrying her wounded sons into bedrooms.

Betty and John kept pace behind. Maizie came from the kitchen door with a kettle of boiling water.

"Jacob, you and I and Maizie will see to Ham. Julie, Betty, and John can take care of Print. Con and Jonas, take some of the boiling water you'll find in the kitchen to Julie. And post sentries on the porch." Louisa's voice remained calm, but she moved swiftly. No one got in Louisa's way when she ministered to a sick or injured family member.

In a shorter time than seemed possible, Zeke was back with Dr. Samuels, who briefly checked both the wounded and returned to Hamilton's bedside. He worked doggedly to remove both bullets from the comatose young man.

Louisa acted as nurse, handing the doctor instruments or clean rags or maintaining pressure on a bleeding vessel. One bullet was extracted, but the other was too close to Ham's spine.

"Thank God he's not aware of the pain," Louisa said. Hamilton lay profoundly unconscious throughout the operation.

Dr. Samuels listened again to Hamilton's chest and said, "We've done what we can."

She nodded and knelt beside her husband, who had begun praying as soon as the doctor arrived.

After a moment, she said, "I'll stay with Ham. Will you go to Print now?"

Dr. Samuels left the room.

Julie knelt beside Print as Zeke stood over them. Blood seeped from three holes in his left hip area and four from the leg, but she and Maizie had his wounds cleansed and ready when the doctor arrived. Uncle

John stood in the doorway as Aunt Betty returned to Ham's room.

Dr. Samuels said, "I'll talk to you about Ham after we see to Print."

Maizie took Julie's hand. "Jacob is praying. God is in control, darling. I'll be with Louisa if you need me."

Julie nodded, not trusting herself to words. She must remain useful. But what was this stress doing to the baby within her?

Uncle John said, "I fortified Print with as much whiskey as I could pour down his throat."

"Let's see what we can do for him. He's lost a lot of blood." Dr. Samuels began probing and removing pellets from Print's hip and leg. "These blue whistlers have spread a pattern of damage. And I see splinters of wood. Something protected him from a full load of that shot. But all of it has to come out."

Julie held the basin while Dr. Samuels cleansed and bandaged the wounds. The doctor finally stood wearily, his hands pressing against his hips to stretch his back.

"Print is one tough *hombre*, but he's not out of the woods, Julie. A bone was chipped in the hip joint, so the biggest danger is infection. We'll have a challenge on our hands to keep him down until the good Lord can heal him, but John's whiskey is doing its job tonight. He's sleeping just the way we want him to."

"Thank you, Dr. Samuels," said Julie. "That was not an easy job you did for Print." Her voice sounded weak. Her chest was so tight she wondered how air could enter.

The doctor motioned Julie away from Print's bedside. "I need to talk to Louisa. I think Print would be better off in town with me since she'll have her hands full with Ham. Print will have plenty of guards." He gazed over the top of his glasses. "Between you and me, I don't see how Ham can possibly make it."

She gasped and he reached out a comforting hand. "One lung is collapsed and that stomach wound pierced the bowel before it lodged near the spine. All I can do for him is keep him sedated. I'll leave laudanum and tell Louisa not to spare it. Infection could set in by tomorrow."

Tears stood in Julie's eyes. "Dr. Samuels, if I know Louisa, she won't allow Print to be moved to town. She'll want both her boys here. Aunt Betty and Uncle John and Maizie and I will stay with her and do everything we possibly can. Will Print recover use of that leg?"

"I would never say Print English couldn't do *anything*," the doctor replied. "A will like his is something to behold; but I know I'm preaching to the choir telling you how stubborn that man can be."

Julie smiled. "His father says he has a hard head. I might just say determined."

Dr. Samuels nodded. "Critical to his full recovery will be the things he does within the next week. If he'll stay put and let some healing take place, I think Print can recover most of his leg function. He did with the other one, and I understand it was a worse wound than this one."

Julie promised to do all she could to keep her man down until Dr. Samuels agreed to let him up. How she would manage, she had no idea.

Maizie returned to Print. "Julie, why don't you make sandwiches for the doctor and yourself. You both need feeding. I sliced up some roast beef and bread for you."

A weary Dr. Samuels followed Julie into the kitchen. She stared in surprise at the window.

Sunlight poured in.

I've been so locked in on Print that I couldn't have said if it thundered. She poured coffee for both of them, and put together cold roast beef and pickle sandwiches. Under the doctor's watchful eye, Julie forced down as much as she could. They ate in silence.

"I'll return sometime later in the day," Dr. Samuels said, still chewing his last bite. "My wife'll know where I am if you need me. Get some rest, Julie. You and the baby need rest."

She headed back to Print's room. The house held the air of a frightened child. An unnatural hush filled its hallways and rooms. Conner and Jonas conferred in the hallway, their faces strained and somber. In the hallway mirror, Julie caught sight of her own pale face and sunken eyes.

When she returned to Print's room, Zeke was settled in a corner on the floor.

"Zeke, please go to your cabin and get some rest. I'll be here with Print. Con and Jonas are next door."

Zeke pulled himself upright. "Miz Julie," he said with a nod as he left the room.

Julie went down the hallway to check on Hamilton before returning to settle at Print's bedside. In the doorway, she stopped and gasped. Something or someone was under Print's bed. She watched for a long moment, but saw no movement until she crept a bit closer.

Zeke's boots. He's still watching over Mr. Print.

From the linen press, Julie took another pillow and blanket and asked Conner to bring a sturdy chair from the living room. He put it in place and said, "Zeke, come out from under the bed. I brought a better place to sleep."

Zeke emerged, his face sheepish. "I'z all right under there, but I thank you, Mr. Con."

Julie took her place in the big bedside chair, but not before handing a pillow and blanket to Zeke.

"You're a faithful friend, Zeke. Are you a praying man?"

"The Lord and I ain't strangers, but I'm not one to ask for much help, Miz Julie."

"We need His help now. Will you pray with me?" They bowed their heads together.

Zeke was up each time Julie or Louisa or Maizie went to Print's bedside. Print lay propped on pillows, pale and taking slow, shallow breaths. Sometimes the interval between would be too long and Julie would be up to check his pulse. Print's heartbeat remained steady and reassuring. She'd nod, and Zeke's lips formed unspoken words.

Chapter 28

The next day at noon, Louisa entered Print's bedroom. "Julie, you must consider the baby. What you've been through is being shared by that little one. Stress is not good for a developing child. You both need rest. Maizie and I are here to see that you get it."

Maizie nodded. "Yes, ma'am. No ifs, ands, or buts, sweet one. You're gonna eat some breakfast and then take a nap in a real bed."

She took Julie's hand and led her toward Louisa's bedroom, motioning to Betty to cut off any retreat. After she had Julie settled, she brought a bowl of oatmeal with rich cream and a glass of milk. Beside it were two oatmeal-raisin cookies. "I'm staying till you finish and close your eyes."

Julie emitted a deep sigh. "I feel like I'm three years old."

Aunt Betty smiled at Julie. "Louisa and I will see to lunch for the men. Please sleep, darling."

An hour later, Maizie entered the kitchen with

a smile. "Julie's asleep and Print is sleeping more naturally." She smiled. "So is Zeke. I'll take him a tray after we eat, and then we'll feed the guards."

Louisa watched the family gather at the table. John and Jacob from Hamilton's room where they'd been praying. Jonas, Conner, and Zeke came from the front porch where cowhands stood watch, rifles at the ready. They all sat together in silence.

After prayer, Louisa raised her head. Tears brimmed in her eyes. "Ham has been my joy and my cross to bear. I've never understood his heart the way I did with you two." She nodded at Conner and Jonas. "He's been Print's more than mine. But too many years separate them. Ham can't keep up with the brother he worships. I've done my poorest work with him, and you know it, Jacob."

He patted Louisa's hand. "You've loved him just as much and just as effectively as you have any of the others. Ham has a different make-up. Wants to grow up too fast. Now all we can do is pray he'll have the years to do it."

Louisa's head drooped and she chewed at her lip. *Ham's wounds are not the kind men survive, but miracles happen. I can't give up hope.*

"Jacob, will you sit with him today and read from the Bible? I've never been sure what he really understands. If he comes around, I want you to make sure he knows about the blood of Jesus—that it's for young and old. Talk to him, even if you're not sure he can hear you. Tell him he can count on Jesus' sacrifice to be enough for him when he needs it."

"Of course, darling."

By mid-afternoon, Louisa was thrilled to see that Hamilton seemed a little revived. He was conscious, though the laudanum made his responses fuzzy. He drank some water and took a small portion of broth that she spooned to him as Jacob read. He replied to Jacob's questions, then closed his eyes as his father read again. Each time she checked throughout the night, Hamilton appeared to be sleeping peacefully.

Her heart sang; but in early afternoon of the next day, fever set in. By nightfall it raged throughout his body. Jacob and Louisa remained beside their son, reading and talking and praying almost constantly for the next full day.

Around the third midnight of his agony, Hamilton Anthony English died just before his seventeenth birthday. He was taken the next day to the little graveyard behind the Crossroads chapel.

In Print's bedroom, Julie said, "I'm going to Hamilton's burial service." She tied bonnet strings beneath her chin.

His dark face etched with weariness and concern, Zeke replied, "You're needed. I'll stay right here. Mr. Print's in the battle of his life, but he's tough and he's in the right. Makes a difference."

"Oh, Zeke. He has to make it. He'll be so disappointed that he can't be there for Ham. I don't think many others will, either. Only a few have come to the house to offer support. I think people are afraid to be seen with us. The English family have become targets for evil."

Print moved restlessly and Zeke jumped to rearrange his pillows. When he opened his eyes, Zeke bent over Print and whispered, "We'll finish this up soon, Mr. Print. Them gougers have about had their run in this county. They'll get their own."

Dr. Samuels followed the family home from the funeral. Julie told him, "Print doesn't know of Ham's death. He's had little reaction to anything asked of or done to him, as you can see, but he's taking soup."

"He's a fighter. I don't want him concerned with anything but healing. He'll have time for Ham later."

Two days after Ham's funeral, Conner came to Julie. "Zeke, Jonas, and I are going out to the scene of the raid."

Print opened his eyes and whispered, "Tell me what you find, little brother."

Conner said, "I don't expect to find much of use, but we need something to do. I'll have a report ready when you wake up."

Julie followed Conner into the hall. He said, "Several of our men remained at the scene to be sure the fire was contained, but I think they pretty well let it run its course."

The blackened ruins of the log bunkhouse were a disheartening sight. The roof had caved in and the smell of charred wood hung heavy in the air. Conner shook his head and rubbed at his burning eyes.

"Have to clear it away and rebuild," he said. "We need to get started before Print sees it. He has enough to deal with. Bad memories here."

Conner worked his way down the west side of the cabin. "Some of these timbers can be reused."

Something gleamed in the grass at his feet. He bent, picked it up, and stood staring at it.

"Come here," he called to Zeke and Jonas.

After a long moment studying the objct, Zeke said, "We'd better get this to Mr. Print. He wouldn't want us to put it off till he gets better. He's gonna want to know when he opens his eyes."

Louisa met them at the door. After one glance at their faces, she turned and went to the door of the bedroom where Print sat propped on pillows swallowing the broth Julie spooned to him. "Julie, come out with me and let the boys see Print."

Conner said, "No, Mother. Let Julie stay, and please bring Father."

Print managed a weak smile. "Look at you. Why the long faces? I'm not done for yet." The faces remained unchanged. "What is it? What's wrong?"

Julie said, "Surely it can wait. Let Print finish eating."

Conner reached into his pocket. He laid the found object on Print's chest.

Print fingered it and asked, "What are you doing with Frank's watch?"

Julie gasped and held her stomach. Louisa shook her head, and Jacob looked stricken.

Print's brow furrowed. Then the little color remaining in his face slowly drained. "You found it up at the pens?"

"On the west side where Ham was shot," Conner growled. "Frank couldn't have been on that side of the cabin any time except with the raiders. You know he never left the porch when he came by earlier. And I saw him put that watch in his pocket just before he left to go to his mother."

Julie sat beside Print and took his hand. "Incomprehensible. Your best friend..."

Print maneuvered himself up and tried to swing his legs over the side of the bed, despite the women's pleading.

"Help me," he demanded. "We're going over there. He'll be with his sick mother. Frank's always been a good son. We're going—now."

Louisa stared at Julie. She shook her head and Jacob nodded. Neither Julie nor Louisa spoke. Print would go, no matter what they said.

In the buggy Print held his body rigid, trying to minimize jolts to his hip. When they arrived, old man Evans sat slumped in a chair on the front porch. Conner put a restraining arm on Print.

"I'll go," he said.

"I'm coming, too," Print growled.

Conner went to the door as Jonas and Zeke helped Print from the buggy onto the porch. Liquor fumes surrounded Tom in his chair. He met Print's gaze, but he didn't call out to his sons.

At Conner's no-nonsense rap, the door cracked open to reveal Tru's surprised face. Conner shoved the door open, pushing Tru back to the middle of the room. The man's right arm was in a sling and his face was marked by a crease.

Conner pushed past Tru, and said, "Frank, come out here. You don't want us back there with your sick mother."

Frank came out of a bedroom smiling. He stared at the faces of the men surrounding Tru, and his expression hardened.

"What can I do for you?" Frank's voice carried a rough edge.

Print didn't answer. He made his slow and painful way across the room until he stood toe-to-toe with Frank.

"Hold out your hand, Frank."

Frank stiffened, but he held out his hand. Print placed the watch there, covering it until the last second. The gold gleamed dully in Frank's palm. His hand began to shake.

"Yours, Frank. I know what it's meant to you since you were a kid, so I brought it back. It's the least a friend can do for another friend."

Conner said, "Your worst nightmare. I bet you hoped you'd lost it on the road."

Tru's wounded arm jerked. His eyes darted from one to another. He sank down on a chair and whispered, "Y'all are four and we're only two. My arm's out of play and Frank don't even have a gun, but it's your move. Do what you came to do."

Print turned his back on Frank. He didn't glance at Tru as he motioned Conner and Zeke to help him make his way outside to the buggy.

Conner followed and whipped the horse away from the Evans' house, his face foreboding.

"That's it? That's your response to a murdering, lying, thieving traitor? What about Ham? Doesn't he deserve some kind of justice? What do you suppose he's thinking of his brave big brother right now, lying out there under the ground in that graveyard behind the chapel. I don't think I've ever been ashamed of you in my life until this moment."

Print blanched. "Ham's dead? When?"

No one answered until Zeke finally said, "He only lived two full days."

Print's head bowed for a long minute. "How about you, Jonas? What do you have to say?"

Jonas didn't reply at once. "I'm not ashamed of you, but I don't understand. Ham would've backed your play any day of the week and would've died for you—probably did."

Print winced and stared at Jonas. "You're right. I failed Ham. I deserve everything you've got to say about that business." He hung his head.

Jonas continued, "I've never known you to be afraid to stand up to any man, or for a cause you believed in. I'm willing to give you the benefit of the doubt until I'm proved wrong."

"Zeke?" Print turned to the friend at his side.

He answered quietly, “Whenever you’re ready, Mr. Print.” Then he said to Conner, “Mr. Con, you’re sellin’ your brother short.”

“I don’t have any answers right now,” Print said. “I’ve always issued orders, thinking I knew how to handle things. I’ve believed all my life I knew how a man ought to act. I taught my way to Ham, and it got him killed.”

Conner’s face didn’t soften. “We need to do something. What are you waiting for?”

“I’m not going to do anything until I think it through. My way got Ham killed and almost got Julie raped and murdered by a maniac. I thought I knew a friend through and through. I’m gutted by Frank’s betrayal. Give me time to think.”

Conner made a choking noise in his throat, and his lip curled. “So, we do nothing while you turn over a new leaf?”

Print continued as if Conner hadn’t spoken. “Frank is worse than Cully and Tru ever were. He used them, twisted them, and turned them loose on innocent people. I wasn’t smart enough to recognize how bad my friend was, even though I grew up with him. I need help here. And I’m going to wait till I know what it is I’m supposed to do.”

Zeke said, “Listen to him, Mr. Con.”

Print said slowly, “Frank will cut stick and run. I know him. Whenever he’s in over his head, he always runs. He’ll pull up stakes and take Tru with him—leave the rest of his bunch to carry the can.”

“And you’re giving him time to do just that,” said Conner. “He must have deserted the military when the going got tough and come here. No telling when. *If* he went into service at all. Tom, as head of the Home Guard, protected him, while he gathered his own little army down there in The Bend.”

Print said, "Has to be true. But he'll wait for his mother to die. We have that long to figure out how to deal with him before he takes to his heels."

Jonas said, "I don't think that'll be long. Dr. Samuels told me he's done all he can for Mrs. Evans, and she doesn't have much time."

Print mused, almost to himself. "I got the feeling from Frank years ago that one of the reasons he stuck with me was that I took his side in any ruckus he stirred up. It didn't matter to me. I kept on being his friend, because I never found another like I thought he was—till I found Julie."

Conner shook his head and muttered. He whipped up the horse and pain jolted through Print in a furious torrent. Conner refused to speak again and left it to Jonas and Zeke to get his wounded brother into the house. Then Conner saddled his horse and left the ranch, telling no one his intentions. Jonas helped Zeke and Julie get Print settled and rode after him.

Chapter 29

As Zeke helped Print back into bed, Julie's stomach clenched. "Your hip is bleeding again." Blood seeped through the groin area of his trousers.

Louisa crooked her finger to Zeke. They disappeared and returned with a basin of hot water and fresh linen strips.

"We'll have to bathe the wounds, son, and replace the dressings. This time, I pray you'll follow the doctor's orders about staying in bed until they have a chance to heal." Louisa sent Julie a knowing glance and began unwinding soiled bandages from his hip.

Print scowled. "Guess I'm paying for my outing to see my friend Frank," he muttered.

Julie's chin trembled. Print was Print. He believed Frank was his responsibility and no amount of urging would stop him from dealing with the problem.

Louisa held up the bottle of laudanum, but he shook his head. "I need a clear mind."

Jacob entered the room with John. “Just finished talking to Sheriff Longworth and Amos. They’ve been out to the pens and found two dead rustlers left behind in the brush.”

Print whispered, “I hadn’t given them a thought.” He flinched as Louisa worked to soften the gauze pad glued to his hip by dried blood. His face was gray and he fisted the coverlet.

Julie covered one of his hands with her own. He winked at her.

Jacob said, “The thing is, I can’t see what the sheriff can do about it. Finding Frank’s watch out there—where he’s been a dozen times before—isn’t clear proof that he was leading the gang.”

Print grunted. Between clenched teeth, he ground out, “But his expression gave him away when he saw his watch.”

John said, “Still not enough for a jury. No telling how long Frank has been in the county. Tom provided the perfect cover.”

“Con said much the same.” Print winced when Julie gingerly began unwinding the dressing on his lower leg.

From the foot of the bed, Zeke muttered, “A man like Frank shouldn’t be breathin’ God’s air.”

Print said, “Zeke, don’ t…”

Zeke stepped out into the hall.

Louisa splashed water into a glass, measured a spoonful of the narcotic left by Dr. Samuels, and stirred it into the water.

Print watched her, shaking his head. “I said no laudanum.”

John mused, “Frank probably found it easy to gain control of those desperate young men who left the army and gathered where they felt safe. I can imagine the ideas he put into their heads. He certainly fooled me. I never believed him capable of such ruthlessness."

Jacob's face seemed to have aged in preceding days. He sighed. "I can't understand what turned Frank. He was like another son to me."

John shook his head. "He was flawed. Unable to feel what others do. Blamed the world for his lack of success, and envied your dream of an empire, Print. He decided to put together his own domain, built on violence and bulwarked by fear."

Print's pain-filled gaze regarded the men. His words came at intervals. "Agree with what you say. Haven't figured out what to do about it." His brow wrinkled. "You know it had to be Tuffy making our affairs known to Frank. A step ahead of us all the way." Print paused for a few breaths.

Zeke had returned. His face unreadable, he nodded. "Had to be, Mr. Print."

Julie choked back tears. *Tuffy! This must be killing Zeke.* "Surely his betrayal was innocent. Tuffy wouldn't have suspected Frank's questions carried an evil intent."

Zeke shook his head. "We'll see, Miz Julie."

"Print, you must get a nap." Julie held Print's head up enough to take several deep swigs from the glass Louisa held. He closed his eyes for so long that Julie thought he was asleep, but he reached for her hand.

"I can handle most of what Frank did." He took a shallow breath. "I understand greed. What haunts me is that Frank rode out to the cabin that morning to be sure you were alone. Knew that killing you would hurt me most."

"Don't talk, darling. Please rest a bit."

Louisa motioned everyone to the door, but John stood his ground.

"The law will have to deal with Frank, and with Tru and Tuffy. Don't take it into your hands."

Print's voice gained strength as the painkiller took hold. "You know how well that's worked so far. Men are indicted and scheduled for trial, then witnesses are murdered or intimidated. The thieves go free. Jurors are afraid to do their jobs."

He struggled to sit up, and Julie pushed another pillow behind him.

"Even old man Evans was no-billed on cattle theft and I had papers signed by his hand," Print added. "I don't know what the answer is, but I'm not sure the law—at least the law we have in San Simon County—is going to be able to get the job done."

The spate of words obviously exhausted him. But he struggled on. "And the Yankee military, when it finally gets here, won't be any better." His voice had become a whisper.

Julie stood and kissed Print's forehead. "You must rest."

He caught her wrist. "What will you do if I have to be the one to kill Frank and Tru?"

Tears blurred Julie's vision. "God has forgiven me for that horrible and willful act. He makes a new path, but I'll always wonder what would have been on the other one before Cully found me."

Print patted the bed. She lay beside him and he drew her head down onto his chest. The others withdrew. It was almost an hour before Print stirred.

"Need more laudanum. I'm going to Hamilton's gravesite."

Julie shook her head. Ice filled her veins. "You can't."

Print caught her chin in one hand. "I got him killed," he whispered, "sure as God's little green apples turn red. You and Mother tried to tell me, but

I wouldn't listen, and now Ham is dead. I've got to go to him."

Julie's heart thudded in her ears. *The worst thing he can do, but this is Print. He'll go one way or another.*

Zeke helped her load Print back into the buggy, with Maizie scolding in the background.

Julie said, "It's something we must do alone, Zeke." He nodded.

At the Crossroads Chapel, Julie drove as near the grave as possible. It was set beneath a sturdy oak behind the tiny church. Print leaned heavily on her in his painful progress to Ham's burial place.

A rustle in the leaves drew Julie's attention. At the edge of the grove, Zeke stood beside his horse.

Somehow Print was able to get to his knees. He remained there, smoothing and patting the raw soil mounded above his brother's body.

Julie stood near, trying to pray. Print's grief washed over her, its weight almost unbearable. She heard a single sob. She wanted to touch him. Let him know she understood, but something stilled her. He had to do it his way.

The light began to fade. Print remained—the most desolate figure she'd ever seen. Zeke stood, watching. Julie finally knelt beside Print and took his hand.

"When your grief is finished, you must forgive yourself. You know what we talked about. It's not an option. I had to forgive myself for murder and you must forgive yourself for Ham's death. It is God's command."

Print squeezed her hand. "Get Zeke over here to help me. Let's go home."

The next morning Print was delirious with fever—a radical downturn in his condition. Pain glazed his eyes and he muttered incoherently. Louisa and Maizie unwrapped the wounds as Julie held Print's upper body. Jacob and Zeke were nearby.

He's so hot. Why did I allow you to talk me into taking you to the grave site?

"Louisa, I'm so sorry—"

"I know how determined Print is. You did the only thing you could." She touched Julie's shoulder. "Two of the wounds are inflamed. See the red streaks? Could be the early stages of blood poisoning."

Maizie's voice shook as she wrung scalding water from a cloth. "We need to act now."

Julie stared at the injuries, unseeing. Her hands began to tremble. He could be dead within hours. She was unable to add any words to Louisa's prayer. Maizie took her hand and voiced them for her.

Jacob stood behind them. "Zeke said Dr. Samuels is out on a call, and his wife has no idea when he'll be available. John is waiting there, and will bring him to us."

Maizie patted Julie's arm. "Let us do this, sweet child. I'll call you when we're finished."

"I must be with him, Maizie."

Jacob said, "You can stay, but it'll take a man's strength to keep him still."

Jacob held Print's head and Louisa was able to help him swallow a generous dose of laudanum. "It may help. We must open and cleanse the worst of Print's wounds, then cauterize them."

Julie gasped. *The pain will be unbearable.*

Maizie brought a small iron rod, which she boiled and then heated to a glowing red in the fire place. "I'll let it cool a bit before it touches him. Don't want to sear too deeply."

Julie stood fixed, a prayer frozen on her lips.

Maizie unbound the injuries, while Jacob held Print. Louisa drained the wounds and cleansed them with whiskey. When she took the iron, Julie pushed forward.

She kissed Print's forehead and took his hand. "He'll know I'm here." Julie began whispering to him.

Louisa approached with the hot iron. "You should leave, for the sake of the baby."

Zeke carefully moved Julie away from Print's bed to the chair. "Close as you need to be, Miz Julie. You pray."

Print's screams reduced her to quivers. Zeke gently pushed Jacob aside as the last wound was treated. Louisa's hands shook so hard she was unable to help Maizie apply poultices.

"Some of the herbs we collect. They'll help. We'll wrap him up again and allow God to do his healing," Maizie said.

Julie stood and insisted on helping them bathe Print's body, with Zeke providing the strong arms needed to lift the comatose Print and change the linens beneath him. She bathed Print's face with cool water and kissed his lips. At last they were finished and Aunt Maizie took away the soiled linens.

John and Dr. Samuels entered as they finished. "Thanks for the ride, John. Not sure I could have done it on my own. Up all night with a difficult birth." He strode to Print's bedside, examined the worst wound, and re-wrapped it. "I could have done no better. Only time will tell now."

Uncle John pulled Jacob and Zeke into the hallway for a whispered conversation, while Louisa and Maizie took Dr. Samuels to the kitchen. Julie sank to her knees beside Print's bed.

How has it come to this?

How could one of God's magnificent English brothers lie under a mound of sod and another be teetering on the brink? Only days ago, they'd been strong and vital. Why did good men undergo such trauma?

Julie's voice shook as she prayed, "Lord, must the sins of our past continue to reap destruction? Please use even our mistakes to bless, Father. All I want is healing for Print. He hasn't yet seen his child." She paused. Her chin trembled. "But I pray that You make me willing to accept Your decision, whatever it is. Your will be done."

Through the night Julie, Louisa, Jacob, and Zeke remained at Print's bedside, dozing fitfully and waking guiltily. Neither Jonas nor Conner came to their brother's bed side. Print slept his fevered sleep, occasionally moaning or calling out some delusional word.

Once, he said Julie's name, and stretched out his hand. She grasped it and held it to her lips, while Louisa soothed him with a moist cloth. Julie released his hand, and spooned cool water between his lips. She whispered to him until he once again settled.

Uncle John returned from town early the next morning with news. "Mrs. Evans died last night. She'll be buried this afternoon."

Julie received the news woodenly. "I don't care if Frank escapes after the funeral. Would his death serve God? The death of one evil man cannot make much difference. There seem to be so many."

"No, darling. We must spare some other soul the agony his actions have caused in this county. Frank must be brought to justice."

Zeke stood. "I'm gonna see to Mr. Con and Mr. Jonas. Them boys don't need to be up to what they have in mind."

Chapter 30

Concealed in a grove of young oak trees the evening of Mrs. Evans' funeral, Conner and Jonas watched the Evans' house. One or the other had been on constant surveillance since the confrontation with Frank and Tru.

Con said, "I'm surprised Zeke hasn't found us."

"Things must be bad with Print. Only thing that could keep him from hunting us down." Jonas' horse snorted and pawed the ground. His rider patted him. "I know, boy. I'm sick of this waiting business, too. Sick of cold food and sleeping in a bedroll."

"Go home, little brother."

"You know I won't. But you've never even told me what we'll do when we get them in our sights."

Conner rubbed the back of his neck. "It's almost over. We'll soon be watching those murdering traitors through our rifle sights. We can haul them to the sheriff to put under lock and key."

"And then what? A trial with lack of evidence? They'll go free."

"Do you want to kill them?"

"Of course not, but if they leave us no choice—"

"No buts. Just hope Zeke doesn't find us first." Conner didn't look forward to a session with Zeke. Not after his harsh words to Print. A spurt of shame shot through him. Sometimes he spoke too quickly. Print had been right not to act in haste.

"Can you imagine how frantic Frank and Tru are?" he asked. "In that house, gathering up what they can't leave behind?"

He pulled his rifle from its scabbard and checked to see that it had a cartridge in the chamber, ready to fire.

Jonas whispered, "Someone's coming out."

Tru carried a saddlebag and Frank a large valise. They entered the barn. Frank came out in the old surrey he often used, followed by Tru on his roan horse. The two men sped into the night.

Jonas and Connery did not try to stop them. Instead, the brothers cut across a field west of the Evans place and traveled to the shallow creek crossing. They concealed themselves in a walnut copse. Minutes later the splash of horses crossing the water galvanized them into action. Rifles in their hands, Con and Jonas broke cover.

"Hold up," said Conner. A rifle lay on the seat beside Frank, but he didn't reach for it.

Jonas pushed closer to Tru, long gun leveled. Frank said, "Boys, you don't want to do this—"

"You two seem to be in a hurry to get somewhere, but the only place you're going tonight is straight to jail. Either throw down your rifle or make your move." Jonas' voice was hoarse.

"We'll do better than that." The words came from a canebrake at the north edge of the road. "We'll send 'em straight to hell, but you boys won't be having any part in the sendoff."

Masked riders emerged, each with rifles or drawn pistols aimed not only at Frank and Tru, but some of them trained on Jonas and Conner.

Tru was forced into the buggy with Frank and a new driver whipped the conveyance away, surrounded by four masked men, two of them holding nooses.

"It'll be three on a limb tonight," said a familiar voice that seemed out of place behind a bandana. "We already have Tuffy up there where Tru and Frank are going."

Shock coursed through Conner. The vigilante was lawyer Ben Truly. Others wearing masks were clearly the Wyatt brothers and Dr. Samuels, but something warned Conner not to speak their names.

Another said, "Zeke, come take the English boys home." Mr. Bowden of the general store.

Zeke emerged from concealment with his rifle leveled at his two young charges. His face was hard.

"You heard the man, fellas. Let's go." Prodding Conner with the rifle, Zeke ordered, "Sheathe your guns, and we'll say goodnight to these genna'men."

The storekeeper said, "Not work you two should have to do. We should have acted before Ham was killed—before other good men and young Teresa were murdered. Before Julie had to shoot Teresa's killer to protect her baby."

Paralysis gripped Conner. Were these men really going to hang Frank and Tru, without even any semblance of due process? Zeke was the only one not masked—the only one willing to own up to his actions.

Ben Truly added, "We should've acted together and not left it to one family to try to stop a murdering bunch of thieves. Tonight, we put a stop to their reign of terror."

Bowden's voice chimed in. "We'll hang those two up there with Tuffy and then break up the rest of them. Their days in this county are finished. Won't leave any for seed. Don't need another crop of this kind."

Conner envisioned the outcome of the night's work: three bodies dangling from a single limb of an oak tree. No prayer to grace the sendoff. His blood had turned to ice. One glance at Jonas' anguished face told him he felt the same. But they had no choice. Zeke meant business.

They rode ahead, Zeke behind pushing them forward like skittish longhorns. The ride seemed interminable. Their parents waited on the porch. Jacob embraced both his sons as Zeke rode away.

After the story was revealed, Jacob said, "Men act together as they'd never act separately. I can see you two are having a hard time with this thing, as we all are. For this very reason laws were created; but these are our friends."

Conner's hands still shook. He was probably as pale-faced and shaken as Jonas. "Yes, good men, as you say; but out there, behind those masks, they weren't the men I knew. I was terrified of them."

"I don't want you boys to tell me—or anyone—who you think you recognized. They were pushed beyond their limits. Their actions will not be condemned in this house."

Louisa said, "Listen to your father. We've seen this kind of thing before. You are well out of it."

"I knew this was coming," Jacob continued. "John learned of their plans. He managed to convince them he'd never tell and they let him stay out of it. But they may change their minds—may one day see him as a threat. That's the nature of mobs."

Zeke led Conner and two Reverse E cowboys to the hanging site at dawn, a short distance from the church graveyard. Conner had insisted that Jonas wasn't needed. Three bodies dangled from the stout oak limb that had supported them through the night. Zeke pushed his skittish horse beneath Tuffy's short body, cut it down, and laid it across the horse in front of him. "Mr. Print said I can bury him on the ranch in his favorite spot."

Conner watched him prod his horse forward with its tragic load. Turning to the task at hand, he found it impossible to focus on the twisted faces of Frank and Tru for more than the instant it took to identify them. He instructed his men to bury the bodies in separate graves outside the graveyard, and to mark each with the cypress shingles he brought bearing their initials. They didn't deserve to be in the midst of decent folk.

Conner rode to Buck Evans' house to tell him about his brothers, uncertain of what he'd find. Had the mob visited him, too? Buck came out into the yard and listened to the tale of the burials, his face hostile.

"Are you English brothers satisfied now? Have you wiped out enough of us Evans and our kin, or can I expect to be next? Or my aged father? Get off my place, Con, and don't ever come back. Leave me to grieve my mother, my brothers, and my cousin Cully. Even your women act out your hate."

Conner didn't answer. Injustice filled Buck's words, but perhaps he might have felt equal bitterness in the circumstances.

"At least you could've placed my brothers next to Mother's grave and spared me the job of reburying them," Buck said. "I'm sure most of the decent folk of the church won't want them near her, but I mean to put them there because that's what she'd want."

"Preacher Cravens may have an opinion."

Buck spat on the ground. "'Course, I may not have the chance. Your mob of Regulators may come here to run me and my wife and kids out of the county. *If* I'm lucky. Or they may hang me, no questions asked."

"It should get easier if you keep your powder dry." The words sounded hollow and insincere. Conner had no assurance. He, too, wondered what the mob would do. He had to talk to Print.

Later in the day, Conner sat beside Print's bed, mulling over the legal and moral dilemma the hangings posed—and his involvement. He was no longer sure how he felt about the justice system. It seemed to have failed his family when they needed it most, and then failed again with the lynching.

Julie had left him alone with Print, saying, "He's beginning to have longer periods of consciousness and clarity as Louisa decreases the laudanum. You can help me feed him."

Conner found himself praying for this same brother he'd condemned a few days before. He wanted Print healed—to wake up and do the big brother thing. He'd felt so righteous convicting Print of giving Frank time to bury his mother. In light of the hangings, he was no longer certain.

What would happen to the men Jacob characterized as friends and good men? Were they changed forever? Was vengeance ever the right solution? Only God had all the facts. God judged rather than avenged.

The mob had lynched an old man who may not have understood how his knowledge of English ranch affairs was being used. There'd been no evidence of Tuffy's involvement in treachery. Conner needed to get Print's take on last night, but he dreaded to break the news about Zeke and Tuffy.

Julie came back into the room with a bowl of broth for Print. "Can you get him upright?"

Print grimaced as Conner propped him with pillows, but then managed a wobbly grin. "Here's my nurse again with more of that dishwater. Where's my fried steak? How can a man get well on swill?"

Conner said, "Shut up, brother, and take your medicine like a man. Aunt Maizie has promised beef steak tonight, if you can stay awake long enough to chew it."

Julie offered a spoonful of the bland broth, but Print took the bowl into his hands after the first swallow, then tipped it to drink its contents.

"That didn't taste too bad, sweet wife. How about another one?"

Julie's face was radiant as she hurried back to the kitchen.

Conner said, "I've got something circling inside me that I can't get my head around. Do you feel up to discussing it now, or should we wait?"

"We can talk, but you might want to ask Julie to wait a few minutes before she returns."

When Conner came back, he blurted, "Zeke let a mob hang Tuffy."

"I know. Zeke came and told me after the night's work was finished," Print said. "I couldn't make much sense of what he said, but he kept pushing till I understood what happened."

Conner shook his head. "How could he do that?"

"Zeke lives by a different code. Treachery is the

same as murder in his eyes. Tuffy violated Zeke's moral code when he sold out to Frank."

Conner's brow wrinkled. "Hard to take. I can't believe—"

"Not saying I think Zeke was right—just that he believed he was."

"But how can a man hang his friend?"

"The same as a friend can betray a friend, I suppose," said Print. "You have to understand, it makes sense in that man's mind, even if it doesn't to anyone else. Even Frank would think he had reasons to turn on me. I know he had goodness in him." Print fingered the patterned quilt covering his legs. "One of Maizie's. Wonder how many she's made?"

Conner expelled a frustrated sigh.

Print whispered, "Frank had a private part of himself he never let me enter. I guess it was in his hidden thoughts where Cain held sway. Remember Cain struck down his brother Abel."

Conner nodded. "Still tough to understand."

"I'm learning that apart from God's precepts there is no right manner of acting. We rationalize what we want to do and twist it to make it seem right, but it's not going to come out how it should. God's is the only route."

Con's eyebrows raised.

"I taught Ham my way instead of God's. Frank and Zeke thought they found what worked for them, but it wasn't within God's law, and none of it came out right."

Print winced as he moved his hip. "You need to make the Word of God the most important thing in your life. Don't wait till you're an old man like me."

Conner nodded. "Yeah, you have a couple of years on me. Last night changed me. I feel differently today."

"Will you go find Zeke? Ask him to come here about supper time. Say if he'll listen to a sermon, he can eat all the beefsteak and fixin's he can hold." Print managed a smile.

Chapter 31

"Well, Zeke. Did you have enough?" Print was propped up on pillows as Zeke moved a tray from his lap to the bedside table.

"Full as a tick," Zeke muttered.

Julie had brought Print's tray early and cut up his steak for him before she went to the others. He listened to the comforting voices of his family as they sat together in the nearby dining room. They were talking about Hamilton and how much they missed him, especially when fried steak was involved.

"Please close the door," Print whispered.

Zeke pushed shut the heavy oak door and returned to Print's bedside.

Print stared up at him. "I'm going to ask you to do something that will go against the grain, but I have to do it. I need you to trust me."

"Ask away, Mr. Print. I can't think of much I wouldn't do for you."

Print nodded. "That's why I can ask. I need you to tell me what the Regulators are planning. I know this thing's not over by a long shot, and I need to know where and when they mean to strike next."

Zeke sat unmoving, saying nothing. Print waited, hoping to find some response in Zeke's fathomless black eyes. At last, his answer came. "Mr. Print, you know I can't do that."

"You can, Zeke. You believe in God, same as I do. I'm now trying to let Him guide me. It will be God who decides how to use what you tell me. I'm trusting Him, just as I am asking you to trust me."

For what seemed like a full minute, Zeke's gaze never wavered from Print's. His mouth opened and closed. Then his expression hardened. "They're goin' after Buck and old man Evans next. Said they can't leave any bad seed in San Simon County. They'll hold off until the men from Mills and Lampasas Counties arrive."

Print drew a long breath. "Buck's wife is a good woman."

Zeke's brow furrowed, but his toneless words continued. "They're gonna round up ever' last one of that bunch in The Bend before the Yankee military comes. Plannin' one grand hangin'. And I'm goin' with 'em, Mr. Print."

"When?"

"Day after tomorrow."

"Thank you, Zeke. You're a good man and probably the best friend I have in this world."

"Is that all, Mr. Print?"

"That's all. Go digest that good beef, and I'll see you in the morning. Please ask Julie to come to me." As Julie entered, Print said, "Close the door. Then come up here on the bed. I need you beside me."

Print held her, kissing her hair, then her face softly. "I've missed you so much."

Julie kissed his cheek. "That works both ways."

Print's voice was soft. "What you said about not putting you first in my life has been on my mind. I can't live without you. I need your spirit, your faith in God and your faith in me. I need you as much as I need air and food."

Julie started to speak, but Print lifted a finger to her lips.

"I don't think I'm putting you before God to love you this way. I think it's because I love Him first that I can love you as I do."

Tears shimmered in her lashes.

"You've become so much a part of me that if I lost you, I'd no longer be me. Perhaps God could still use the piece of a man I'd be, but He wouldn't have much to work with."

Julie nodded. "I don't suppose it's wrong to love this way, as long as we understand God doesn't have to keep the union intact."

Print frowned. *Where's she going?*

"We're made for His purposes," she said. "Not He for ours. Our purpose is to glorify God by our lives and by our deaths. To enjoy Him forever. Think of that, Print. Forever!"

Her smile was radiant and held a hint of mischief. "Now that brings a whole new perspective to mind. I wonder if there's fried steak in heaven, or if you'll be cured of your craving?"

Print chuckled, then winced. "You make me glad I robbed your Uncle John's cradle."

For minutes they held each other, taking comfort in the oneness. Then Print said, "I need you to pray with me. God has laid a big thing on me and I don't know exactly how to start. I'll have only one chance at it and many lives are involved. I can't mess it up."

He explained and they prayed.

Early the next morning Jonas and Conner loped along the road to town.

"It'll take me half an hour with Ben," Jonas said. Wait in the walnut trees till you see us go by, and then hightail it to Doc Samuels'. We don't want them to see each other on the road."

Once in town, Jonas hustled up the steps to the lawyer's office. He opened the door without knocking, and Ben stared up uncertainly. His right hand moved toward a desk drawer.

Must have a pistol there.

"What can I do for you?" Caution edged Truly's words.

"It's Print, Ben. Sent me to bring you. Maybe feels he won't make it. Will you go with me now?"

"Makes me sick to hear, but I'll be glad to see that his affairs are in order." Ben pulled a binder from his desk's deep side drawer. "Let's go."

When the two passed his place of concealment, Conner galloped to Dr. Samuels' house. "Julie sent me. Must not be going well for Print. She said to beg if I must."

It'll take a harder man than the Doc to resist Julie. Conner took Samuels directly to Print's room, where Ben leaned close to Print, obviously straining to hear his whispered words.

Samuels pushed Truly away. "Let me up here." He opened his medical bag, an expression of concern on his face. As he bent to listen to his patient's chest, Print grabbed his hand in a strong fist.

"Not as bad as you think, Doc. I need you all right; and you, too, Ben, but not for what you think."

Conner motioned Jonas to stand with him in the doorway. Both wore their pistols.

Print said, “Doc, you and Ben have to take control of this situation and keep it sane. Otherwise, events might set this county back fifty years. Your lives and those of your families could be ruined. You know what I’m talking about.”

Neither man said a word, both faces inscrutable.

“Ben, you know that legally you don’t have a thing on Buck. As far as I know, he never was a part of what Frank and Tru were doing. His only crime is bearing the name of Evans.”

Ben no longer met Print’s gaze.

Print continued, “And Tom is almost seventy years old now and never draws a sober breath. What good can it do for that worthless old man to strangle to death at the end of a rope?”

Dr. Samuels shifted his feet.

Print continued in a quiet voice, “Another old man who may not have been so bad has already done just that. We have no proof that Tuffy knew he was doing more than helping Frank run off a bunch of my cattle. He was with me on the drive when Frank turned Cully loose on Julie.”

The men gawked at Print. Ben’s cheeks were hollowed and dark circles rimmed his eyes. Dr. Samuels’ shoulders sagged.

Print gauged his next words. “I owe my life to you, Doc, and part of my business success to you, Ben. I know your hearts—and the desperation that drove you to act.”

Sitting taller in the bed, he continued, “Frank turned his maniac cousin loose on Julie and it was probably Frank’s gun that killed Ham. It’s almost certain Tru killed old man Crawford. Shot him in front of his wife, and he may have had a hand in other murders. Hanging Frank and Tru was justice, and not many people in the county would disagree."

Ben's hand cupped his mouth. Doc Samuels nodded, his eyes on the floor.

"But it's not the same with Buck and old Tom. Nor with that gang of desperate young men down in The Bend."

Ben said, "What happened to Frank and Tru was an execution of known killers, but Tuffy should not have swung from the same limb. I was too weak to stand against it." His voice cracked with the last admission.

Print swallowed hard. "Both of you know the difference between a bunch of scared, confused boys and the few really bad men who are among them. Zeke will know if you don't."

He paused, searching their faces. Neither spoke, but both squinted at him. Samuels blew out a noisy breath.

Print said, "You can take them by surprise, as many men as you'll have. What you do with them afterward is what you must decide. You can stop this thing before it becomes so bad no one can. Count on the Sanders brothers to help you."

The two men exchanged a darting glance.

"Tell me your plan fits with the Word of God," Print pushed. "That it's the only way to handle this mess. I need to hear it from you."

A moment of silence. Dr. Samuels finally murmured, "I've been afraid to say anything, to tell you the truth." His voice strengthened. "I imagine you feel the same, Ben. But it may already be out of hand. I'm not sure we can stop it. It may be worth our lives to try."

"It's not too late." Print leaned toward them. "It's never too late to try. If you get the Regulators together, I'll go with you to reason with them. We can straighten things out so that decent people can feel safe again. What do you say?"

Dr. Samuels uttered a shaky laugh. "You think you're made of iron, but I know the condition of your hip, and unless you let me examine you now, I'll never agree. As your doctor, I can't. You look like a half-starved barber's cat."

One corner of Ben's mouth turned up and he said, "And unless you answer some questions for me, as your lawyer, I can't vouch for your sanity in making such a plan. But I'm on board. We've got to stop acting like judge and jury in matters better left to the Almighty."

Print glanced heavenward. "Thank God. We can sway Zeke to our view. He and his pistol are big persuaders. My father and brothers, John Denton, and the Sanders brothers, as well as some of our cowboys, can take on anything if we're acting in the right motive."

"No more hangings," said Conner and Jonas as one.

Ben nodded. "No more."

Chapter 32

In the months that passed, changes surrounded Print. Some he orchestrated, and some he watched in amazement. His wife had swelled before his eyes.

Soon his son would be born.

Print kissed Julie at the door one evening in early November and gave her a careful squeeze. He loosened his embrace and studied her radiant face.

"More beautiful than ever, sweet wife."

"Hmph. If you can appreciate a grumpy walrus. Everything that goes wrong seems to set my teeth on edge."

"I have something that may help." He pulled a paper from his pocket. It was folded to form an envelope and closed with a wax seal, now broken.

"Mother sent along a letter from Con and Charlotte. They're settled in Austin, and he's training in Rufus Emerson's law office. Pretty high-powered stuff."

Julie shook her head. "Never thought Con would be the one to leave the ranch. Jonas was the one interested in law, and now he's firmly settled in the cabin Con was building, talking about studying animal husbandry and bringing in Hereford cattle."

"I thought it would be longhorns all the way for the four of us. Then..." Print fell silent for a long moment, remembering the death of his youngest brother. "Ham never had a chance to choose, but he would have stuck with me."

Julie gave him an extra-long hug. "We'll read the letter later. I'm hungry and I'm sure you are, too. Maizie brought supper again. Fried steak for you."

After a few bites, Print said, "Julie, I wish you'd feed Little Print some of this good beefsteak instead of that chicken and dumplings your Aunt Betty made. Chicken three times this week. He may cluck like a hen when he tries to talk. A man needs *beef*."

"Elizabeth Louisa and I are quite happy with chicken, carrots and tiny potatoes. Women cannot live on beef alone."

"Please don't call our son by a girl's name."

Julie laughed. "Your mother says it's a girl."

"What can she know? We should have a boy first. Every girl needs an older brother. Bert taught you a great deal."

"And some of it I'd have been better off not knowing—like rock throwing."

"If he hadn't taught you how to throw a rock, we might never have met. I'm pretty sure I wouldn't have noticed a skinny red-headed kid unless she did something awful, like putting herself in a peck of trouble."

Julie's smile was serene. "Oh, you'd have noticed me. You did your best to ignore me that night of the rain dance and escape with your brothers, but you couldn't help yourself. *Auburn* hair has its allure."

Print grinned and suddenly sobered. "Honey,

how much longer do we have? You've developed a real bay window. I'm afraid you're going to pop if Little Print doesn't hurry up and move out of there. You're a small woman."

"Stop right there, Print English."

"I've never seen a mare so pregnant. I think you ought to come down to the barn with me. I can fix you up in a twinkling. I've helped many a mare to domino."

"Don't be crude. Pregnancy isn't like a drawn-out domino game. And the only helpers I need are the good Lord and his assistants Louisa, Maizie, and Aunt Betty." They both laughed.

"I'll clear away and wash up," Print said. "You stay off your feet."

"I'll wash and you can dry."

"I don't mind doing *wo-man's* work. It's fun with you. Can't imagine trying to explain that to Zeke, though."

Julie finished the last dish, sighed, and rubbed at her aching back as Print wiped the table. *Reassuring to know Aunt Betty is staying with Louisa as the due date approaches. Louisa says it's past time. Elizabeth Louisa English must be another small lady with a mind of her own.*

The three women saw to Julie's every wish and a few she never had. Three chicken dishes in a row. No wonder Print was worried about her nutrition, being the beef-believer he was.

As Print put away the last dish, he said, "There's a full moon tonight. If I carry enough pillows onto the porch, do you think you and Print Jr. can be comfortable? I've always felt guilty about robbing you of that moon on our wedding night."

"Ease your mind, darling. The entertainment you provided that night was almost as good."

"Almost! If you weren't in your present condition, I'd show you *almost*. You didn't have any complaints that night. All I heard were sounds of contentment."

"I'm sure you're right. You always are." Julie smiled up at her husband. "It might be chilly outside, but we can put our chairs together and snuggle under the fluffy. It should be fun. Maybe even a bit romantic, don't you think?"

"Doesn't seem to me like you need any romance for a while. I've taken care of that rather thoroughly for now. I want you to sing to me."

"I'll sing, but first I want us to tour our beautiful house."

"Again? It's been finished for a week and we've had a tour every evening."

"I never tire of seeing it."

The cabin had become a spacious home, with three new bedrooms added, and the original cabin now a large living area, leading to an expanded dining space and kitchen on the north end.

"The nursery is my favorite," Julie said. "The old cradle that you boys used is perfect with the coat of white paint Maizie added. Aunt Betty is sewing curtains and Louisa is tying rugs."

Print grunted. Curtains couldn't hold a cattleman's interest. He wouldn't see these until after the baby came. The frilly things would be too final a pronouncement on Print's hopes for a son.

After he holds his child, he'll find it impossible to think of anything but the tiny wonder of his daughter, Elizabeth Louisa. We'll call her Bets. Uncle John says a tiny girl needs a short name.

Print reached for the big feather comforter atop the wardrobe that Julie called her fluffy. He headed for the bed and its four downy pillows—three of which Julie put to use each night, and all four when she could manage to nab the one from beneath Print's head.

"Okay, I'm ready for some singing."

Julie sang Print's favorites. The coverlet hadn't quite stretched over her expansion and two chairs, but she was quite content on his lap. She leaned back in his arms, secure and content. How she loved this man!

Print toyed with an auburn ringlet and occasionally rubbed her tummy. A calf bawled from the corrals, and the minutes stretched into an hour, with an occasional favorite song. A Milky Way-streaked sky awaited the rising of the promised full moon as they talked of inconsequential things.

Julie tapped Print's arm. In the deepening dusk, three white-tailed deer had emerged from the oak trees and stood like arranged statues. Poised on delicate legs, gazes fixed, they appeared prepared to run at the slightest movement, yet curiously ready to stand watching.

Print smiled and whispered, "Need to spread some windfall apples out there." He stirred, and the deer melted into the gathering twilight.

"Amazing how God works," Print finally said. "This beautiful evening is a gift. It reminds me to give thanks for God's continuing healing after Ham's death."

"A mercy of His grace. And I'm so grateful The Great Hanging never took place." Julie said. "I still grieve for Tuffy. Incomprehensible that Zeke could have been part of it. Do you ever talk about what happened that night?"

"Not to Zeke. Everyone concerned finally agreed it was better to take the bad guys to Austin for trial and let the young deserters go home, instead of hanging them. But, as I told you, it was touch and go with some of the vigilantes for the better part of an hour."

Julie said, "Thank heavens they made the right decision. Without your insistence, it might have gone the other way."

Print nodded. "Watching Tuffy die must have helped Zeke see the light. It didn't take much persuasion for him to agree. Doc and Ben were strong persuaders, but it was clearly Zeke's opinion that counted most with the vigilance committee."

He expelled a long breath. "I pray the worst is over, but there'll be strong opposition to military law when it comes to the county. We'll see occupation. The war isn't over in the minds of a lot of people, northern and southern." He tucked the fluffy more snugly around Julie, then tipped his head back for a moment.

"What are you thinking?" Julie asked.

"I'm glad that old Tom Evans was able to die peacefully. Buck may never know how close he came to hanging. He's still bitter—not without cause—but it could have ended horribly."

Julie agreed drowsily. From beneath the warmth of the fluffy, her mind wandered. She stirred from Print's lap, and moved over into the other chair, meaning to take only a corner of the coverlet, but Print wrapped her in the whole thing.

"Do you want to give young Print a chill? We can go in whenever you're ready."

The moon was now a surge of brilliance, fully risen, a golden orb hanging tantalizingly near. Its light streamed across the porch, illuminating Print's face and his worshipful dark eyes.

They still turn me to jelly.

Julie had seen them dance with mischief, burn with anger, and simmer with passion, but it was their melancholy tilt that melted her heart. Aunt Maizie was right in her estimation of the one who owned her heart. Print was a *real man.*

She answered, "Not yet, please. Let me stay a while longer with you in this perfect spot. That man in the moon seems so near I can almost hold his hand. But I'd rather hold yours. I wouldn't trade you, Print English, for any man in the world."

Print appeared uncomfortable with the praise, but he needed to hear her words.

"I've watched you change under God's direction from a fine man into an exceptional one. I've shared with you in the work He's accomplishing in both of us. I've grown with you, but you've far outstripped me in becoming a servant of the Lord."

Print snorted. "Julie—"

She touched her finger to his lips and he held it there. "You find a need and offer help anonymously. Buck will never learn from me that you paid the back taxes on his father's place to preserve it for him and his growing family. But I know, and you weren't the one who told me. Nor will Polly ever know who built the new houses in Gallo."

He kissed Julie's finger. "Small potatoes, compared to what God has done for us."

Julie said, "Strange to think of Con and Charlotte married and living in Austin."

"Not to Jonas. He's enjoying being on his own in the cabin Con was building and helping Zeke gather a herd."

"So generous of the family to give Ham's portion of the ranch to Zeke. I know it was your idea."

"He's never had a home of his own." Print grew silent.

An owl called its mournful hoot and Julie waited.

Something was on Print's mind.

He toyed with her thumb. "My dream of an empire is dead. We have more than enough. I'll stay busy maintaining our herd, making improvements, and helping Jonas establish his Herefords. But I'll never give up longhorns. I can't imagine driving short-legged Herefords across the distances my longhorns can cover."

"You have a considerably bigger dream now. God thinks on a much grander scale than we do." Print fell silent. So many changes in his life.

Before Julie's black depression he'd been willing to celebrate God's story, but had refused to live it. He knew the words, attended church, said his prayers, sang the hymns, and gave his tithe. Willing to give his money, but not himself. What had happened inside him, once he surrendered, was amazing. His thinking had changed. What made him happy—

"Print, are you listening?"

"I'm listening, sweetheart. Just thinking about some of what you're saying."

She said, "I'm reminded of the tale of a sculptor's cleaning lady who swept up chips of marble night after night as the artist carved a bust of President George Washington. When the bust was almost finished, she said to the sculptor, 'I think what you've done is wonderful; but how did you know Mr. Washington was inside that stone?' I know what she meant."

Julie smiled dreamily at him in that way of hers—the smile that made his knees go weak.

"You've taken on a new image, Print. I've asked God how He knew the *you* I see today was inside the man I married. I think of you now as one of God's loving handprints in this world. What an adventure it is living with you and God. And there's more to come."

Print kissed her open palm. "I want to grow old with you, but our love will never grow old. You'll keep it young. You've been surprising me since I first saw you throw that rock."

He scooped Julie up into his arms, fluffy and all, and carried her through the doorway of their ranch house on the hill. "Here we go, Miz English. This had better be the night you get busy birthing Little Print."

THE END

Also by
Marilyn Read and Cheryl Spears Waugh:

Women of Monterey series

Book 1: Seek a Safe Harbor
Book 2: Dawn's Light in Monterey

Please visit Cheryl and Marilyn at
Inspired Women of the Southwest.
www.InspiredWomenoftheSW.com

Marilyn and Cheryl greatly appreciate all reader feedback! Would you consider leaving a brief review of this book on Amazon, Goodreads, or any other book review site?
We thank you!

Lightning Source UK Ltd.
Milton Keynes UK
UKHW011552250820
368764UK00002B/62/J

9 781950 481217